I0747932

FOUND IN MAGIC

IN MAGIC SERIES
BOOK THREE

KJ WARAWA

MYSTIC
CITY
PRESS

PROLOGUE

Twenty-Two Years Ago

The bad men told her if she cried again, they'd hurt the other children. She pulled the covers over her head and cried as softly as she could, hoping the blankets would muffle any sound.

They said her family was all dead and that they were her family now. Them, and the other kids who would soon come. She even had a new name—Morgana Smith. That's what they called her and if she didn't answer to it, they hit her or drained her magic. It hurt. Then she was weak and could only sleep.

Her daddy told her she only had a little bit of magic right now because she was little, and she would get more when she was a teenager. He said that's how it worked with all people born with magic. But that was a long time away. She wished she had her full magic now—then she could flash home.

One day she would be powerful like him and Mommy. Maybe someday she'd be able to flash as far as Daddy and

Mommy. She shook her head, it hurt too much to think of them.

She squeezed her eyes shut to stop the tears and tried to think of something else. Second grade. That was a good thing to think about. She was going to start second grade after the summer holiday and she had a lot of friends at school. She liked playing with them at recess.

Then she remembered she wouldn't be going to school with her friends. Her throat felt tight, and her stomach hurt. She wiped away the new tears. There had to be something she could think about to make her happy… Cupcakes.

She loved cupcakes. Chocolate ones with lots of sprinkles. Her mommy would conjure them. No, she wouldn't think about her family. She'd remember the ingredients and one day she would make them herself.

She yawned and hugged her pillow. Maybe she could think of other recipes and not think about the bad men.

Eighteen Years Ago

Morgana struggled against the ropes holding her wrists to the wooden arms of the chair. She knew it was useless. The bad men had used the special magic rope and it stopped her powers, the meager amount she had. Someday she would show them they couldn't tell her what to do.

Her powers were supposed to be getting stronger now because she was eleven. That's what Mirek said and he was fourteen and knew a lot more than she did. He kept track of things like that and knew how old everyone was.

They'd been told to call him Mark, but he'd refused to answer to it. At first, they would punish him, but he didn't care. He took the beatings until Zeus and Snake finally gave up and he got to stay Mirek.

She shivered at the thought of the bad men. They weren't always around, but they scared her and she hated them. She'd tried to fight them, but then they'd hurt her by slapping her around or by draining her magic.

So many days, like today, she felt useless and wondered why she was even alive. She wasn't good at anything and when she tried to help, she always caused trouble. Even cooking didn't make her helpful—she'd forget an ingredient or burn something.

Zeus reminded her every chance he got that her weak magic made her useless.

Every day had become the same—trying to escape punishment and failing. Her life had become a monotony and the days, weeks, and months melded together. She only knew the seasons were changing because she was sometimes allowed outside into a small backyard. They had been somewhere with cold winters and hot, sticky summers. Morgana liked the fall the best—cool breezes and leaves changing colors on the trees she could see over the back fence. Until everything had changed.

A couple months ago, she'd moved with the other kids to someplace hot. Everyone in the new compound spoke Spanish and she didn't understand very much of it. Mirek thought they were in Mexico since he remembered reading about it for a school project and they'd passed a landmark he saw in one of the books/

She'd learned some Spanish from watching *Sesame Street* and *Dora the Explorer* when she was little, but that was a long time ago. She couldn't remember the last time she'd watched TV.

At their old place—in a basement—they got to watch movies all the time. When their tutor wasn't there and they didn't have to study, she watched princess movies. She wished she was watching a princess movie now, and not sitting in a room by herself.

Sometimes Zeus or the other men would leave her tied up for what felt like hours. Letting her mind wander was the only thing that kept her sane. Her memories were becoming harder and harder to hold onto—she didn't remember much of her family anymore. And every time her power was drained, she felt groggier and knew she'd lost another memory.

Letting out a big breath, she looked down at her wrists. She could see still healing wounds and old scars underneath the rope. She used to fight to try and to get free, but it had been useless. The only thing she'd managed to do was hurt herself, so she'd learned to sit and wait until someone came for her. She wished for it and feared it at the same time.

Footsteps sounded outside the door and she lifted her head, then shuddered as Zeus walked in. "Morgana, I heard you've been defiant again. We can't have that."

She was pretty sure he meant she hadn't been following his men's stupid orders. And she wasn't going to. She lifted her chin and stared right into his eyes.

She'd learned years ago that Zeus hated when someone didn't respond to him. Even though he hadn't asked a question, she knew from experience that he wanted her to say yes.

"I've been tolerant with you, Morgana, but my patience is running thin. Today you're going to learn when someone tells you to do something, you will do it immediately." He stepped further into the room and towered over her. "I heard you hate spiders."

She lasted three minutes before her screams could be heard throughout the compound.

*M*organa Smith had been free for 320 days.

She was physically free and yet she felt just as trapped as she'd been for over twenty years.

But she wasn't free from the relentless pounding in her skull that threatened to drive her insane and prevented her from sleeping. She wasn't free from the feelings of shame that came with her magic being so weak it was useless. She wasn't free from the missing memories and the worry of not knowing who she was or where she came from.

The lack of memories was the worst. She could only remember the last year before she'd been rescued, the year she'd spent with Zeus. After her rescue, she'd learned his real name had been Louis Copeland, and the day he died was one of the happiest of her life. At least, from the life she remembered.

Every day she woke and wondered if it would be the day she remembered something about her past. And every night she went to bed disappointed, wondering who she was and where she belonged and if there were people who missed her. People she'd miss if she remembered them.

Ben Davis, the head of the FBI's magic task force, told her that over the past twenty to thirty years, there'd been dozens of magic families killed after their magic was siphoned. The magic task force knew that children were taken, but they had no idea how many. If civilian police or FBI were alerted to the crime first, the information didn't always make it to them, so he feared that there were even more missing children than they knew about.

Ben had his team investigating the missing children's cases, but so far there was no one fitting her description. Even photos age-progressed by twenty years hadn't come close.

As she watched the sun start its rise over the Rocky Mountains, she wondered if today would bring answers. She'd been in Blue Mountain, Colorado, for almost two years now and each day she watched the sunset, she wondered the same thing. Her first year there, she was trapped inside without windows and hadn't felt the sun on her face.

Since her rescue ten months ago, she'd watched it rise and felt its warmth every chance she got.

Blankets had become one of her favorite things. She couldn't remember having a special one growing up, or more than one at a time. Now she had lots to wrap herself in when the weather was cold. Blankets someone had conjured because she couldn't. She couldn't even conjure a cup of coffee.

Today a sweatshirt was enough to protect her against the chilly end-of-August morning. After several hours of fighting against the constant throbbing in her head, she'd finally given up and had come down to her usual spot and curled up on a chair.

She loved the back patio of the Williams's restaurant, The Magic Plate. The Williams family owned three tall buildings they were renovating with offices and shops on the bottom level and condos on the higher floors. Meredith, the cousin in charge of all the renovations, had shown Morgana around the buildings. She'd fallen in love with all the plans for making the buildings into a community—something she'd yearned for.

Guilt swamped Morgana when she thought about the family's generosity—they'd rescued her, given her a condo, and a family. They didn't even expect her to work, but she did anyway, helping in the bakery owned by Reece, one of the cousins, and the restaurant.

"Figured I'd find you up and thought you might need this."

Morgana looked up, shielding her eyes from the sun with one hand. Rowena stood beside her with two mugs of coffee. "Thanks," she said, taking the proffered drink. She inhaled deeply and took a tentative sip as the steam hit her face.

"Couldn't sleep?" Rowena asked.

Morgana shrugged and sipped her coffee. Rowena, along with her cousins Meredith, Jo, and Jo's brother Reece, were in a similar situation as Morgana since they too were all learning more about who they were. The cousins knew where they came from, but last year they'd learned that they had been spellbound since they were children. They had grown up not knowing they were magic. They hadn't even known magics existed.

The knowledge had changed all four of their lives, especially Jo's and Rowena's. Jo now worked for the magic council and Rowena had decided to change the direction of her practice. She was still a psychologist but now worked almost exclusively with magics. Morgana was one of them. Sometimes.

"I've got an early client this morning, so I can't stay long, but it's nice to have company," Rowena said.

Morgana eyed her friend suspiciously. "Just coffee and

company, or are you going to put on your psychologist hat because I haven't made an appointment with you recently?"

Rowena chuckled. "Just coffee and company… for now."

Morgana snorted and took another sip. "It's been quieter since Jo and Simon left for Budapest, but it's nice having Jack and Meredith back from their honeymoon."

"I expect we'll see them at dinner tonight, and Reece is around somewhere too. As much as I love my cousins and their partners, I can't keep track of them anymore with everyone able to flash here and there."

One more thing Morgana couldn't do—flash. She looked down, letting her hair fall over her face to hide her shame.

Rowena took a sip of her coffee and then turned wide eyes to her. "Oh, Morgana, I'm sorry, I didn't mean that the way it sounded. I didn't mean to boast. Not everyone can flash."

"It's okay. Maybe Jack and Meredith and the other council leaders will figure out what's wrong with my magic. Or maybe they won't." She didn't want to give up hope, but how long should she hold out? Another month? Another year? Forever? At what point would hope in the hopeless start to hold her back?

She looked out over the mountains, loving the way the sun reflected off the peaks, and decided to enjoy the moment. "Is Meredith organizing the dinner tonight or does she need help?" As soon as the words were out of her mouth, she looked at Rowena and they both burst into laughter. "Right, dumb question." Meredith was an organizer extraordinaire and made it seem effortless. "Well, maybe I'll still ask if I can help."

"Good idea. I think it's going to be a large crowd tonight and I love seeing who shows up."

Weekly family dinners in the restaurant were a tradition and it seemed the invitation was open to all the magics the

Williams family knew. Morgana liked meeting new people and catching up with those she'd met in the last year. One person in particular—Damon Stone. He never seemed to miss a weekly dinner if he could help it. He was best friends with Meredith's husband, Jack, and had grown up with all the cousins.

He was sexy and bossy, friendly and annoying, giving and controlling. Yes, he was good-looking, but the bossiness was enough to cancel out his hotness. She'd been bossed around her entire life and now she refused to let anyone else control her. Damon seemed to live to tell her what to do. Ten months ago, she promised herself she would never be controlled again.

No one said she had to be at the dinner, but it was the one time each week when she felt like she had a family she belonged to. There'd been so much loss and turmoil over the last year, and she wasn't the only one who clung to the normality of the dinners. It was a time to be with friends and family and cherish the time they had together.

One of the people they'd lost had been Meredith's mother, Elise. The fact that she'd died while rescuing Meredith and Morgana from Louis Copeland still sat heavy with her. Several months before, Jo and Reece's mother had died. But at least amidst all the tragedy, Reece had been saved from his death bed after a he'd been struck by spell while unbinding another one.

She took another sip from her mug as movement caught the corner of her eye.

The coffee mug slipped from her fingers, shattering on the patio.

Brown liquid oozed into the cracks between the tiles, but Morgana gave it only a fleeting thought. Her entire focus centered on the black spider crawling across her left white sneaker.

The world around her receded as her gaze stayed locked on the spider. Rowena's voice was distant, as if she was calling to Morgana through a long tunnel.

Her vision blurred and there wasn't one spider anymore; there were dozens of them as she was thrown back into the past.

She'd been tied to a chair. Her ankles and calves secured to its legs, her arms fixed to the rests, and another rope around her torso.

At first it was just a dozen or so spiders, sending threads of terror spiraling through her body. When she was scared, her magic came close to the surface, and with just a small spell, someone could siphon it from her easily. They then took the little power she had within themselves. Morgana would be weak for days, sometimes weeks, until her magic regenerated.

The special magic rope limited her movement and prevented her from using her magic but still allowed her captors to drain it from her.

Zeus would conjure spiders onto the floor and then direct them toward her. When she wore shorts, she'd shudder at the feel of their legs inching up over her skin, like small, hairy predators invading. As horrific as that was, long pants were worse. The little creatures would get trapped between her clothing and her skin, invisible attackers working their way up her body.

The older and stronger she became, the more spiders they had to use to incite fear in her. The more fearful she was, the easier it was to drain her pitiful amount of magic. Her heart would start pounding so hard she could hear the blood passing through her ears—a literal thump, thump, thump— and looking down she would see her chest moving up and down through her clothing. Her arms trembled, causing the magic rope to rub back and forth across her wrists, tearing her skin like jagged little teeth. Sweat broke out on her skin, prickling at her forehead and running down between her small breasts. Her vision would become darker and narrower and a voice in her head whispered, *"This is what dying feels like and you are going to die alone."* There was nowhere to escape to and nothing to slow the panic that overtook her.

She refused to die. It had taken months, but she'd practiced over and over until she'd learned to shut her mind off to the little crawlers. She'd go someplace deep in her thoughts where all feeling melted away.

The tactic had worked until they'd switched to biting spiders. They bit into her flesh, small bites over and over again, never-ending, like they would consume her one bite at a time. The death of a thousand tiny bites.

She would scream until her throat was raw and her voice was too hoarse to make a sound. The pounding of her heart would worsen. Her breathing would feel restricted and she'd shake uncontrollably as the spiders climbed higher. They continued onto her chest and neck and eventually onto her face, forcing her to shut her mouth and squeeze her eyes shut tight.

She would sit silent and unmoving, her eyes watering from squeezing them so hard, and wonder if the torture would ever end. That was when the biting would finally stop.

After one particularly brutal session of enduring hours of bites, she laid on the cool bathroom floor, her stomach empty after she'd puked for what felt like hours, and a realization came to her. The more she moved and screamed, the more agitated the spiders became. They were attacking what they thought was a threat in order to protect themselves.

From then on, she never moved.

DAMON STONE LEANED his hands against the brick wall of the Williams's building and stretched his calves, swallowing a groan.

"Too much for you, Damon?" Meredith asked from beside him.

"No."

"Really? The look on your face says something different," she said, elbowing him playfully in the side. "And I had to slow down the last couple of miles."

"Bullshit." He laughed, bending to elbow her back. He'd known Meredith for as long as he could remember, but they'd become closer friends in the last year. "I've just been sitting too much lately."

"Yeah, right." She laughed again as she reached for the door of The Magic Plate. "I said you didn't have to come with me, remember? I'm perfectly safe running on my own. I did it for years when Jack wasn't around, you know."

"I know." He grabbed the door from her as she walked in and followed her into the air-conditioned interior. The place was empty at the early hour, but the quiet was sometimes a welcome reprieve from the craziness of his life.

They always ended their run at the restaurant, more times than not grabbing a drink or breakfast. Sometimes others joined them. "Maybe I'll just join you and Jack more often to give you a run for your money." It would give him an excuse to run into Morgana—which would be both a pleasure and a torture. He was drawn to her in a way he'd never been drawn to another woman before, but she frustrated the fuck out of him. She was beautiful to look at with her long, straight blond hair, light gray eyes, and curvy body, but he wasn't a shallow man. He was attracted to more than her looks. The juxtaposition of her shyness and strong backbone was sexy as hell. She was also kind, and sometimes when she concentrated, she bit into her lower lip and all he could think about was picking her up and taking her someplace where they could be alone. He'd soothe that lip of hers with his own.

"Sure, fit us into your busy schedule, Mr. Businessman."

Meredith's comment brought him back to the present and he had to remember what he'd last said. Joining their run. Right. "Funny coming from you, Kettle." Meredith was busier than several people combined between running her business and co-leading the North American magic council with Jack. They both chuckled since they knew he was right.

"Want to just conjure a coffee and sit out back? I think Rowena said she'd come for a coffee before her first client."

"Sure, lead the way."

Meredith pushed open the door at the back of the kitchen that led to the patio, and the sight greeting them had all thoughts of coffee fleeing his mind.

Rowena was kneeling in front of Morgana, talking softly, but not touching her. "You're in Blue Mountain. You're safe, Morgana. What you're seeing isn't real." Rowena repeated the words again and again, offering Morgana reassurances.

Rushing to Morgana, he knelt down beside Rowena on the brick patio. He reached up to touch Morgana on the leg, but Rowena gently knocked his hand down and shook her head at him.

Morgana's light gray eyes were open and unfocused. It was as if she had gone somewhere deep into her memories.

His protective instincts kicked into high gear whenever he was with Morgana. He wanted her to be safe and happy. Yes, he wanted that for everyone, but more so for Morgana. Seeing her happy settled something inside him. He had to force himself to keep his instincts in check and not pick her up and carry her away.

Seeing her like this made his instincts worse and harder to resist. Her skin was paler than usual, and the ever-present lines of pain bracketing her eyes were deeper. Her long blond hair hung in a braid down her back and wisps floated around her angular face. "What happened?"

"I think she's having a flashback," Rowena said, glancing at him before looking back at Morgana. "Morgana, it's Rowena, your friend. Damon and Meredith are here too. We're at The Magic Plate in Blue Mountain. We're having coffee on the back patio. You're safe. Listen to the sound of my voice."

Rowena continued the explanations, but Damon wanted to push his friend out of the way and hold Morgana. He wanted to be the one to help her through her troubles, defend her against physical threats, and hold her to reassure her that she was safe and that nothing from her past could harm her here.

Time seemed to crawl by as he watched Morgana. Finally, she blinked, slowly coming back to them.

He'd been struck by Morgana's beauty from the moment he'd laid eyes on her, but it wasn't just her blond hair and light gray eyes. There was something about her that just spoke to him. His magic essence had stirred the first time he saw her, as if reaching for her—like she was a part of him— even though they'd never met before. A first for him.

Female companionship was a regular occurrence in his life—he was a healthy and attractive male in his thirties, after all—but he'd never been drawn to another person like he was to Morgana. He got a sense like he'd always known her.

"Rowena? Damon?" Morgana turned her head from side to side then dropped her face in her hands. "Oh my god. I'm so sorry."

He pulled one of the patio chairs over and sat, careful to keep his knees from touching Morgana's. Resting his forearms on his thighs, he hunched over, making himself appear smaller and hopefully less intimidating. He was a big guy and sometimes it was a disadvantage when he wanted to appear non-threatening. "No, Morgana. You have nothing to be sorry for."

"I need to go." She pushed out of her chair and hurried to the back door of the restaurant.

He was out of his chair, ready to go right after her.

"No. Let her go," Rowena said, her hand on his arm.

He was torn between yearning to help Morgana and listening to Rowena's advice. "She's scared and embarrassed."

"Damon, conjure yourself some coffee," Meredith said, pulling up a chair next to his.

He would have preferred a good scotch, but six-thirty in the morning was a little early for alcohol. Coffee would have to do.

The three of them sat in silence for a moment as they drank their coffees, but the itch to go after Morgana wouldn't leave him. "Rowena, are you sure I shouldn't check on her? Her headaches are getting worse. Maybe she needs someone to look after her, at least until the headaches stop."

"I know. She's holding so much in, and except for some superficial stuff, she won't talk about it. But, Damon, we can't force her. Morgana has to do this on her own time."

Even with her own comforting words, Rowena looked worried, like she wished she didn't have to follow the advice she dished out. But he knew she was right. It just went against every cell in his body to sit back and not persuade her to get help.

"Damon, don't do it."

He didn't have to ask what Meredith meant. "I won't use my specialty to persuade her."

Meredith looked skeptical. "You promise? I'm sure you used your persuasion on me when I freaked out after learning I was magic."

Rowena frowned. "Is that true? Did you use it on us?"

He just shrugged. He enjoyed life too much to admit to a very powerful magic woman that he may have used his magic to persuade her to listen when she didn't want to. He wasn't dumb.

"I'll let it go for now, but if she doesn't come down for the dinner tonight, I'll check on her," he said.

Meredith snorted. "I'm not sure that was much of a promise, but okay."

He stayed for a few more minutes to chat, then flashed home to get ready for work.

While he was showering, Morgana's image popped into his mind, like it'd done every day for the past ten months. But not just in the shower, also in his dreams or in the middle of a meeting. Even when he was reading a book, he imagined what it would be like having her nestled up against him. They'd both be reading and then they would stop to talk about their stories. They would kiss—could see them acting out some of their favorite love scenes.

Grabbing the body wash, he soaped himself up, then turned the water to cold and rinsed off quickly. He wouldn't jerk off to Morgana's image.

He respected her and refused to let her become an obsession. He just worried it was too late.

2

"*Hey*, gorgeous!" Morgana looked up as Reece left his office and came to stand in front of her. "You don't have to keep working, you know. You've done a lot today," he said, giving her one of his heart-stopping smiles.

After her flashback this morning, she'd escaped to her apartment until her headache had calmed down to just below a tortuous level. Then she'd gotten ready for the day and headed to the bakery to help out.

Reece understood what it was like to need to hide from others. He'd been spellbound last year while they were trying to remove another spell that had been placed upon him. The second spell had almost succeeded in killing him. Their mutual loss of control and power was something that few people could understand. She felt the shared experience had created a special bond between them.

The craziness of all the spells that could be put on a person was mindboggling. No one had been able to detect any spells on her: not Jack and Meredith, nor their counterparts around the world. Her magic was just weak, and she had headaches like millions of other people in the world.

It was something she just had to accept. She returned to the bowl and poured the batter into cupcake molds before acknowledging his comment. "I know. I just like it here."

"It's a good place to hide, you mean?"

"Yes, that too."

"Believe me, I get it."

Morgana loved hanging out with Reece. He was easy to get along with and he wasn't hard on the eyes either—bulging muscles all over and a smile that could make the most jaded woman smile in return. She hadn't known him before the second spell, but Jo had confessed to Morgana one day that she was worried about her brother. He'd become obsessed with working out and learning everything he could about magic. How that was a bad thing, Morgana didn't know. She liked this version of Reece and the banter between them was fun and flirtatious, but that's as far as it went. They'd both admitted their feelings for each other were more like those of a brother and sister.

They worked in silence for several minutes. Reece's baking skills were amazing, and she'd learned so much from him when she'd first arrived in Blue Mountain and even more in the last two months since he'd come out of the coma and grown stronger. Her own baking was decent, but her cooking kicked ass, although she stuck mostly to Mexican dishes, which were her favorite.

Reece playfully bumped her hip to nudge her out of the way as he placed a pan in the upper oven while she pulled one out of the lower oven. "Headaches still bad?" he asked.

"The same."

"Then what happened? You're a bit more sullen than usual today."

"Sorry."

"Morgana, I keep telling you, you never have to be sorry. You've been through a lot."

"Right." She set the pan to cool on a rack and took the full pan to the oven. "I had a flashback today and Rowena was there. Then Damon and Meredith walked in on me freaking out."

He looked at her in understanding. "Again, you don't have anything to be sorry for. Those things happen, and PTSD is a sneaky bastard. You never know when it'll creep up on you."

"I know… Did what happen to you?… being in a coma… did it affect you like this too? Do you think you have PTSD?"

He squeezed the back of his neck and rotated his head from side to side. "Yup, I've had my moments."

"Okay." What else was there to say? She wasn't going to ask someone to talk when she didn't want to talk either.

"We're ready for tomorrow and the family dinner will be soon. Why don't you take off? I'm going to head out soon too. My staff can close the bakery."

"Okay." She sounded like a broken record. "I'll see you in a while."

She waved to the front bakery staff when she left and headed to her apartment. The bakery was in the bottom of the first of the three Williams's buildings, and she lived in the third, so it wasn't far. If she could flash, she'd be there in a moment, but instead she had to take the elevator. Her apartment was a beautiful and spacious unit on the ninth floor with a view of the park across the street. She'd forever be grateful to the Williams family not only for welcoming her into their family and feeding and clothing her, but also for giving her a space of her own.

She was putting on her shoes to go down to dinner when there was a knock on the door. Since only the Williams family or people vetted by them could get through the spells around the building, she expected it was one of the W's—

shortened from the Little W's. The name always made her smile.

Fiona, Damon's mom, had said they had started calling the cousins by the shared nickname when they were younger because it was easier than listing all their names. It could refer to two, three, or four of them. To Morgana, it spoke of a connection and a past, something she couldn't remember having herself. She wondered what that would feel like—to have a nickname and to belong.

She pushed the thought from her mind as she pulled open the door and swallowed her gasp, ignoring the tingle of excitement low in her belly. "Damon, why are you here?" He was wearing a suit and looked good enough to eat. It was just too bad that, like a decadent dessert, he wasn't good for her.

"I wanted to check on you. See how you're doing."

"I'm fine. Are you going to the dinner?" Shit. She shouldn't have asked. Now he probably thought she wanted him there. She did, kind of, but he didn't have to know that. "I mean, if you're going, I'll meet you down there."

"Morgana, can I come in?"

She stepped back, let go of the door, and walked to the kitchen island. The great big piece of granite was enough to put a bit of distance between her and Damon. And by not shutting the door, maybe he'd take the hint.

Nope—gah! He shut the door and perched on a kitchen stool on the opposite side of the island.

"What do you want, Damon?"

"I'm worried about you. How are you really doing?"

His concern made her feel like bitch since she'd been trying to get rid of him. But if she was around him too often, she feared she'd be putty in his hands. Then it wouldn't be long before he became bossy and controlling like every other man in her past. Spending more time together would only encourage his bossiness.

Or he could kiss her. She'd like that, but then the bossiness might follow. It was probably better not to invite too much conversation. "I'm fine."

"You don't have a headache?"

"I'm fine." She sighed. She was being childish, but if she gave Damon an inch, he'd take a mile and break her down until she was swooning in his arms. That wouldn't do. Not only was he too persuasive and strong enough to control her, but her headaches were getting worse, making it harder for her to come up with the strength to resist him.

That was another problem. Even if Damon wasn't controlling, which he totally was, she couldn't burden him with her problems. It was probably time she left Blue Mountain. The last thing she wanted was to become an even bigger burden on the Williams family. She'd mooched off them enough already. Her migraines and headaches were getting worse, and she feared she was dying.

Damon got up and walked around the island. "You're not fine, Morgana. The headaches are wearing you down, and now you're having flashbacks."

The flashbacks weren't new, but that was another thing he didn't need to know about. "Damon, you can't fix this. Besides, I'll be okay."

He placed his fingers under her chin and gently tilted her head up. She was five foot three, but Damon was a giant. His shoulders were so wide they would have blocked her from seeing the sun if they'd been outside.

"I want to fix this. I hate seeing you in pain."

He was being too nice and if he continued, she'd be the one reaching up for a kiss. "I'm not a real fan either, but you can't do anything to help. Meredith and Jack and some other council leaders checked me out and if they can't find an answer, no one can."

She should step back so he'd drop his hand, but her feet

seemed to have a mind of their own, staying firmly planted in front of Damon.

Her eyes stayed fixed on his face and she watched his expression soften. She wanted him to kiss her, but she shouldn't.

He'd be both forceful and gentle in his kiss. She didn't know how she knew; she just did. If she went up on her toes, maybe he'd take the hint and lean the rest of the way down.

He tilted his head slowly toward her. Her wish was going to come true. She could already imagine the feel of his lips on hers. Just then, his lips touched hers in the softest of kisses and she opened her mouth to invite him in. He moved his hands to her hips and tugged her body flush with his. A moan escaped her at the feel of his hard length against her stomach.

No. Would she never learn? She couldn't start anything with a man who could control her, especially one who had the magical power to make her do whatever he wanted.

She took a step back and he dropped his hands. "I need to finish getting ready for dinner." Her voice sounded breathless to her own ears. She took a deep breath and stood straighter. "I'll meet you downstairs?"

He opened his mouth like he was going to protest and then nodded and flashed away.

Sagging back against the kitchen island, she brought her fingers to her lips. She could still taste him and found she had been right—he was the most decadent of desserts. A dessert that would be no good for her because a treat like that always tasted good while you ate it, but then regret set in later. He couldn't help it—it was just his nature. But that didn't stop her from wondering what it would be like to have someone. Someone who was always there for her. Someone who cared when she was in pain and wanted to comfort her.

Her parents had probably loved and cared for her, but she

couldn't remember them. The W's cared, but having someone like Damon care for her and love her would be so much different. Love? Could someone like Damon—bigger than life, successful, and controlling—care for her?

Oh my god. What was she thinking? Of course, he could care for her—while he controlled her.

She turned around and headed back to her bedroom to finish getting ready for dinner. It was definitely time to start thinking about leaving Blue Mountain, Colorado, and Damon behind. He was making her so crazy she didn't even know what she wanted or needed anymore.

Morgana sat at the end of the line of tables, closest to the kitchen. Another few minutes and she'd have been there long enough for etiquette's sake to make her escape.

It wasn't that she didn't love the family dinners and being included in them; she absolutely did. But her headache was now at the point of inducing nausea. If she didn't escape soon, she might end up more embarrassed than she was after her morning flashback.

"...headache?" Rowena asked.

"Oh sorry, what did you say?" She needed to pay better attention to the people talking to her or they would know something was up.

"I asked if you had a bad headache. Morgana, are you alright? You seem distracted tonight," Rowena asked, interrupting her thoughts.

"I'm fine, just tired. I got up early this morning to watch the sunrise and then I worked with Reece." Rowena had seen her up early but didn't know that Morgana never slept much anymore. No one did since she didn't tell anyone.

Rowena leaned over. "I think you're safe to leave now. You've stayed long enough, no one will say anything," she whispered.

Morgana hadn't realized she'd made her desire to leave so obvious, but she'd take the reprieve. "Thanks." Rowena was one of the nicest people she'd ever met. Morgana just wished she could open up to her about her past like Rowena wanted her to. "I'll see you later."

There was a connecting walkway between the two buildings, and a stairway off to the side of the kitchen would take her there. She looked down, hoping to avoid eye contact with anyone. She was almost at the door when she bumped into a hard chest.

Morgana looked up from a T-shirt stretched across a fit chest. "Oh, Isaac, sorry, I didn't see you."

He laughed and leaned down. "Because you had your head down and were trying to escape."

Startled, she opened her mouth to come up with a lie and saw him wink.

"Hey, I'm just teasing. This isn't my family either, and as much as I love being included, so many people at once can be overwhelming."

She smiled at him and focused on the door near the kitchen. Almost there.

"Wait," Isaac said, moving to stand in front of her.

"What's up?"

"Morgana, you know I'm a magic tattoo artist, right?"

"Yes. Well... I mean, I know you're magic and that you're a tattoo artist."

He laughed. "True. But what I meant is my specialty is magical tattoos. I can't draw them on non-magics, of course..." He ran one hand through his hair and huffed out a breath.

"What he means is he can create memorial tattoos with

embedded memories and tattoos with magical properties," Kate said, coming up beside Isaac.

"I know what I do, Kate."

"Hmmm," Kate said under her breath.

Morgana sensed some tension between the two, but her brain felt like it was trying to ram its way out of her skull, and she didn't have the energy to figure out what was going on with the two artists.

She half-turned toward the kitchen, pointing to the door. "I'm, ah, just going to go…" She let the words trail off as she again tried to make her escape.

Isaac reached out and briefly touched her arm before dropping his hand. "Sorry, Morgana, I wasn't clear. As Kate said, I can imbue magical properties in tattoos, and because of that, I can sense things in people. There've been several times where I've had a driven compulsion to put a particular tattoo on a person. I have that compulsion with you."

"What? You want to give me a tattoo?"

"It's more than that. I'm sensing something different in you and I'd like to discuss it with you."

"Different how?"

He ran his hand through his hair again, but he didn't appear nervous. "Will you come to my studio tomorrow? I've got appointments all day, but I can fit you in at seven p.m. if you'd be willing to talk to me."

Morgana had nothing against tattoos, had even thought about getting one, but Isaac sensing something in her made her nervous. What if she really was dying and he could tell? Did she want to know that right now? She would definitely need to leave Blue Mountain if she was dying. She didn't want to be a bigger burden than she already was.

She must have hesitated too long because Isaac spoke before she could think of a clever way to back out. "I've got to go, but I'll see you at seven tomorrow," Isaac said, walking away with Kate without giving her a chance to decline.

Well, she could always cancel on him tomorrow.

She turned and was almost at the door when she felt a sensation glide over her back, like warmth and lust all mingled together. Shit. Only one person gave her that feeling —Damon.

Why now? She'd had enough for one day and her head was killing her. Just as she reached for the doorknob, a large hand covered hers. "Morgana, let me escort you upstairs."

Oh for goodness' sake! She whirled on Damon and almost nose-planted right into his massive, solid chest, he was so close. She gave him a shove with both hands, but he didn't budge. "For Christ's sake, Damon. I'm a grown woman. Lots of people with headaches and no magic can get to their apartments on their own!"

She spun around and yanked on the door so hard it almost smacked into her. Damn, she really had to get a grip.

Damon didn't follow her and she was almost disappointed.

No, dammit! She didn't want him to follow her. He needed to leave her alone. What was with her today? She was so confused. She told herself she'd feel better once she had a good night's sleep.

She let out a laugh in the empty hallway. Right, like she ever got a good night's sleep. Passing through into the next building, she pressed the button for the elevator and luckily didn't have to wait long.

If sleep wouldn't come, she'd just relax, which was almost as good. When she'd first arrived at the Williams's, Meredith had given her a tablet loaded with some amazing romance novels, and she'd barely made a dent in the list of books. There'd be something on the tablet to take her mind off her never-ending headache and all her other problems.

Stepping out of the elevator when it reached her floor, she headed to her door, then stopped. Damon was standing in front of her apartment, one shoulder leaning against the wall.

His showing up was becoming a habit she wasn't sure she liked. "What do you want, Damon?"

"I heard Isaac and wanted to make sure you were okay with what he said."

She walked into her apartment and didn't even try to get him to stay outside. She didn't have the energy and it would have been futile anyway.

Maybe she would like him showing up if he acted like he cared about her and didn't want to control her.

"I'll go with you tomorrow to Isaac's."

Guh—so much for him being caring and not controlling. He was making her feel like she was some weak woman who couldn't even make it to an appointment and back on her own. She was better off going back to hating Damon's habit of constantly showing up. "No, Damon, you won't. I'm not a child and I don't need you babysitting me. I keep telling you, but you can't seem to get it through your thick skull!" She shouted the last three words, but then took a deep breath and calmed herself. Since she'd been in Blue Mountain, very few people had incited her temper, but Damon seemed to push all her buttons. And not always in a good way. "You can't force yourself on me, Damon."

"I would never force myself on a woman!"

"Oh, for goodness' sake! I wasn't talking about sex. And yes, you force yourself on me all the time. You've forced yourself in here twice today!"

"I care about you," he said softly as he moved around the kitchen island and stood in front of her. They stood much like they had before dinner.

The urge to kiss him hadn't gone away, but the need to be

independent was stronger. "Damon, please do not show up at Isaac's tomorrow. I need to go on my own."

"Will you text me when you're finished?"

She hadn't expected him to acquiesce so quickly, and it almost threw her for a loop. If he was willing to drop some of his controlling tendencies and come halfway, so could she. "Sure, I'll text you when I get back home."

Lifting her chin with his fingers like he'd done earlier in the evening, he tilted his head toward her. His eyes were such a dark brown it was like she was looking into a pool of chocolate when he focused his intense gaze on her. She loved chocolate.

"I want to kiss you, Morgana," he whispered as he lowered his head.

She tilted her chin up in expectation. "I want you—" No, no, she didn't. If she didn't get him to leave soon, he'd break down every single one of her defenses. She took two steps back. "Good night, Damon."

"Good night, Morgana," he said quietly before he flashed away.

"Gah!" she yelled at the empty room. She refused to be controlled again, but Damon was becoming harder and harder to resist. Tomorrow, she'd come up with a plan to leave. But tonight, she had a steamy book with her name on it.

An hour later, she threw the tablet on the nightstand as she stumbled out of bed and rushed to the bathroom. She sunk to her knees and flipped up the toilet seat just in time. She gagged, her throat rippling as she gripped the porcelain bowl. The convulsions started deep in her stomach, and she lost all control of her body as it took over.

She didn't know how long she heaved. Her throat was raw, tears streamed down her face, and the stench of vomit filled the small room.

She grabbed the sink and dragged herself up, then washed her face and brushed her teeth. The bathroom's small fan was quiet when she flipped it on. She hoped it would blow away the horrid smell.

After turning off the bedside light, she crawled into bed and pulled the blankets up to her chin, curling into herself. She'd see Isaac tomorrow and she hoped he wouldn't tell her she was dying like she suspected.

3

"What have you been up to?" Damon's mother asked.

Damon lifted his wine glass and took a sip of the pinot grigio. Wine wasn't his preferred drink, but he liked it enough and enjoyed sharing a bottle once in a while with his mother.

They were at a back table in a cozy Italian restaurant his mother had been coming to for years. They often dined at The Magic Plate, and his mom never missed a weekly family dinner if she could help it, but he expected that going there so frequently would be tough on her now that her close friends were dead. With the death of Meredith's mother, Elise, coming only a few months after Jo's and Reece's mother, his mom was the only one left out of the four women who had been close friends for years.

"Work is good. Busy. We're just in the process of doing our due diligence to invest in two more startups." He pressed the button on his phone where it sat next to his water glass. The screen lit up—no messages.

"Damon, honey, what's going on?"

He lifted his eyes from his phone and feigned innocence. "What do you mean?"

"You've checked your phone every few minutes since we sat down. Do you need to be somewhere?"

"No, it's fine." Guilt washed over him. He was too distracted and not giving his mom the attention she deserved. No one was guaranteed more time with anyone, he knew that better than most—except for maybe the Williams family. He had to cherish what time he did have with his loved ones and not let a certain beautiful, blond, stubborn woman distract him.

"Then it's Morgana."

His hand jerked and he discreetly used his magic to wipe off the spilled liquid before he put the glass down. "Why do you say that?"

She smiled at him, one of those indulgent mother-to-son smiles that said he was being obtuse. "You've been half in love with Morgana since the moment Jack and Meredith rescued her."

"I wouldn't call it love, but I do care about her." He took a sip of his wine and didn't say anything else. Better to be quiet and thought a fool than to open one's mouth and remove all doubt, as the saying went.

He got one of those *I don't believe you* looks that only a mom could give, and then she turned the conversation to her work, telling him about the businesses she was helping as a consultant.

So many of his friends no longer had their mothers. He'd forever feel the loss of his father but was grateful for how close he was with his mom and sister.

Losing his father had hit him hard, but not knowing what had happened to him was the worst part. His mom believed his dad was dead, and anyone who had known Curtis Stone knew he never would have voluntarily left his family. But his body was never found. There had always been a small inkling of a thought in the back of Damon's mind that his dad wasn't dead.

Maybe it was the lost teenager inside Damon, but he still hoped to one day have an answer to his dad's disappearance. It was something he couldn't let go of.

He shook off the dire thoughts and focused on what his mom was saying.

After they finished dinner, they ordered a peach pie to share for dessert. The home-grown fruit was a specialty at the restaurant and too good to pass up when they ate there.

"Did I ever tell you the story of when I first expected your specialty was persuasion?"

"I don't think so. Tell me." He'd heard the story a hundred times but wouldn't deny his mom the pleasure of reminiscing. Even if his friends had been around to hear his embarrassment, this wasn't one of those stories that made him cringe.

"You were with Jack, of course. The two of you could get into more trouble than any two kids I've ever met." She chuckled, obviously remembering the two of them when they were younger. "We were up at the lake with the Williams, Davis, and Hughes families, so you must have been around ten or eleven..."

He'd been eleven and remembered the day like it was yesterday.

Watching her, someone would think she had pushed a lock of hair out of her face, but they'd be wrong. His mother was subtle and elegant in her movements, but she'd magically dried her tears and glamoured her cheeks. Of those twelve adults who had been together that day, including his parents, his mom and Ben and Stella Davis were the only ones still alive.

So many in their lives had died so he tended to worry as

soon as something wasn't right with someone he cared about. Like Morgana's headaches. No one else seemed to think her headaches were unusual, but he sensed that they weren't normal—they caused her far more pain than a regular migraine. He didn't know how to help her and that wasn't a position he was used to being in.

"Meredith and Molly looked up to you and Jack. Even though you considered them almost babies since they were so much younger than you boys, I think you both still wanted to impress the little girls."

They'd been six to his and Jack's eleven.

His mom kept going. "The two of you decided you'd build a swing set, but of course, it didn't go as you originally planned. The plan became more and more elaborate as the day went on."

He still had the plan tucked inside a book in his room.

"You didn't want any help, and when your dad started to stand up to offer a hand, you magically pushed back, and your father plopped right back in his chair. I didn't know what had happened until later. He told me you'd pushed him back with persuasion. Your magic was still so new, and your father was such a powerful magic he could have easily ignored your push, but he didn't. He was so proud of you…"

She took a sip of her wine and flicked her hand like before, as if tucking back a strand of her hair. "Anyway… because you and Jack didn't have much magic, you had to conjure the swing set one piece at a time. Well… it had morphed into a swing set slash play structure by the time it was done. It was an enormous project, and you and Jack had to rest and recharge your magic in between conjuring pieces, but the two of you were so determined. When we went up to the lake a few weeks later, you pushed Molly on one of the swings for hours…" Her voice trailed off as if she was lost in the memory.

"Thanks for telling me, Mom." He reached across the table and gave her hand a quick squeeze. "So, has Kate showed you any of her work lately?" he asked, changing the topic to something that wasn't painful.

His phone vibrated and he looked down at the new text.

Morgana: Home. DO NOT come over. I'm fine.

He chuckled. Maybe he needed to use a bit of his persuasion on Morgana. He'd been trying to avoid it because he didn't want to take her personal choice away from her. But she was stubborn and someone had to figure out what was wrong before it got worse. All he wanted was for her to let him help when she needed it. She could be hurting herself more and putting her health at risk by not accepting help.

After dinner, he dropped his mother off at her house and walked her up to her door.

"Thanks, honey. I had a lovely evening."

"Me too, Mom. I love you." He kissed his mother's cheek and waited until she unlocked the door.

"I love you too. A bit of advice before you go…"

He didn't think he'd like what was coming next.

"Make sure Morgana is not just another acquisition to you."

He frowned, surprised by the comment. "What?"

"You've always been competitive, and I want to make sure you're not going after her because she's a challenge."

"I'm not." He wasn't, was he? No, he liked her.

"I hope not, and don't push her."

"I won't."

His mother laughed and patted his chest. "Yes, you will. But try not to do it too much. You could push her away. I don't know what she went through or how long she was held captive, but she's had everything taken away from her. I expect she'll need time to figure out who she is and to get her independence back. No matter how much you may want to rush in and save the day… don't."

"I'll try." He felt like a little kid again, promising to be nice to the girl next door.

He left his mom and drove downtown to his condo. Driving was a fun hobby since he could flash wherever he wanted, but it also helped keep up appearances with non-magics, something all magics needed to keep in mind to avoid being detected.

He parked the Jaguar beside his Land Rover, the vehicle he used for Colorado's winters, and made his way to his penthouse, purposely walking by the cameras so he was seen.

Once inside his apartment, he headed straight for his bedroom. The night was still early, but he'd had a long day. All he wanted to do was relax with a book. Although popping in to check on Morgana would be better, he could still hear his mom's advice in his head and resisted the temptation.

He got ready for bed, plugged in his phone, and picked up his eReader off the bedside table. Reading was one of his greatest pleasures and reading romance books was his dirty secret, although he'd let the cat out of the bag with Morgana a couple months ago.

One summer when he was in his teens, he'd been bored and had picked up one of Kate's romance books laying on the coffee table. Since then, he'd been hooked. The stories were about people and their struggles to overcome troubles and mistakes, and not just about romance. He loved the inner monologues and how people sorted out their problems. Throwing in some kidnappings or vampires just added some spice to the mix.

He'd switched from paperback to digital a long time ago, so he always had a book with him in public without anyone ever seeing the cover. The last thing he needed was one of his executive team members seeing him read a book with a half-naked man on the cover. Not that they would be bothered if they thought he was gay, but the teasing wouldn't end if they found out he read romance books.

Romantic suspense novels were his favorite, but he didn't mind a good paranormal either. He was three chapters into a new book when his phone pinged. His first thought was of Morgana.

Reaching for the device, he saw a text from someone on his management team. He sent a quick reply and was about to put the phone back on the charger but stopped.

Morgana had said not to come over. But she didn't say he couldn't check on her.

Hi, how was the appointment? He typed the words and paused. Five simple words shouldn't be too pushy. He pressed send and waited. After a couple minutes with no reply, he shoved his disappointment aside and went back to reading but kept his phone in his lap.

Ten minutes later his phone pinged again.

Morgana: Good.

God, the woman was infuriating. One word? He didn't deserve more—at least three or four words? No employee of his would've ever sent a text like that. They knew to answer his questions with some detail. Not go overboard, but give enough information that he didn't have to ask simple questions in return about what they meant.

What should he text back? She obviously wasn't going to elaborate. If he asked for details, would that be pushing? Fuck. He never hesitated or worried when he was communicating. He was a successful, commanding businessman and he'd always had a way with women. Morgana, though, made him feel like an insecure teenager.

Maybe he wasn't looking at her simple response in the right light. Maybe she'd been sleeping or she had one of her painful headaches. If she was hurting, he should go to her.

She couldn't blame him if he wanted to check on her welfare, could she? If no one else knew how bad her headaches were or that she had one, he was the only one who'd even know to check on her. Did that mean he *should* check on her? Fuck. He was a wreck. *No pushing.* He repeated it in his head like a mantra.

Goodnight, Morgana

Short and simple. Since he wasn't twelve years old, he never used text speak, unlike some of his staff.

The three little dots came up on his phone and he had to force himself not to hold his breath.

Morgana: G9

Not even a full word this time, only slang, but at least she hadn't ignored him. Since he hadn't seen her today and a couple of text messages couldn't possibly be seen as pushy, he'd check on her tomorrow. Going slow was going to kill him.

4

*M*organa walked into Isaac's studio the next day feeling even more nervous than she had the night before.

She'd spent all of yesterday fretting that Isaac was going to proclaim he'd sensed her imminent death. It was the only explanation she could come up with for her worsening headaches.

As soon as she'd walked into his studio last night and said hello, she'd burst out with her thoughts. "I'm dying, aren't I?"

He hadn't laughed. "I don't know." He pulled over a stool. "Why don't you sit down? I want to explain how getting a tattoo works." She sat on the stool, and he pulled over another, sitting in front of her, close but not touching.

He talked to her about the process, how he usually listened to what a client wanted and drew it right then, often using images from the net. "I usually charge for my time, and that includes drawing, but I'm not going to charge you."

"Why not?"

"Because this is different. I asked you here and I'm

compelled to tattoo you; I'm not sure why yet, I just feel it. Morgana, I want to give this to you and heal you if I can."

Her eyes started to well with tears, so she only nodded. Thinking about being healed had become a far-off dream. Her migraines were so bad that some days she thought she'd be better off dead. She'd never had suicidal thoughts before, at least in the last two years that she could remember, but some days the pain was more than she could handle.

"I need to sit quietly so I can soak in your presence to see what it tells me. It may take a bit." He closed his eyes.

Totally weird, but then, she wasn't an artist. Plus, he was magic, and she'd heard from one of the cousins that he was really powerful.

Ten minutes later he opened his eyes. "I don't think you're dying, but something evil is inside you."

She gasped and jumped from the stool. "Holy shit, I knew it!" She paced in the small space, looking at but not seeing the designs on the wall.

"Maybe I didn't say that quite right." He came over to her and placed a hand on her shoulder, stopping her pacing. "I think I can help you."

"Really?"

"Yes, but it means I'll need to tattoo you."

"Okay. When? Tonight?"

"Not tonight. I'm sure you're eager to get started right away, but it's been a long day for me and I don't know what the tattoo is going to look like yet."

"When will you know?"

"I'm not sure. It will come to me when it comes to me and though I usually can't say when that is, my magic essence is pushing me with urgency, so I have a feeling it will be soon."

Morgana gave him a small smile, hoping her disappointment didn't show. She'd worked up the courage to let Isaac tattoo her and hopefully cure her, but now, once again, she was going to have to wait for answers. She didn't understand his process, but maybe it was another artist thing. She'd have to trust that Isaac knew what he was doing.

He walked over to the desk in the corner and shook the mouse, waking up his computer. "I'm hoping the design will come to me tonight. I've had a cancellation tomorrow, can you come at one p.m.? If the design doesn't come, I'll contact you."

"I'll be here."

Last night and that morning had seemed to last forever as she waited for one p.m., but now it was time. "Isaac?" she called out when she walked in. The door to the studio had been unlocked, but the place looked empty.

"Come on back, I'm in the last room."

The night before, they'd only been in Isaac's office and she hadn't seen the rest of the place. She passed a bathroom and three small rooms, each containing shelves of ink and what looked like massage tables.

Stepping into the last room, black and white sketches on the far wall caught her eye. "Hi. Wow, did you draw all these?"

"Yes, some for clients, and others just needed me to reveal them. Have a seat."

Morgana took a stool, just like the one in his office last night when she thought he was going to tell her she was dying. She still wasn't convinced she wasn't.

"Coffee?" Isaac asked as he conjured himself a mug.

"No thanks. Water?" Caffeine probably wasn't a good bet with how jittery she already was. She accepted the bottle of water Isaac held out to her after conjuring it.

"Your tattoo came to me last night in my dream. It's going to be large." He picked up a piece of paper from the counter and passed it to her.

She glanced down at the drawing and felt a sense of awe.

"It's beautiful," she said in a whisper, not wanting to break the moment. The image would be inked on her body forever, whether it helped heal her or not. When she'd woken up after her restless night of sleep, she'd known she'd accept the image no matter what it looked like. If she didn't, she'd always wonder if it could have helped—if she survived.

At first glance she saw vines and flowers winding in a circuitous path along the paper. The longer she studied the drawing, the more she picked out. Tiny fairies peeped out from behind leaves and held something small in their palms. "Are those thorns?" she asked, pointing to part of the drawing.

"Yes, they represent the evil that will be pulled out of you."

"Wow." She looked at the paper again, trying to imagine how it would look on her body. And no matter how hard she tried, she couldn't. She was just going to trust Isaac. It wasn't lost on her how big a risk she was taking putting herself in someone's hands, but whether it healed her or not, she loved the design. "This came to you in a dream?"

"Yes. It's only happened two other times in my life. One was a huge back piece – a lioness and her two cubs for a woman dealing with some trauma in her past."

"Did it help?"

The corner of his lip lifted in a small smile, dropping some of the seriousness he seemed to wear like a shield of armor around him. "Yes, it did."

"Where would you tattoo this? Uh, on my body I mean... I don't know the lingo."

"I'd like to place it on your torso, on the left side. Some say the left is your feminine side and it carries the energy of desire and correlates to your past experiences. I'll place a smaller design—this portion here"—he pointed to a smaller drawing on the bottom corner of the image—"on your right side. That will give it balance, forcing the evil out of you, and not allowing it to shift. I see this image being in bright colors."

"Okay, I'm in."

"Then let's get started. I'll print the images on transfer paper and position them where we want them on your skin.

"Since you're magic, I would normally have no problem using my magic to dull your pain, but I don't think I should. I'm worried if I do anything to interfere with the inking process that it will alter the power I expect the tattoo will have on you. Just let me know if it becomes too much. We'll take breaks, and depending on how it goes, we'll get the outline done today."

"Okay, I'll let you know, but I think I have a pretty high pain tolerance." She didn't tell him why—that it had been put to the test for years with different types of torture. She wasn't ready to tell anyone all of that yet.

It wasn't long before they were ready to start.

Morgana laid on her back on the massage table and Isaac rolled her away from him until she was in the right position for him to reach the area he'd be working on.

"You ready?"

She let out a long, slow breath. "Yes," she said, but she didn't know if she was telling the truth.

DAMON FLASHED to the hallway outside of Morgana's apartment, hoping for a good reception. She'd popped into his mind a hundred times during the day, and he reached for his phone to text her almost as many times. But he'd refrained and hadn't texted her since he'd said good night the night before.

He'd convinced himself that since he hadn't come over last night it wouldn't be too pushy to pop in today. He knocked on the door and waited. After a minute he knocked again, but she still didn't respond. It hadn't even occurred to him that she wouldn't be home. She never ventured out very far, usually staying within one of the three Williams's buildings.

He flashed to the back of the kitchen, out of sight of any non-magic staff that might be around, and then checked the front and the back of the restaurant. No Morgana.

Next, he flashed to Jack's place and ended up staying for a drink because he was trying not to panic and jump to the worst-case scenario. Meredith reached out to her cousins and reported that no one had seen Morgana all day, which happened occasionally but wasn't the norm.

By the time he made his way back up to Morgana's place forty minutes later, he was sure she'd be there since she wasn't at The Magic Plate or with the cousins. The logical part of his brain told him she could have gone to a movie or shopping. He just couldn't imagine her going alone.

His knock was greeted with silence once again. Pulling on his magic, he scanned the interior of the apartment for signs of life. It was a bit invasive, but he was too worried to care. He just got the feeling that there was more going on with her than anyone realized. With her not answering, he was only just under panic mode now.

He sensed one person inside. There wasn't a spell on the door, so it was child's play to magically pick the lock.

The foyer was dark when he stepped inside. "Morgana?"

It was one thing to push himself into her apartment, but another to interrupt her and invade her privacy if she was doing something she didn't want him to see.

At the hallway that led to the bedrooms and bathroom, he called her name again, then listened.

He heard a sound that seemed to come from the last bedroom. His steps were silent as he walked to the bedroom and stopped outside the door that was a few inches ajar.

He listened again and this time he heard a pained moan. "Morgana?" Fuck privacy, she was hurt. He barged into the room and the smell of vomit wafting from the attached bathroom hit him as he entered.

Morgana was curled up in a ball on the bed, blankets pulled up to her chin. Kneeling beside the bed, he called her name again. "Morgana, it's Damon. Can you hear me?"

Her lashes fluttered. "Damon?" She opened her eyes and then squeezed them shut. "Light. Hurts."

If he hadn't been right next to her, he would have missed her whispered response. The curtains were mostly closed, but a small sliver of light came in from the streetlights outside. He flicked his hand toward the curtains, closing the gap. Then he turned toward the hallway and disappeared the light. He did the same for the bathroom light and made the bedroom door quietly swing closed.

"The room is dark now," he said, keeping his voice low. He pulled on his magic again and sent some to his eyes to heighten his vision in the almost complete darkness.

Her long blond hair fanned out like a halo and contrasted with the deep shadows below her eyes. He watched as she slowly opened her eyes, blinking several times. "Water?" she asked, her voice an almost imperceptible croak.

He conjured a glass of water and helped her sit up to drink. After only a few sips, she flopped back against his arm, and he lowered her to the mattress before placing the glass on the nightstand. "Morgana, what's wrong?"

"Just a headache."

"A headache made you throw up, drained you of energy, and requires you to be in complete darkness?" She winced as his voice rose on the last word.

"It happens."

"You mean this isn't the first time?"

He laid the back of his hand on her forehead; she didn't feel hot. "I'm not a great healer, but maybe I can take some of your pain away."

"No!" She lifted her head to look at him and winced. "Don't, please. Jack and Meredith tried, and the pain got worse. I just need to sleep."

It ate at him that there wasn't anything he could do. The last time he'd felt this useless had been years ago when his father had disappeared. Not one time since that day had he been in a situation where he didn't have some kind of a solution. But neither his magic nor his money could take away her pain.

"Okay, I'll just stay then in case you need anything."

"Go."

"No, Morgana, I can't leave you like this."

"Yes, leave. I need sleep."

"You sleep and I'll be here in case you need something."

"No."

He wanted to pull on his hair and scream. This woman was so infuriating. He didn't understand why she wouldn't accept help. "Where's your phone?"

She stuck one arm out from under the blankets and pointed toward the dresser. He retrieved the phone and pressed the lock screen to check that it was charged and put it on the nightstand beside the glass of water.

"Here's your phone. Don't hesitate to call me if you need anything."

Her eyes were closed, and lines of pain were etched across her face. He knelt beside the bed again, getting close to her. "Did something happen today?"

"Tattoo," she said without opening her eyes.

"Let me see. Is it infected? Why didn't Isaac stop if your headache was getting worse?"

"Go, Damon."

"Let me see your tattoo. I should check it."

"No. Go."

He couldn't go. Something inside him was pushing him to stay. Fuck. No one ever told him to go—they listened and followed directions. This stubborn woman was driving him crazy. Turning the lights off and getting water wasn't enough. With her pain being so debilitating, she needed more than water and sleep and he was going to find out what.

"Go," she said again, her eyes still closed.

He wavered, then remembered his mother's words. He had to respect Morgana's wishes, even if went against every fiber of his being. "Fine, I'll go, but call me if you need anything." He kissed her on the forehead and then left the room, closing the door softly.

In the living room, he looked around at how Morgana had made the place a home. Pictures of her and the cousins lined the bookshelves, along with knickknacks and books. He picked up her tablet laying on the table and saw it wasn't locked. Her reading app was open so he perused the titles and chuckled as he recognized some of his favorite romantic suspense authors.

He put the tablet back on the table and paced to the window. The impulse to ignore her wishes and walk back into the bedroom to watch over her all night beat at him.

Leaving while she was in her current state was out of the question. What if she worsened? She might need something. Sinking down onto the couch, he conjured himself a scotch and soaked in the silence. A few minutes later his phone pinged. He debated ignoring it. If it was work, it could wait, but what if it was Morgana? He'd told her to call if she needed anything.

Morgana: Go home.

How she knew he was in the living room, he didn't know. Her magic wasn't strong enough for her to detect him. Maybe he was becoming predictable.

Damon: I'm going. He sent the text and flicked his hand toward the apartment door, making it open and close. Then he sat on the couch for hours, listening for her. At four in the morning, he went to her bedroom and quietly opened the door. When he heard her soft, steady breathing and knew she was asleep, he shut the door again and flashed home.

He'd check on her again tomorrow—today.

5

*M*organa ushered in the morning with coffee and vomiting. Now she was back at Isacc's bright and early because he usually didn't work in the mornings and could fit her in. Pushing open the studio door, she had an odd mix of anticipation and trepidation sparring in her mind. She didn't feel great but definitely better than she had last night; sleep had helped and even though her stomach was empty, she wasn't nauseous any longer.

She wanted to have the tattoo finished to see if it brought any relief, but she wasn't sure she would live through the experience to find out. "Isaac?" she called out.

"In the back."

Isaac looked up from a drawing when she walked in. "I'm going to add six small sunflowers to your design," he said in way of greeting. "They're good for the cardiovascular system if you ingest them, but I'm hoping by adding them to the tattoo, they'll help with blood flow to push the evil out of you."

"If that's true, then it feels like you already added them." She huffed out a harsh laugh.

"What happened?"

"I barfed up lots of evil last night."

"Was the headache worse too?"

"It definitely wasn't better."

"You okay to continue?"

Morgana doubted it, but she had to do something because she couldn't keep living this way. "Yes, let's do this."

Isaac nodded and went to the shelves full of ink and started pulling down bottles. "Okay, I'll draw the sunflowers freehand and weave them into the vines down your left side. Climb up onto the table in the same position you were in yesterday," he said once he had everything ready. "I want to check that you're healed."

Morgana stripped off her sweats and hoodie to reveal the same shorts and bathing suit top she'd worn the day before. Isaac had conjured her a body pillow and blanket to hold against her front the day before, and besides providing warmth, they preserved her modesty when he had to undo her top so he could tattoo where the string had rested.

He'd asked to heal her yesterday before she left his studio, but she'd been hesitant. If he didn't heal her, she'd have to wait two to three weeks before the next appointment as her skin naturally healed. From the way she'd been throwing up lately, she didn't think she'd live that long.

It wasn't that she didn't want him to heal her. It was the unknown of whether the healing would make her headache worse, like it had when others had tried. He'd promised to only heal at skin level. He'd healed her skin when she'd left the night before and whether it made the headache worse or not, she didn't know. All that mattered was that her skin was healed and they could continue.

She climbed onto the table and Isaac handed her another blanket and body pillow. "I disappeared the ones you used yesterday, for sanitary reasons—you know, blood and all—so these are new."

"Thanks," she said as she arranged herself comfortably on the table to begin another long session.

"Everything looks good. Healed. You ready?"

"As I'll ever be."

The first press of the tattoo machine was the toughest, just like the day before. She soon settled into the strange scratchy sensation and slight pain.

Isaac had jazz music playing in the background and she let her mind drift as he worked. No one specific train of thought stuck—her mind wandered, like continual tabs opening on an internet browser.

She still wasn't convinced she wasn't dying, but last year she hadn't thought she'd even live this long. Between the rollercoasters of boredom and fearing for her life, she never knew what to expect from day to day.

Images from the day of her rescue popped into her head; she could picture Meredith coming to rescue her mom. Morgana wondered if her own mom would have been something like Meredith's. Would she have been willing to die for her?

Another browser tab opened in her mind and this time she saw her first Williams's family dinner and how easily she'd been accepted into the large group. She was sure they would miss her if she left, but she'd been in their lives such a short time, they'd get over her. Her leaving wouldn't be like losing a family member.

"Okay, let's take a break. We've been at this for two hours."

It took a moment for Isaac's words and the loss of feeling of the tattoo machine to penetrate her bouncing thoughts.

After he helped her off the table, she used the washroom and then walked over to the large mirror on the wall.

Isaac was the most talented artist she'd ever seen. The fairies looked so real as they peeked out amongst the leaves. The colors were vibrant, seeming to explode off her skin. "It's beautiful, Isaac," she said quietly, in awe.

He handed her a bottle of water as he inspected his work. "How's the head?"

"Not bad." Her headache had been getting worse, but it wasn't as bad as it'd been the night before.

Morgana climbed back onto the table and hoped she'd make it through the rest of the session.

They took breaks every hour and were in their fifth when her headache worsened, the pain no longer in just her head. It radiated down her neck and shoulders. Little zings of pain flared over her upper body. She squeezed her eyes shut and blew out her breaths in small pants.

Isaac stopped working. "It's getting worse, isn't it?"

"A little." She hoped he wouldn't call her out on the lie because she didn't want him to stop. If he stopped, it might not work, and she didn't know if she could bring herself to come back and withstand the intensity of her worsening headache all over again.

"You said trying to stop the pain made it worse, but what if I sent some soothing calm into you?"

"I don't know."

"How about if I try just a bit and see how it goes?"

"Sure," she said, still panting.

He'd finished the large tattoo on her left side and now was halfway through the smaller one on her right, having finished the outline the day before. While still lying on her side, Isaac placed one hand on her hip and the other on her shoulder. "Let me know if it's too much."

Cool air flowed through her like a breeze on a warm sunny day. The muscles in her arms and neck relaxed like an elastic going slack and she felt her headache ease from a twelve out of ten down to an eight. Hopefully, it would be enough to get her through.

"Better?" Isaac asked as he sat back on his stool.

"Much. Thank you."

"Okay, let's get this finished."

A half hour later, her headache ratcheted back up to a nine. She needed a distraction. "How did you learn this was your specialty? The magic part, not the tattoo part, I mean."

"For me, they're one and the same," he said as he moved to the final portion of the tattoo, located a few inches above her hip. "I was born with an artistic ability, and I've sketched for as long as I can remember. My dad was a tattoo artist, so I've always known this is what I wanted to do."

"Does your dad create memorial tattoos and imbue special properties in them too?"

"Yeah, that's where I got my talent from. He was an amazing artist."

"Was—? Oh, sorry, you don't have to answer that."

"It's okay. He died when I was twenty-three—a car accident."

"I'm sorry."

"Thanks."

"Are you an only child?"

He hesitated and she wondered if she'd asked something too personal. People had asked her the same question and she never knew how to answer. Was she an only child? Or did she have a whole slew of brothers and sisters out in the world somewhere?

"I had a brother, but he died." He put down the tattoo machine. "That's it. Let me clean you up so you can see, and then I'll heal your skin."

Morgana knew when a topic was closed. She adjusted her bathing suit top and took Isaac's offered hand to help her step off the table.

Her feet hit the floor and her knees buckled. She dropped to the floor like a hundred-pound bag of flour and grasped her head with both hands.

"Morgana?"

Her headache went from a nine to what felt like a nine hundred in a split second. She panted like she was about to give birth, and the breathing did shit to help. "Pain," she said, the only word she could gasp out.

Isaac knelt in front of her and gently placed his hands on her shoulders. She felt the cooling air like before, but it didn't offer her the same relief.

"S...sick," she said before clamping a hand over her mouth.

A large bowl appeared in front of her and she grabbed it with both hands as her body revolted. Convulsions surged up her throat, the muscles spasming as her body purged bile from her empty stomach.

Tears streamed down her face and her nose ran, upping her embarrassment level as she leaned over the bowl. It felt like forever before she regained control of her body.

"I'll take that," Isaac said, and the bowl disappeared. He handed her a damp towel and she wiped her face.

"I...I'm so sorry. I didn't mean—"

"Stop," he said quietly, interrupting her. "There's nothing to be sorry for. There are clean toothbrushes in the bathroom cabinet above the sink, or I can help you."

She looked up from where she was still kneeling on the floor. Isaac waved his hand in front of her and she felt a clean, minty taste in her mouth.

"I didn't know that was possible." She accepted the hand he held out and he hauled her up, guiding her to a chair.

"Really? You weren't taught that when you were little?"

She shrugged. Maybe she had been, but she'd never know.

"I think you should call someone to walk you home, or maybe carry you."

"No, I'll be okay." She didn't want to confess to this kind man that she was tired of being a burden when he'd just taken two days out of his life to work on her for free. Then had to deal with her puke. Talk about a burden.

"You're not okay, but I get it. Let's deal with your tattoo and then I'll walk you home. It's not like it's far." He looked down at her and grinned; his shop was housed in the bottom of the building next to hers.

Once he healed her skin and she'd put her clothes on, he wound his arm around her and helped her get to the elevator in her building. "You sure you don't need me to go up with you?"

"No, I'm okay."

"If you say so, but Morgana…"

She tilted her chin up to meet his eyes when he paused.

"None of this is your fault. I know what it's like to feel guilty for something, but you didn't cause this."

Giving him a small smile, she walked onto the waiting elevator.

If only Isaac was right—but he wasn't. She didn't remember all of her time in captivity, but she somehow knew she'd brought this on herself. There was something truly wrong with her, and not just the evil Isaac's tattoo was trying to purge.

6

*M*organa was sure she was dying.

She had managed to stumble into her apartment when she got home but couldn't make it to her bedroom, her legs too weak to carry her. Using her furniture as crutches, she'd inched her way to the sofa and collapsed.

Her throat was raw from puking and her entire head pounded like her brain was trying to break free from her skull. Even her eyelids thumped with the beat. She hadn't been able to sleep, only lay helplessly like a small child.

For ten months, she'd wished she could remember her life from before Copeland had brought her to Blue Mountain. But now she wasn't so sure trying to remember was worth it. Whatever evil was crawling through her body must be inside her because she'd done something equally as evil to deserve the slow, torturous pain that was eating her alive.

Copeland used to sneer at her, telling her she was useless and evil. Useless she began to believe, but not evil. She'd been unkind to the healer and probably to others. But she hadn't wanted to believe that she'd been evil like Copeland.

Maybe he'd been right.

A memory of Copeland popped into her head. He'd moved her to Blue Mountain, Colorado, but at the time, she hadn't known where she was. Just that it was a new place. She shuddered at the remembrance.

She'd arrived in the pitch darkness of night, but then lost all track of time. The room was stark white and small with no windows. The only furniture was a twin bed, pushed against the back wall, with one pillow and a single, thin blanket.

One of Copeland's men brought her a meal and escorted her across the hall to a bathroom twice throughout the night. Fear and boredom clawed at her in equal measures.

But fear took over when Copeland walked into the room hours later. In the doorway behind him, she saw artificial light illuminating the hallway and figured it was nighttime again.

"Are you enjoying your new accommodations, Morgana?"

She stayed quiet. There was no right answer to his question, there never was.

"You brought this on yourself, Morgana. If you were nicer and not so selfish, I wouldn't have had to separate you from the others."

She didn't know who the others were. It was as if her past had been wiped clean when they'd arrived the night before. She couldn't call forth a single memory of who she'd been prior to Copeland bringing her here, wherever here was.

They'd traveled in the dark of night on a private plane, but she hadn't seen an airport or gone through customs. It occurred to her that even though she didn't remember anything, she knew who Copeland was and what he was capable of. It felt as if only specific memories had been embedded in her brain. She knew he'd never hesitate to use his magic to his advantage, and he must have used it to get them here.

"I promise I'll be nice. Please, just let me out so I can see the sun," she said quietly, hoping her voice didn't display any resemblance of a demand.

"See? Selfish. It's always about you. You don't care about

anyone but yourself," he sneered at her while he half turned toward the door.

How could she care about others when she couldn't remember anyone else? "I don't know what I've done. I don't remember." Her voice was almost a whine now, but she couldn't help it. "If you tell me what I've done, I'll try to fix it. I'll do whatever you say."

"Of course you will, or I'll bring out the spiders."

One second she had no memories and the next she had a memory pop into her mind, as clear as if it had happened just moments ago. In the new memory, she was strapped to a chair and felt a sickly sensation of thousands of legs all over her as spiders crawled up her body. She gasped and her chin shot up as she looked up at Copeland.

"That's what will happen if you defy me, Morgana. Now, come here."

She hesitated for a moment. Within seconds, another memory popped into her mind, worse than the first, and she scrambled off the bed. Standing in front of Copeland, she kept her eyes lowered.

"That's better," he said as he placed his hands on her shoulders.

A tingling sensation started deep within her as her magic essence, what little there was of it, stirred. The feelings intensified and her knees buckled. Copeland's hold somehow kept her upright as the stirring of her magic turned into pain.

Her mouth opened and she felt the scream rip from her, but there wasn't any sound.

"I won't have you screaming the place down," Copeland said, his voice commanding but quiet. "I will take your magic when I want, and you will be grateful that you're still alive."

He pulled his hands from her shoulders, and she fell forward, catching herself on her hands and knees. When she had enough strength to lift her head, Copeland was gone.

Before the image had even begun to fade from her mind, Morgana shoved to her feet and prayed her legs would work. She raced to the bathroom as fast as she could, falling into the wall twice as she stumbled along the hallway.

Shoving open the door, she dropped to her knees, heedless of the hard tile floor, and flipped up the toilet seat. Heaves engulfed her as she leaned over the porcelain bowl, but she had nothing left to expel.

How could she have forgotten that he'd drained her magic almost daily? Was she now losing memories from the time with Copeland? What was next? Would she lose the memories she'd made after being rescued? Maybe the evil was attacking her mind as well as her body.

With no strength to get up, she wiped her mouth and nose on her sleeve and lay down on the tile. The cool surface felt good on her face but did nothing to relieve the pounding in her head and the aches in her body. Nor could it wipe away her feelings of hopelessness.

She hadn't fought Copeland. She'd just let him take what he'd wanted again and again. The only time she'd ever done anything was when she said she was injured, and that had likely gotten the healer killed. A sudden thought occurred to her—was she a murderer? If Copeland's claims about her being evil were true, then maybe the evil wasn't something foreign to her, but part of who she really was.

What would the cousins think if they learned how truly selfish and weak she was? How could she stay with the people who'd welcomed her into their family when she didn't deserve them? And what about Damon? He was caring, and honorable, and strong—even when he acted controlling—far more than she deserved.

If she had the strength, she would get up and get her tablet from the living room. She'd start looking for a job and eventually find a place to go. Some place where no one knew her history and pitied her or learned about the horrible things she'd done. But would she die alone if she left? Maybe that was part of her punishment.

Pushing onto her arms, she tried to get to her hands and knees, but her elbows buckled, and she crashed to the floor. The pounding in her head increased and she screamed, not able to hold back the agony.

She grasped the sides of her head and squeezed, but the pain only increased until her vision blurred, her arms lost all strength, and she fell back to the floor.

The bathroom came in and out of focus as she lay there, barely able to move. She lost all track of time as she breathed through the pain.

This was it. Isaac's tattoo hadn't worked, and she was going to die.

Dying on a cold bathroom floor by herself, was not how she thought she'd go. There were worse ways and places to die, but she didn't want to take her last breath alone, even if she deserved it.

Rolling onto her back, the small movement zapped so much of her remaining strength. She laid still for a couple minutes, trying to catch her breath, but the pounding of her headache didn't ease. Flopping like a fish running out of air, she struggled to get her hand into the pocket of her sweatpants. She lifted her butt while trying to find the pocket opening and after several attempts, pulled out her phone.

She was too weak to do anything more and rested her back on the tile floor, closing her eyes. After about a minute —thought it could have been an hour—she brought the phone close to her eyes and squinted against the light to focus on the screen. It took her three tries to select Damon's name in her contacts as her fingers shook and her vision blurred.

Morgana: Help.

Typing that one word and pressing send took the last of her energy. She closed her eyes and let her hand fall to the floor, the phone making a small thud as it hit the tiles. If someone was going to watch her take her last breath, she didn't want it to be one of the cousins. They'd already been through so much. But was she right to put Damon through that? It was too late to decide now. She hoped he was strong enough to get through it.

The sharpest of pains tore through her head and body, cutting off all conscious thought as it engulfed her. She opened her mouth to scream, but no sound came, her throat silent in her pain.

Then it stopped.

A sudden small sting pinched her right side and then it was gone. All that remained was a strange sensation in her head and body, like a lightness she'd never felt before. She rolled her head to the side and glanced up at the toilet and bathtub as if the porcelain fixtures would have the answers. After several seconds, she realized what the strange feeling was.

She no longer felt any pain.

Her head wasn't pounding. The usual tightness in her shoulders and neck was gone.

Rolling over to her side, she got up on her hands and knees and waited for the ever-present pain to come back. A minute later when the lightness continued and the pain hadn't returned, she stood. Her legs didn't have any of their usual stiffness.

Morgana turned toward the mirror. "Oh shit!"

7

*D*amon nodded at Jack. "Great. I'll put together the paperwork." Jack had just accepted an opportunity to invest in one of Damon's new ventures.

"Thanks, appreciate it."

"It's been a while since we've had the chance to talk face to face. It says something about life when all we have time to do is send paperwork back and forth." Damon picked up his drink and swirled the dark liquid inside the glass before taking a sip.

"Yeah, that's on me. With work and the council, I've been busy."

"You going to keep working with the FBI now that you have the council?" Damon asked.

"At least for now. Having my boss and the Special Agent in Charge of our division both be like father figures works in my favor when it comes to the council. Plus, you know Ben and Frank have been pushing me to start up a new council for years. I don't think they expected me to quit the FBI right away, but they'd be supportive if I did."

"True." Damon took another sip of his drink and pulled

out his phone to check the time. He'd texted Morgana hours ago but hadn't heard back from her. There was a message notification. He opened the app and his breath hitched.

Morgana: Help

Fuck! The text had come in ten minutes ago and he hadn't felt it vibrate. He stood, almost knocking the stool over. "I've gotta go."

"I've got this," Jack said, already pulling out his wallet. "Your mom?"

"No. Morgana." Damon gave Jack a nod and rushed to the bar's front door. He'd driven to the local pub but flashing to Morgana's would be faster. He'd get his car later. Morgana had never reached out before, and the message was too cryptic for his liking.

Rushing to the back of the building, he threw up a light protection spell in case there were security cameras around and flashed to the Williams's building.

He flashed right into Morgana's apartment, landing in the foyer.

He frowned when he saw Meredith standing by the sliding glass doors looking out, her hair long and glossy in the low light coming from a lamp on a side table. "Meredith? Did Jack call you?"

She turned around and Damon felt his world tilt.

From the back, she'd had a striking resemblance to Meredith—same build and hair—but he knew it wasn't her now that she was facing him. She wasn't identical to Meredith and there was something else that was different, perhaps how she carried herself.

"Morgana?" He walked toward her, his steps slow as he waited for his world to right itself.

"It's me." She bit her lower lip and her gaze darted around the room before settling back on him.

The mannerisms were all Morgana but that was where

the similarities ended. Her hair was still long, but her straight blond locks were now brunette; her gray eyes were now hazel. Even her body shape was different.

"What happ—" He cut himself off as Meredith's yell came from behind him.

"Morgana! Jack said Damon—"

Damon and Morgana watched Meredith as she came toward them, the same realization dawning on her expression. "Oh my god!"

Meredith reached forward tentatively, as if worried her hand would touch a mirage. She laid her hand on Morgana's arm. "Molly?" Meredith asked.

So many times when Molly and Meredith were little, Damon had been caught off guard as to who was who when he wasn't fully facing them.

"Meredith, I asked you to wait," Jack said as his feet touched down beside them. "We don't know what's—" Jack stopped talking abruptly and looked between the sisters. "What the hell?"

Morgana glanced between them like a deer caught in a car's headlights, as if not sure of what to do.

Meredith's eyes welled with tears as she wrapped her arms around Morgana and then lifted her eyes to her husband. "Jack, it's Molly. Can you believe it?" Meredith turned back to Morgana. "I mean, it is you, right? Not many people have the ability to become someone else like Simon."

Damon watched as Meredith turned to her husband, as if he would tell her what she wanted to hear, and Morgana bit her lip again and looked at him with wide eyes.

He could only imagine what they must be feeling, being sisters, as his emotions were practically boiling over. He grasped Morgana's arm and gently pulled her away from Meredith, hoping she'd let go. "Let's sit down. This is a shock for everyone." Damon wanted to push everyone out of the room and have Morgana to himself, but if she was actually Molly, and he thought she was, these people were her family.

He was going to have to be sure because he'd seen Simon Hughes, Jo's husband, take on someone else's appearance, but his gut was telling him this was his Morgana.

"Morgana! What's wrong?" Rowena called as her feet touched down in the foyer, Reece landing next to her. "Meredith said you were hurt."

He knew the exact moment when Rowena and Reece spotted Morgana. Both their heads swiveled back and forth between Meredith and Morgana, like spectators at a tennis match.

"Molly? No, that's not possible! What on earth is going on? You're in Morgana's place, does that mean…" Rowena's voice trailed off as she walked over to the group.

"I am Morgana." Morgana's words were barely above a whisper and Damon could swear he saw guilt written on her face.

"Hey, beautiful, it's okay, come and sit down." Reece walked up to Morgana and guided her to the sofa, gently forcing her to sit, before sitting beside her.

Damon wanted to push Reece out of the way and take his spot. He wanted to be the one to comfort Morgana, but he let her family surround her… if this was her family. He took the chair kitty-corner to the couch.

Rowena sat in the opposite chair and Jack leaned against a wall, pulling Meredith's back into his front and wrapping his arms around her. He couldn't imagine what she must be feeling with seeing her twin, almost a mirror image of herself, after burying her over twenty years ago.

Damon lifted his chin at Jack. "Jack? Are you thinking about Simon?"

"Hey! Damon, how can you say that?" Meredith didn't wait for him to answer and spun around to face her husband.

"You can't think that Morgana—er, Molly—is just someone with Simon's specialty?"

Jack held Meredith's arms and his gaze softened as he looked into her eyes. "I don't know. I didn't think that what Simon could do was even possible until I saw it myself."

"Beautiful," Reece said, ignoring the others and getting Morgana's attention. "Tell us what happened."

Morgana fish-mouthed a few times and Damon thought he was going to crawl out of his skin, seeing her so lost. He conjured a glass of water and kneeled in front of her. "Here, have a drink and take your time."

She took the glass from him and as she drank, he used his magic to move the large heavy armchair next to the couch. He ignored Jack's chuckle as he sat in the chair, focusing his attention on Morgana. When she was finished with the water, he disappeared the glass and reached for her hand. He took it as a good sign when she didn't pull away.

Morgana gave him a small smile and then looked at the others in the room before turning her body toward him. She fish-mouthed again, and Damon gave her hand a small squeeze to urge her to continue.

"Isaac gave me a tattoo." She turned her head to look at Jack. "He'll be able to tell you if this is the tattoo that he put on me, Morgana. He said that not only did he embed healing into the tattoo, but he can also sense when he needs to give a tattoo to someone."

She turned back to Reece. "Anyway... He said he felt evil inside me, and he needed to give me the tattoo that came to him in a dream. He started last night and healed my skin so he could continue today."

"Last night when I saw you... had the tattoo made you sick, not your headache?" He shouldn't have left last night, and he should have gone with her to finish the tattoo. His magic was scratching at him to find a way to protect her.

Protective instincts were innate with him, but he was feeling them on a whole new level.

"I think so, but I'm not sure."

He leaned closer to her, still holding her hand. "What happened when you texted me?"

"My headache got worse when Isaac finished the tattoo and then I felt weak, so he helped me get home. I think I slept for a while and then I went to the bathroom because I was nauseous again."

Damon wanted to have it out with Isaac for not calling him when Morgana was too weak to get home on her own, but he knew that was irrational. She was a grown woman and could make her own decisions. Yet he wanted to take care of her and know every detail about what had happened. Considering how she sloughed off her pain the night before, he got the hint she was likely glossing some things over, but he wouldn't push. For now.

"When did you become Molly?" Meredith gave her head a small shake. "Wow, that sounds so weird, but you know what I mean."

Damon glanced at Meredith and could see excitement written on her face, even with her still leaning back in Jack's arms. He turned back to Morgana and squeezed her hand again, hoping she found his touch reassuring.

"The pain became really bad... that's when I texted you," she said, looking at him. "Then the pain just stopped. I felt light. I didn't have a headache or any of my usual pains. When I got up and looked in the mirror, I looked like this." She waved her hand in front of her face.

"We hadn't sensed a spell on you, but obviously there was one," Jack said. "I'll have to talk to the other council leaders and figure out how we could have missed such a powerful spell. Later. Anyway... I'm guessing Isaac's tattoo broke it, which allowed you to become your true self—Molly."

"And perhaps the headaches and pain were because as Molly, you're taller than Morgana, not to mention your hair and eye color are different," Meredith said and pulled away from Jack.

Damon reluctantly let go of Morgana's hand as Meredith walked over and knelt beside her sister. She put her hand on Morgana's face. "Molly," she said quietly.

Morgana gaped again and Damon knew that while Morgana looked like Molly, she probably didn't recognize that girl inside her. "How about we still call you Morgana for now?" he asked, and he knew it had been the right suggestion to make when Morgana let out a breath and gave a small nod.

Meredith nodded as well and went back to stand with her husband. They were all in unchartered territory, and it wasn't like they were all going to be able to pick up where they'd left off over twenty years ago.

"What about my brother Dylan and Rowena's brothers, Taren and Mirek?" Reece asked. "Since you're alive, are our brothers?"

Morgana's eyes widened and then she squeezed them shut as a tear fell down her cheek. "I don't know. I don't remember."

Damon felt his heart break for her. Not being able to remember her past was one of the things Morgana struggled with the most. She hadn't said so in so many words, but he'd figured it out over the past ten months.

Her tears almost did him in. Fuck giving her space, that was not what she needed right now. He lifted her up and sat down on the couch with her in his lap. When she moved to get up, he whispered, "I've got you" in her ear, and she settled back in his lap. He felt complete for the first time in forever.

"My brothers are dead," Rowena said in a way that left no room for argument.

8

"*How* do you know that?" Reece asked, forcing Morgana to ignore the warm muscles under her thighs and focus on Rowena. She loved the feeling of being on Damon's lap. Yes, he was being controlling, but right now she'd take the comfort. Worrying about his attitude could come later.

Rowena closed her eyes for a moment, as if fortifying herself and then looked at her cousin. "I can't tell you how, I just know. My brothers are dead," she said, her voice huskier than usual.

Damon gripped Morgana's thigh, holding her in place as she reached forward and squeezed Reece's hand before letting go. He looked as if all hope had suddenly been sucked out of him.

"What about Dylan?" Reece asked.

Rowena shook her head. "Sorry, I don't know about him. Just that *my* brothers are dead."

If they were dead, why was she alive? And why had she been made to look like someone else? All the memories taken from her had to have been taken for a reason. Copeland had never missed a chance to remind her she wasn't a good person, that she was selfish. Maybe she'd done something and she was the reason the others were dead. Oh my god... how could she live with herself if that were true?

"Rowena, I'd like to know why you're so sure. but we can save that conversation for later. Morgana's transformation is huge, so let's not worry about the others right now since we don't have any answers," Jack said, pushing away from the wall and holding Meredith in his arms. "Why don't we let Morgana relax and adjust to the shock and we can talk more tomorrow?"

Damon gave his best friend a nod before looking at the others in the room. "Good idea. I'm sure Morgana could use some time on her own to digest everything that's happened."

That was an understatement. She felt like the floor had shifted between her feet and she was teetering on the jagged pieces, not able to get a firm footing. Tomorrow might bring even more questions than answers, but she'd welcome the reprieve from the questions for as long as it lasted.

Meredith put up a bit of a fuss, wanting to stay, but Jack finally convinced her to wait until tomorrow. Each person hugged her and flashed away. Everyone except Damon. She stood in the living room wondering what to do next. It seemed weird to pick up her life from where she'd left it earlier in the day when she wasn't ever the same person now.

Damon took her hand in his and gave her a slight tug. "Come sit in the kitchen with me as I make us dinner. I'm guessing you haven't eaten. And we can talk."

Her stomach growled and she looked down at it, wondering when she'd last heard the sound. For months, she'd been so focused on controlling the pain and staving off the nausea that came with it that she'd never really been hungry. She'd had to force herself to eat most days.

Damon rifled through cupboards and drawers without asking where anything was, pulling out a couple of plates and cutlery. "I'll conjure something. What do you feel like eating? I can conjure a mean steak and potato."

"I think I'd like comfort food."

"What's your favorite?"

Smiling for the first time all day, she looked up at Damon. "Chilaquiles." Opening the fridge, she pulled out four tomatoes and a bowl of cooked, cut-up chicken. Placing them on the counter, she pointed to the cupboard and then pulled out a skillet from the bottom cupboard. "Can you grab that bag of tortillas and a cutting board? They're in the pantry."

"Sure."

Working side by side, Morgana cut the tortillas into wedges and showed Damon how to fry them, flipping them once, until they were lightly browned and crisp.

When he had the hang of the chips, she picked up a tomato, and the sight of her hand startled her. She dropped the tomato on the counter, not caring when it rolled to the side, and flipped her hand back to front and front to back, again and again. It wasn't her hand. At least, not the hand she'd known for almost two years.

Her fingers were longer and her skin was darker, more-olive toned, like Meredith's. Oh my god, she wasn't Morgana anymore.

Pushing past Damon, she ran to her bedroom.

"Morgana, what's wrong?"

Ignoring Damon's call, she pulled on the walk-in closet door and stared at herself in the full-length mirror.

She'd been in such shock earlier and because Damon was on his way, she hadn't stopped to think about the change.

The mirror reflected someone who looked like a stranger. Her long blond hair was gone and now it was a deep chestnut brown. Wavy, where it had been straight. Running her hands through its length, she pulled her fingers to the ends and they fell just short of where her muscle memory told her the strands finished.

Stepping closer to the mirror, she examined the eyes staring back at her. The light gray color had been replaced by hazel. She lifted her hand hesitantly, as if waiting for the image to disappear, and touched the glass. Even her cheekbones and lips were different. Closing her eyes, she ran her fingers along her face, feeling the differences in her features.

Then she stepped back and grasped the bottom of her hoodie. She had to get it off. Now.

Tugging on the hem, she ripped it over her head and struggled as it caught on her hair. Rushing now, she finally freed her hair and threw the hoodie behind her. A feeling of compulsion to reveal this new person consumed her as she shoved down her sweatpants and stepped out of them, kicking them to the side. Standing in just the bathing suit top and shorts she'd worn for getting the tattoo, she again faced the mirror.

Watching herself in the mirror, she ran her hands over her torso, along her breasts, and down her ribs. The tattoo was beautiful and bright under her fingers, the little fairies peeking out from behind the leaves and vines. She trailed her fingers lower and across her stomach. It was flatter than it had been, and now longer, like she'd been stretched. Her legs were longer too and her hips not quite as curvy.

Dropping her arms to her sides, she stared at the woman facing her. She was nice looking but so different. Not the woman she'd known for as long as she could remember.

Oh my god, she was gone.

Morgana was dead. Did she ever even exist?

She fell to her knees and put her face in her hands as the realization sank in. Her throat tightened as memories from the last year played in her mind. Brushing her hair in the mirror, running her hands over her body as she washed herself.

It had all been a lie.

Tears welled in her eyes and her nose felt stuffy as she tried to swallow against the tightness in her throat. She felt wetness hit her palms. Dropping her hands, she looked down at them. Tracing the finger of her left hand along the palm of her right, she moved the moisture around.

Lines on a palm were such a small thing, and yet she'd never paid them much mind before. They were just something that was always there. She thought she would have always been able to recognize her own hands, but not now. Looking at the lines, she couldn't say what was different, just that they were. Were some lines longer or shorter? Were the creases deeper now?

How many other small things on her body had changed? Her ear lobes? Her toes?

For over two years, she'd been lost, wondering who she was, but forging ahead to find a new self. Then everything she'd known had been erased in the blink of an eye.

Yes, she'd wanted to remember where she came from, but not by eliminating who she'd become. Not by seeing a stranger when she looked in the mirror.

Was she just supposed to be Molly now? But Molly had died at age seven. If she really was Molly, Morgana hadn't been that person for over twenty years and her memories as Molly were gone. The spell had likely erased them, but the *how* didn't matter right now.

She felt Damon move in front of her and looked up at him.

He reached out with his hand, gently wiping away a tear on her face before she felt a coolness across her cheeks, disappearing the rest of the dampness. "I don't know how, but you'll find your way," he said quietly, his voice husky when he spoke.

"I'm not Morgana anymore, I—" Her voice broke into a sob and she couldn't finish.

"No, you're not."

He moved from his haunches and sat on the floor, pulling her onto his lap. He leaned against the wall and held her as she sobbed into his shirt. His scent surrounded her, giving her a sense of safety in the emotional chaos.

He'd always tried to give her that, even when she'd pushed him away. She sucked in her breath as another thought occurred to her. "You liked Morgana," she whispered against his shirt.

"Yes." His voice sounded even huskier than it had before.

Her eyes welled again as more of the truth settled into her. "Morgana is dead."

"Not all of her."

"Everything I was, was a lie. I'm not some mysterious woman with a haunted past anymore. I'm not a curvy blond." She pulled back so she could see his face. "You thought Morgana was beautiful. You told me."

He nodded and closed his eyes for a moment before looking down at her.

Morgana couldn't let it go and pushed him even when a part of her didn't want the truth. "You were falling in love with Morgana."

"Yes, I am falling in love with you."

9

*D*amon held Morgana until her tears stopped and she sniffed against his wet shirt. He'd suffer wearing a wet shirt every day if he could hold her like this.

He conjured a tissue into his hand and held it in front of her. "Here."

She blew her nose and he disappeared the tissue.

Running his hand down her hair, he let the dark, silky strands slide through his fingers and looked down at her. With her face hidden in his shirt, he wouldn't have recognized her. For over a year he'd had his eyes peeled for a blond whenever he'd gone to the Williams's buildings. Women dyed their hair all the time, but this was different. It wasn't just her hair that was different—no part of her looked the same. Even her height had changed.

He felt a hole form inside of him for the woman he'd lost even as she lay in his arms.

When he'd walked to the bedroom door and saw her standing at the mirror, a feeling that he couldn't quite explain came over him. Grief, perhaps. Grief for the woman that had been and was no more. She was still beautiful, just different. The tattoos etched along her sides accentuated her small waist and shapely hips and added to her beauty. Damon was determined to get to know everything new about Morgana's appearance.

Pushing up, he pulled her with him. "Why don't you put your sweats back on and I'll meet you in the kitchen? We'll finish getting dinner ready." Eating wouldn't solve their problems, but it could give her a sense of normalcy and help calm her. He turned his back to Morgana and forced his feet to move, taking himself into the kitchen.

Turning on the stovetop he'd shut off when Morgana had rushed from the kitchen, he went back to frying the tortilla wedges.

A minute later, she walked into the kitchen fully dressed and he watched her pick up the knife and turn it over in her hand. She hesitated before going back to chopping up the tomatoes and onions and fetching the rest of the ingredients.

When she'd rushed to the bedroom, he'd followed her and stood quietly as she'd looked at herself in the mirror and then frantically stripped. Immediately, he'd known what she'd wanted—to see herself and see how much had changed.

His first instinct had been to go to her and reassure her that everything was going to be okay, but he didn't. She'd solved one problem but added another in its place—she knew where she came from, but it didn't answer who she really was inside. He didn't know how long, but it would take time to adjust to such a big change. She'd be forever changed, and not just her appearance. And he'd be there for her.

He placed the tortilla chips on a paper towel before putting the next batch in the pan, concentrating on his task. "Do you cook a lot?"

"Not as much as I'd like since it's not as fun to cook for one, but sometimes I go down to the restaurant and help out."

"Is that where you learned to cook chi-la…" He grinned at her and raised his eyebrows.

"Chilaquiles. It's pronounced chee—luh—kee—layz." Damon gave the pronunciation a try. She playfully bumped his hip. "Your accent needs work, but you got it." She finished chopping the vegetables and put them in her food processor, waiting until she finished and it was quiet enough to speak to continue. "I don't remember where I learned…"

Her voice trailed off and he wanted to know what else she was thinking, but she'd already been through so much today. He would wait for her to reveal her thoughts in her own time. The wait might test his patience, but he'd somehow find out more if he needed to.

"Maybe your memories will start to come back now that the spell is broken. That's the way it was with the W's. Their memories came back a bit at a time."

She nodded at him and dumped the blended sauce into the now-empty skillet.

Maybe she didn't want her memories returned. He could understand that, but a selfish part of him wanted to know everything that had happened to her—what she'd suffered, what made her tick, and who she was now. She'd told him once that she was worried about what her memories contained, but he wasn't. He knew deep down that the little girl he'd known was in there and that little girl had been a good person. No matter what she thought, she was still a good person, and it didn't matter if a bad situation had made her do desperate things. It wouldn't change how he felt about her.

Morgana had never been the chatty type around him, but he didn't like this new sullen version of her. He couldn't blame her, but a change of subject to lighten the mood wouldn't hurt.

"Did I tell you about the latest app that I want to fund?"

he asked, interrupting what could be her downward spiral of thoughts.

She shook her head and gave him a small smile before he launched into an explanation about the new app.

Her mood changed like a switch had been flipped and he basked in her laughter. He could be pushy, but he could also read her well.

Earlier, when Meredith had called her Molly and she hadn't known what to do, he had. Like now, he knew she wasn't ready to think about her lost memories. He could hope that most of her changes were on the outside, but deep down, he knew that was naïve. The physical changes she'd gone through would affect her emotionally, and that was bound to affect her personality. Little Molly had been impulsive and gregarious... maybe now that the spell was broken, Morgana would be too.

When he'd finished his story, they plated the food and sat side by side on the stools at the kitchen island.

They ate in comfortable silence for several minutes until out of the corner of his eye, he saw her glancing over at him.

"Okay?" he asked, turning toward her.

She nodded and continued to eat so he let it go. Patience, he reminded himself. She'd tell him when she was ready.

When they finished their meals, he pushed his plate away and turned toward her. "That was excellent, thank you. And thank you for teaching me."

She looked down as her cheeks flushed. "I'd cooked the chicken yesterday to make the dish, but then I'd felt too horrible to cook."

"Speaking of that, let's talk about how the spell broke." Damon waved his hand at the dishes, and they were now clean, even the skillet. She watched as they floated one by one into the cupboard and drawers.

He didn't give her a chance to protest, taking her hand in

his as he'd done earlier in the evening, and walking them over to the couch. "Let's get more comfortable."

She pointed at her armchair still snugged up against the sofa and raised her eyebrow at him. "Can you return that?"

He wasn't going to apologize for moving her furniture to get closer to her. Raising his hand, he moved the armchair back to its proper position.

"Thanks." She curled up onto one end of the couch, facing him, and he sat a cushion away.

He wanted to pull her into his lap and yet also give her space. Conflicting emotions were foreign to him, and he didn't like it. State what he wanted and go after it—that was his standard operating procedure—in both business and pleasure. But Morgana brought out feelings in him he couldn't ignore and that made her even more special, no matter what she looked like. Never before had he been this conflicted around someone—perhaps he'd have to get used to it.

He felt like a high school boy on a first date instead of a successful businessman with a woman he'd known for months. He had to get back to thinking that way—step one: make the other person comfortable. Step two: find out what they were thinking and wanted. Step three: identify the gap between their wants and his. Step four: determine a way forward so both parties were satisfied and they got what they wanted.

Sometimes the other party's wants and his were mutually inclusive, and the solution was simple. Other times he needed to use a little persuasion for the other party to be open-minded enough to realize they could both win.

If they both couldn't come out with some kind of win, he'd drop the deal, but even that sometimes took some persuasion. He wasn't an ass and didn't conduct his business that way. Being cutthroat and winning, even at a detriment to the other party, would be easy, whether they were magic or not, but that wasn't his style.

Morgana wasn't a business deal, but he could treat their relationship like one until he won her over and she understood how he really felt about her. So he focused on step one.

He smiled. The hazel color of her eyes was still a shock but no less beautiful. "I noticed you didn't have any wine; can I conjure you a glass?"

She gave him a small smile. "That'd be nice. Thank you."

Holding out his hand, he conjured a glass of white wine almost filled to the brim. "That should tide you over for a bit."

"I should hope so." She huffed out a laugh and his eyes followed her hands as she carefully brought the glass to her lips to take her first sip. Her lips were plump and red as they wrapped around the edge of the glass. He'd already tasted those lips once and he wanted to do it again.

He conjured himself a glass of scotch and rested it on his knee after taking a drink.

Step two: find out what she was thinking and what she wanted.

Morgana had been right when she'd asked if he'd been falling in love with her. It was in that moment that he'd accepted the truth—he had. She thought she was someone different now, but he expected that the innate things that had made her Morgana were still there. Only time would tell if the impulsive and fun, outgoing little girl that Molly had been still existed inside Morgana. He'd liked her then and had been drawn to her energy, even though they'd only been twelve and seven.

Fast forward over twenty years and he'd been immediately attracted to Morgana, even when he didn't know who she was. Blond hair or brunette, curvy or slender, light gray eyes or hazel, it didn't matter.

"What are you thinking about? The change?"

"I'm just wondering what my life will be like now. How it's going to change now that I know I'm a Williams."

"I think it will take time to figure that out. There's no rush."

He leaned further back into the cushions, hoping he looked relaxed when what he really wanted was to pull her into his lap and kiss the fuck out of her. Would it feel different kissing her now? What would she feel like pressed up against him? His body heated up at the thought and his pants felt tighter. Time to change the subject.

He took a sip of his drink and blew out a breath, forcing his body to relax. "What was it like when the spell broke?"

"There was intense pain. I thought I was dying, that's why I texted you." She looked down and her hair covered the blush rising up her neck.

Pride swelled inside him at the thought that she'd thought of him first. "I'm glad you texted me."

She gave him a small smile. "When I looked in the mirror, I realized I'd changed. I was in shock."

She paused, and he didn't think she'd continue until she looked him straight in the eyes. "At first it didn't even dawn on me who I was—I just looked different. It wasn't until everyone called me Molly that I figured it out."

When she'd turned to face him, he'd known immediately who she was, but then, he'd been friends with her twin for decades. The resemblance was uncanny.

"Will you show me your tattoo?"

She looked startled at the change of topic. "Ah— didn't you see it earlier?"

"Not really. I was more concerned with what you were going through and I was watching your face."

He could see her indecision as she decided what to do.

"Please," he whispered. The compulsion to know more about her—everything about her—was back.

"Okay." She stood and pulled her hoodie off, revealing the blue bathing suit top that he'd seen earlier.

Inching forward on the couch until he was sitting right in front of her, he lifted his hand and ran one of his fingers along a tattooed vine. "It's beautiful. I just hated that you were in such pain." He could hear the awe in his voice as he studied the design on her skin. It didn't detract from her beauty, only enhanced it.

"Getting the tattoo itself wasn't too bad, it was the headaches that sucked."

His finger hovered over a butterfly that looked like it was resting high up on her ribs. "It's all amazing, but this butterfly is stunning."

"It's a sunflower. Isaac weaved six of them through the design."

"I see five sunflowers and a butterfly."

"What?" Morgana twisted her torso and peered down at her skin. "Oh shit, it is a butterfly. But I swear it wasn't earlier."

"Well, it's beautiful." Placing his hands on her hips, he leaned forward and kissed the butterfly and then each of the fairies. Her breath hitched, but she didn't back away. He moved his lips across her torso and let his hands gently trail after his kisses. After his lips caressed her on one side, he moved to the next. Her breath quickened as he kissed her colorful skin.

Holding her hips, he guided her back a step and stood. Even with her newly added height, he still towered over her. "You're beautiful," he said softly as he bent forward, wrapping one hand around the back of her neck and using his other hand on her hip to pull her forward.

"I want to kiss you, Damon," she whispered before licking her lips.

It felt like time had stopped and he'd been thrust into his favorite novel when she braced her hands on his shoulders and raised her lips to his. They were warm and pliant, and she opened, inviting him in. She tasted like wine and sunshine and felt better than any description he'd read in any of the romance books they both enjoyed.

He let her lead as she tasted and teased his mouth. Her hands gripped his shoulders, her fingernails eliciting a delicious sting as they bit into him. She pushed her lower body against his, and he called on more patience than he knew he possessed not to take over and make love to her.

A lustful groan escaped him and he felt her smile against his lips. He pulled back only enough to look into her eyes. "Maybe we should stop."

Morgana stilled and her eyes widened. "You don't want this?"

"Oh, angel, I want this more than anything, but I need you to be sure too."

"Angel?" Her voice was breathless.

"Yes, angel. Because to me, you are one."

"I'm sure. I want you, Damon." She kissed him again. It was slow and heated. Not like she was testing the waters, but instead plunging right in.

He trailed his lips across her jaw and down her neck. "There's no rush, I can kiss you all night."

He felt her swallow against his lips as he caressed her neck. "I want more. Please, Damon, make me feel good and forget everything for just a little while."

Reaching around her neck, he lifted the thin string holding her bikini top in place but didn't pull. "I want this to be all about you tonight. I want to pleasure you. We can stop at any time. All you have to do is say so."

"Please, Damon."

He pulled on the string and the two triangles fell forward, revealing the most beautiful breasts he'd ever seen. "Gorgeous," he whispered as he took a step back and sat on the couch. Holding her hips, he brought her forward and only had to reach up a few inches to take one of her perfect nipples into his mouth. She whimpered and threaded her fingers into his hair.

Using his mouth, he lathered attention on one breast and then the other. The small moans she made and her quickened breathing spurred him on. "I've wanted you for so long."

She stiffened in his arms. "Not this version of me."

"Any version of you, Morgana. I've been drawn to you since we first met." He continued to trail his lips along her body as he spoke. "Blond or brunette, gray eyes or hazel, curvy or thin. It's all you."

He lost track of time as he worshipped her, running his hands and lips along her body, spending time on each spot before he moved on. Watching and listening, he paid attention to her cues, wanting to pleasure her.

"More, Damon."

The plea was ambrosia to his ears. He spun her around and pulled her between his legs so her back was flush with his chest.

"What about you?" Her words came out breathless.

"This is about you." He was so much taller than her that when sitting down, he was able to rest his chin in the crook of her neck. Licking the sensitive spot between her shoulder and neck, he slid one hand from her hip across her stomach and slipped his fingers beneath the elastic of her sweatpants and panties. He felt her shiver and grip his forearms for balance before her body melted into his touch.

He loved the feel of her soft and supple skin under his fingers. Moving lower, he felt the heat of her core as he cupped her mound and applied light pressure, rubbing in soft, circular motions. He continued, unrushed, until Morgana groaned and pushed against his hand.

Using his fingers, he parted her folds and pressed his thumb against her clit. He rubbed in small circles. "You're so wet, but I want you wetter. I want you so turned on that you see stars when you come."

She rubbed against his hand and he inserted a finger; her muscles gripped him tight. He knew exactly when he'd found her G-spot—her breathing sped up and she undulated her hips, her knees weakening. Wrapping one arm around her waist, he held her up and continued his sensual torture.

"More, Damon. Harder."

He used his thumb and fingers and increased the pressure until she clenched around him and called out his name. He withdrew his hand and turned her around to face him. Cupping his hand around the back of her neck, he pulled her down to him and kissed her with everything he had.

His cock strained against his pants and he knew he'd be relieving himself as soon as he got home, but it had been worth it to bring her pleasure.

Letting her go, he held her until her breathing returned to normal. When he felt her stiffen in his arms, he knew what was coming. He should have stopped sooner, but he didn't regret it. "Morgana?"

"I'm good. I wanted it," she said, pushing away from him and righting her clothing. "But just because I let you pleasure me doesn't mean I'll suddenly become your docile little woman."

It took tremendous willpower to hold back his laugh, knowing she wouldn't appreciate it. He looked up into her eyes from his seated position, giving her the power. "I'd never consider you docile, Morgana, and I don't want to control you. I want to pleasure you and get to know you."

A few minutes later, she rushed him out the door. He'd wanted to kiss her again but instead forced himself to leave. She had to be feeling raw from everything she'd gone through and what they had done but at least she'd been comfortable with him for a short time. He could take baby steps. Now it was time to move on to step three and figure out the gap between what they both wanted.

One thing he already suspected was that she was the one for him and he'd work hard to make sure she saw that he was the right one for her too.

10

*O*rgana wiped her damp palms on her jeans as she approached Meredith's office door. She'd put Meredith off a day already, saying she wasn't ready to talk to anyone. She'd spent a lot of the day before thinking about Damon and what was going to happen to their relationship, yet she didn't have any answers. So much of her life in the past ten months had been consumed with just dealing with her headaches. The pain might be gone, but so much had changed when it left, and now she didn't know how she was supposed to act around anyone.

Meredith already knew that Morgana hadn't remembered her, but was she now supposed to be her loving sister? She liked Meredith—just as she liked all the Williams cousins—but she didn't feel the twin bond she'd heard so much about. Maybe when she saw her now, the bond would come.

Looking at the solid door, she straightened her shoulders and knocked. When Meredith called out to enter, Morgana walked in, gathering as much confidence as she could muster. It wasn't like she didn't already know Meredith as a friend. Finding out they were sisters shouldn't make a difference in how they interacted, but she feared it would.

"Molly, I'm so glad you could come." Meredith's voice was higher pitched than usual and far too enthusiastic for a meeting.

"Ah, it's Morgana." The guilt that had been constant since the spell broke pushed down on Morgana's shoulders. For almost two years, she'd yearned to know who she was, and now that she did, it didn't feel natural, like she was pretending to be someone else. She didn't want to go by her real name. Molly felt like a stranger to her. Definitely fucked up. "Ah… it's what I'm used to."

"Right. Please, come and sit down." Meredith gestured to a sitting area with wing-backed chairs and a small table between them. They both sat and stared at each other for a moment.

Meredith broke the silence. "Can I conjure you a cup of coffee? Tea? Soda?"

"Coffee, thanks. With some milk." Morgana took the proffered mug from Meredith and took a sip. Meredith made the same for herself and the silence stretched between them once more. They hadn't been like this before the spell had been broken. Morgana was a bit closer with Jo but she'd been friendly with Meredith and Rowena as well. They'd talked about everyday things, nothing too deep, but enough to keep a conversation going.

Resting her mug on her knee, she looked over at Meredith. Her sister. That was still taking some time to get used to. They looked so much alike now, both in their coloring and the shape of their features. She could see they weren't identical, but close to it. Should the twin bond come now? Morgana felt so lost. They stared at each for a minute before she broke the silence this time. "It's a bit awkward, isn't it?"

Meredith huffed out a laugh. "Yes, it's not every day that the sister you buried over twenty years ago comes back from the dead."

"Or that you learn that the unknown woman who rescued you from a psycho is your twin." They grinned at each other. "So now what? I mean, we already know each other, and I still don't remember the past."

"Has anything new come to you about your time with Copeland?"

Meredith's expression was so hopeful that Morgana wanted to tell her something. Anything to give her closure or maybe hope. She could tell her that Copeland had drained her magic almost every day, a painful and life-sucking torture, but Morgana didn't want her sister's pity. "No," she said, shaking her head.

"Oh, okay. Well... I know you like to cook. Do you know who taught you?"

Oh god, this wasn't going to go well. "Sorry, I don't. I'm guessing whoever took care of us."

"I know it's only been a day, but do you know what you want to do now?"

Morgana tensed. "Do you mean when I leave? Do you *want* me to leave?"

"Oh no! Of course not." Meredith's eyes grew wide. "This is your home. It's been your home for the last year and now even more so. One fifth of everything is yours."

"One fifth? I don't understand."

Meredith waved her arm around her office. "This—well, not my office exactly, but all the Williams's holdings—one fifth of it is yours. It's split equally between Jo, Reece, Rowena, me, and now you."

"Oh god, I can't take what you've built."

"Morgana, we didn't build it, our parents did. Sure, when

we took over, we made it grow because our mothers didn't do much when they were on their own and raising child— Shit." Meredith put down her coffee and rubbed her temple before giving Morgana a sheepish grin. "You know what I mean."

She reached across and patted Meredith on the knee. "I get it."

Meredith wiped the back of her arm across her forehead in a mock gesture. "Phew. I thought I had screwed up again." Meredith stood and walked to her desk. "Let me show you. I printed off some spreadsheets." She grabbed a huge stack of papers from her desk and Morgana felt tension ripple down her spine.

"I can also put some of our projections on my white-board," Meredith said, looking over her shoulder "so you can see where we're taking the business. I'd love your thoughts and ideas—I mean, maybe not yet, since you don't know the business yet, but you will. I want you to be a part of it, like the rest of us."

Morgana felt like her head was going to explode, but not from a headache for once. "Ah…"

"I'm moving too fast, aren't I?"

"Maybe a little."

Meredith came back to her chair and picked up her coffee.

When the silence edged toward awkward again, Morgana knew she had to make a move. Meredith had invited her to talk, so Morgana needed to get them going. "Can you tell me about when we were little? Since I was tak… since I left—" Shit, this was harder than she thought. "You know what I mean… we weren't together after we turned seven, and I don't know if you remember anything from back then."

"I know what you mean. And yes, I remember some

things." Meredith looked over at her desk and then looked back, a nervous expression on her face. "I brought a photo album."

"Really? Well, bring it out. Let's walk down memory lane!" Morgana laughed and realized she was actually happy. Her head and body didn't ache, and for the first time she remembered in decades, she had a family. It was awkward and they wouldn't pick up where they'd left off, but she now had a sister and cousins.

She wanted to grasp onto the happiness and hold tight, and yet it felt like nothing had changed. Well, her appearance had changed, but really nothing else had in the last two days. In one way, she still felt like she had before the tattoo, just without the headaches. She'd still taken so much from this family. To now jump in and take more—one fifth of every-thing—just didn't feel right. This time with Meredith she'd take, but the rest could wait.

Meredith picked up the album off her desk and placed it on the table. She waved her hand at her large wing-back chair and it slid over next to Morgana's so they could sit side by side. "We were like this as kids too."

"Like what?"

"I was the planner, always looking ahead. I swear I had my first day of school clothes picked out a month in advance. You were more of the spur-of-the-moment type. You'd tumble out of bed and just make a decision."

Morgana smiled. "Well, it's good to see some things never change."

Meredith picked up the album and turned to the first page. "This was our dad. He was so tall, at least it felt like that when I was little. He was just the type of person who seemed bigger than life. He would walk into a room and command it without even trying. We both thought he was more than just magic." She wanted to remember him so badly, but looking at the picture was like looking at a stranger.

A picture of their mother was next and Morgana ran her finger along the edge of the photo. The woman in the photo was so much younger than the person Morgana had seen at Copeland's apartment, though it was obvious they were the same person. Meredith looked so much like her. Morgana startled, realizing that she now did too. "I didn't remember her," she whispered. Morgana blinked back tears and swallowed, forcing her throat not to close, and looked at her twin. "I'm a shitty sister because I didn't remember you, but what kind of daughter does that make me that I didn't recognize my own mother?"

Meredith's eyes were bright with tears, but she didn't wipe them away. "It makes you no different than us. I didn't recognize you either, nor did Mom."

Morgana squeezed her eyes shut and took in a deep breath to steady herself. She'd always wondered if her family was looking for her, wondering where she was. The truth was a bittersweet pill to swallow—they hadn't looked. From day one of her being taken, they'd thought she was dead and life went on. There was no going back and picking up where they'd left off.

There wasn't a twin bond with Meredith because it had been severed with her supposed death. She gave her sister a watery smile. Maybe it wasn't too late to forge a new one. She pointed to the next picture… "Is that Dad too?" Even saying the name felt strange, but she'd push forward.

Meredith laughed. "Oh my god, yes, he…."

Morgana listened as Meredith described who was in each photo and where the photos were taken. There were more than a few tears from each of them, but it was a start to getting back some of what they'd lost.

DAMON REACHED for his phone again and checked it—no messages. He hadn't seen Morgana since he'd left her place two nights ago and she'd only texted him once. Promising to give her space was one of the hardest things he'd agreed to do lately.

The current business proposals he should be reading were spread out beside him on the bed. His eReader lay untouched next to them. Nothing could retain his interest for long as thoughts of Morgana continued to occupy his mind.

When he closed his eyes, he could still see the expression on her face as an orgasm shattered her. It was one of the most beautiful sights he'd ever seen. Her head thrown back, her dark hair a current around her, and the small sounds she made as she took what he gave.

For months he'd pictured her blond hair and light gray eyes—her image popping into his mind at all hours of the day. Now he needed to change the image in his mind's eye. She was even more beautiful than she'd been before but it wasn't her looks that he'd been falling in love with. It was her strength hidden under a layer of insecurity and kindness.

Already thinking about step three—where the gaps were between their end goals—he knew it was the subtleties that were going to be the hardest to detect. And if he missed any, he could screw up step four: determine a way forward so both parties were satisfied and they both got what they wanted.

He wanted her to let him in, so he could get to know her better and love her. Did he love her now? He wasn't sure, but he knew he was on his way.

Morgana hadn't said exactly what she wanted, but he

knew in his heart that she wanted to be loved too. She also needed her independence. That was going to be the tough one. He knew he could be a controlling bastard. Unknowns were his kryptonite. He'd recognized it in himself years ago, not long after his dad went missing. From then on, Damon had started to make sure he knew where everyone in his life was and that they were safe. Sure, he couldn't control friends like Jack, but Damon made sure his mother and sister were always safe, and he controlled his work environment as much as he could, and that included taking care of his employees.

What would he do if a business venture he was courting asked him for space? He knew the answer without giving it any thought—respecting their wishes was one thing, but backing off completely was another. Too much space and the person would start to have doubts and it opened up room for other ideas to percolate. He'd slow down the courting but wouldn't stop completely. After all, how would they know what they could have together if he didn't show them?

That's where he'd been going wrong with Morgana—he wasn't showing her what they could have together. Now came the tricky part. The courting without making it obvious what he was doing.

He picked up his phone, contemplating his next move. In the one text he'd gotten from Morgana, she said she was going to meet Meredith. She was now probably all up in her head about their meeting. And if he knew Meredith the way he thought he did, she'd have planned the next six months of Morgana's life down to the hour. There were probably even spreadsheets and whiteboards involved. He could imagine Morgana freaking out right about now and he knew just the thing to help her relax.

Damon: What are you doing?

After a minute without a response, he tossed the phone

on the bed and picked up his eReader. A sense of déjà vu washed over him as he waited. In business, he managed just the right amount of patience to get what he wanted, but his patience went out the window every time he waited for Morgana to respond to a text.

The words on the page swam in front of his vision as he waited. His phone pinged when he was just finishing reading the same page for the third time.

Morgana: Reading. Wyd?

For a woman who had been in captivity for almost her entire life, she'd sure picked up text speak quickly. Too quickly for Damon as he stared at the letters and finally figured out what she was asking.

Damon: I'm reading too.

Since she was willing to respond to his text, she couldn't be that into her book. Maybe she needed a distraction or a friend to talk to. Without overanalyzing his actions, he hit the call button.

"Hello?"

Her voice was quiet when she answered, but just hearing it soothed something inside him. "Just thought I'd say hi and see how you are."

"Hi."

"Hi... Now that we've gotten that out of the way... How are you?" There was a pause on the other end of the phone. Shit. He'd moved too fast again. Maybe something more specific would be better. "How was your time with Meredith?"

He could hear some rustling in the background and thought she might be in bed like he was. A beautiful image, but not one he needed if he was going to concentrate on her words.

"It was okay, but strange."

"How so?"

She sighed and he wished he could be there for her. He wanted nothing more in that moment than to hold her.

"I've known Meredith for almost a year now, but it was like we'd never spoken before. At first it was really awkward."

"She has memories of Molly and she's probably trying to reconcile the seven-year-old version she knew with who you are now."

"After I was rescued, Jo told me all about the spellbinding my mother and aunts put on the Little W's." She chuckled softly into the phone. "I know that everyone has dropped the *Little* now, and it's just the W's, but I love that they used to refer to Meredith and my cousins that way... I would have been a Little W too." Her voice wobbled as she said the last words and a sound came through the phone, like a tissue being pulled from a tissue box. "Anyway... I know any memories the W's had that were connected to magic were wiped out."

"Yes, the mothers didn't want them to know anything about magic, which meant erasing any memory that could raise suspicion of its existence. Because of that, Jack and I made ourselves scarce in those early years. It was difficult to remember what not to say and do. More than once, we had to erase their memories and cover up something we'd done. It was both tougher and easier not to be around them. And we were all mourning the loss of the dads, you, Mirek, Taren, and Dylan."

"I don't remember any of them..."

He heard Morgana sniff, and his heart broke for her. "You were little. Plus, you were spellbound."

"Still makes me a shitty cousin for forgetting them. So, what were you reading?"

She wasn't ready to listen to reassurances, so he'd let her wallow for a bit and accept the change of topic. "A romantic suspense. Just finished reading a sex scene." That was a lie. He'd been at the climactic moment when the heroine was kidnapped and trying to rescue herself. That scene would probably hit a little too close to home and wouldn't help him with his agenda.

Throwing the sex scene comment out there could be risky, but he wouldn't haven't gotten where he was in his life if he hadn't taken some risks. Calculated ones.

"Was it any good?"

"Yes. Steamy. The guy was away on a trip, so they had phone sex." He figured in for a penny, in for a pound.

"Hmm."

Shit. That didn't tell him anything and now the silence felt heavy. "Morgana, you still there?"

"Yes."

Okay, back to simple answers. He'd bet money that this wasn't the real Morgana. No, this was the learned Morgana —the one who had to be careful with how she answered questions for fear of reprisal. He decided it was time he take another risk and said what he was thinking. "It's okay to like it. It can be fun and steamy."

"Ah, I've never done it before. I've only had a phone since I got here…"

Her voice trailed off. He hoped no phone sex meant since she hadn't had any in-person sex since coming to Colorado either. His hand had been his only companion since she'd walked into his life months earlier. "Would you like to try it?"

"Now?" Her voice rose an octave, but whether it was from fear or excitement, he didn't know. He hoped it was the latter.

"Sure. Why not? You can't see me, and I can't touch you, so you've got nothing to lose and you might enjoy it." If she said no, he'd let the topic go. But if she said yes, he was one step closer to closing out step three—figuring out the gaps in what they both wanted. Or in this case, what they both enjoyed. Since they hadn't talked since the other night, they hadn't brought up what they'd done together. But he'd relived the moment a dozen times in the last two days. He'd hoped since she'd answered his call and was even contemplating phone sex that she'd thought about them too.

"Okay," she said so softly he almost didn't hear her.

"Okay? I need you to be sure, Morgana."

"I'm sure... just embarrassed."

"There's nothing to be embarrassed about. I guarantee you'll like it." And he would too, if it didn't kill him. He couldn't remember his dick ever being this hard from just a conversation. The other night didn't count since he'd had his hands all over her—now he was only hearing her voice and he felt like he was going to shoot his load. "Are the lights on?"

"Just the bedside one."

"What are you wearing?"

A small laugh escaped her. "Isn't that like some cheesy line men always ask?"

"I suppose it is. I just want to make sure you're comfortable first."

He heard rustling and figured she was getting ready. "I'm in my panties and a tank top. What about you?"

"Sweatpants." He ran his hand down his abs and held in a groan as he palmed his cock. "Are you lying back?"

There was more rustling. "Yes."

"Close your eyes, angel." When she didn't respond, he worried she was second-guessing her actions. "Push your tank up above your gorgeous breasts." He kept his voice low and tried not to sound too forceful. He must have succeeded because he heard the whispers of movement.

"Okay."

Shy, conditioned-to-be-quiet Morgana was back. He was going to work his damnedest to get the impatient, fearless

Morgana to appear. "Put a finger in your mouth and get it wet. Then rub it over your nipple to make it hard." Her breathing increased and he imagined what she looked like while she carried out his directions. Fuck, this was going to kill him. It would be a self-inflicted death because he couldn't stop. "Wet your finger again and tease your other nipple." He heard her suck her finger and then make the same mewling sounds she'd made the other night when he'd brought her pleasure. "Now pinch your nipples and make them really hard."

What he wouldn't give for video calling right now, but he didn't need her to withdraw like she had before. "Angel?"

"Mmm hmm?"

"Feel good?"

"I wish it was you."

He stroked his cock from the base to the tip, his leaked precum lubricating his hand. "Pretend I'm with you. Suck on your finger again." He paused to give her time. "Now run your finger through your pussy... Are you wet?"

"Mmm hmm."

"That's it. Drag your finger up to your clit and rub it in circles like I would." Her light breaths floated across the phone line. "You're so beautiful."

"You can't see me." Her voice had become husky.

"I saw you the other night and I know how beautiful you are. And even more than your looks, it's what's inside you that makes you so beautiful. You're kind and giving and so strong."

"I don't feel strong."

"You will. I'll help you see what I see." He paused, listening to her breathing and giving her time. It would be so easy for him to flash right into her bedroom and be with her, watching her pleasure herself. But he knew that would be too much for her. "Are you stroking your pussy? Add another finger." He closed his eyes and squeezed the head of his cock to prevent him from coming too soon. It was becoming a common occurrence around Morgana.

Her breathing sped up and he knew she was close. "Rub your clit harder now."

He heard her groan and he fumbled with his phone, catching it before it fell to the bed. He didn't want to miss hearing her come.

"I... I want..."

"What do you want, angel?"

"I want you to come too."

He squeezed the head of his cock again, trying to slow down his eruption. "That's not going to be a problem. Are you close?"

"So close... so... oh... yes..."

"Keep touching yourself, angel. Pretend it's my fingers on you. Next time I want to taste you. I'll run my tongue all over your pussy while my fingers hit your G-spot."

He heard her panting now.

"I'm coming!"

Damon stroked his cock four more times and let himself go over the edge with her. His come spurted over his bare stomach and he could have sworn he saw stars behind his closed eyelids. That was the best orgasm he'd ever had with his own hand.

He waited until her breathing slowed before speaking again. "Angel?"

"I'm here."

"Don't get inside your head. You gave yourself pleasure. It was natural and beautiful."

"I'm embarrassed," she whispered.

"You shouldn't be. You are exquisite."

"Okay."

He wasn't sure she believed him, but he'd work on that.

When they said their goodnights and hung up, he thought about their wants and recognized a gap between them. He wanted Morgana with everything she had, and he was damned sure she wanted him too, but she wasn't willing to admit it yet. Step four would be to figure out how to get her to see what he saw.

11

*N*o matter how hard Morgana tried, she couldn't remember the time she'd spent with her cousins when they were little. The spell had been broken for almost a week and flashes of memories had come to her—cooking in a large kitchen; a small, cramped room; spiders—but none of her sister or her cousins.

She'd been with Ben, Frank, and Jack for hours now as they asked her question after question. Damon had stayed quiet by her side, and after the first few minutes, he'd rested his hand on her thigh. She'd clung to the touch like a lifeline, him grounding her in a way she hadn't expected.

They'd met at Ben's house instead of the FBI offices, because it prevented her from being seen by the non-magics in the office and them asking questions. She didn't care where they'd met but wished the questioning would stop.

Across the table from her, Jack scrubbed his hand across his face. "Let's go back to what you remember from Copeland's. I know we've gone over it already, but let's do it again. Sometimes revisiting memories is when we pick up details we missed the first time around."

"From the beginning?" Morgana heard the wariness in her own voice and winced. She did want to be helpful, but she was tired and so frustrated that her memories hadn't returned.

"Jack, why don't we take a break? How about some fresh coffee?" Damon squeezed her thigh and stood before Jack had a chance to respond. "I'm sure everyone could use a break."

Damon offered her his hand and she let him pull her up. "Thanks." She squeezed his hand, and then dropped it, turning to Ben. "May I use your restroom?"

"Of course. Second door on the left," he said, pointing toward a hallway.

Morgana locked the bathroom door behind her and took a deep breath before turning around to look in the mirror. It'd been almost a week since the spell broke and looking at herself in the mirror still felt like she was looking at someone else. The shock that she'd had the first couple of days had slowly disappeared, but the sense that she wasn't herself remained.

She used the toilet and washed her hands, careful not to look at the mirror again. Reaching for a towel, she dried her hands and the sight of them jarred a memory.

"Watch me," the woman said in heavily accented English.

Her hands kneaded the dough over and over again. She stopped and added some flour and repeated the process. "You go."

Morgana's hands weren't as large as the woman's, and she struggled to get the dough to fold the way the woman had. Her hands were covered in flour and she had bits of dough under her fingernails.

She worked with the woman for what felt like hours, making buns and loaf after loaf of bread.

"Good," the woman said, praising Morgana.

The memory faded and Morgana sat on the closed toilet

lid. How old had she been? Her hands weren't that of a small child but not an adult's either, so maybe eleven or twelve?

"Morgana? You okay?"

She started at Damon's voice. She unlocked and opened the door, facing him. "I'm fine."

"Really? I've been taught that whenever a woman says she's fine, she's really not fine." He wiggled his brows and the gesture coming from the serious, brick house of a man was comical.

She chuckled and pushed at his chest, walking out of the bathroom. "Yes, really, I'm fine."

"Okay, but before you go…" He stopped and put his hand on her arm.

"What?"

Holding her by both arms, he turned her back toward the wall and leaned in. "This." Lowering his head, he took her mouth in a kiss that made her want to melt. Her hands went to his chest, feeling the warmth of his muscles as his hands caressed up and down her arms.

She'd barely opened her eyes and registered the kiss was over before he took her hand in his and walked them back toward the kitchen.

As they passed what looked like an office or den, a gallery of pictures on a bookcase caught her eye. Walking toward the pictures, she had a weird sense that the pictures were somehow important to her lost memories. More than just family photos, but a glimpse into the past that she needed to see.

There were pictures of Ben's and Stella's kids through the years. She'd met the two boys, now grown, at family dinners over the last year. A picture of Ben and Stella on their wedding day made her breath hitch. Ben was holding a small girl in his arms.

Morgana stepped closer to the picture. The little girl was

maybe four or five years old with longish blond hair, and she had one hand wrapped around Ben's neck and the other reached across his chest to hold Stella's hand.

Ben had mentioned losing a child in a fire. She wracked her brain for the details she'd heard. Something about a bunch of people gathered to listen to a seer after the fire that had killed the Williams's men and children.

The little girl had been the only one who had died in that second fire.

"That's Julia," Damon said, coming up to stand behind her. "She was only five when she died. I was twelve or so, so I don't remember exactly, but I think Ben and Stella's wedding was a couple of months before the fire. Stella was pregnant with Nate when Julia died."

"Two fires within the same year?" She spun around and tilted her head to look up at Damon. "It wasn't a coincidence, was it?"

Damon placed his hand at the small of her back and guided her out of the room. She was letting him do that a lot lately. It seemed so innocent, but if she wasn't careful, he could easily take over more things until he was controlling every aspect of her life. His hand at the small of her back could be seen as just a thoughtful gesture, but what if he used it as a subtle way to control her? To guide her only where he wanted her to go? Shivers ran through her at the thought.

"You cold?" He turned toward her and ran his hands up and down her arms, warmth seeping into her from his heated hands. Now that the spell was broken and memories were coming back, maybe her magic would come back too. He probably hadn't even realized he was using his. It was just so natural for magics. But not her.

Neither said a word about the kiss as they took their seats back at the kitchen table and he conjured them more coffee and some cookies.

Ben and Jack took their seats again, but Frank was missing. "Frank got called into the office," Ben said, as if reading her mind. "As the Special Agent in Charge of our division, he's not usually involved in individual cases like this, but because this involves the magic task force and because you're a Williams, he wanted to be here. We'll fill him in later."

Morgana nodded and looked down at the mug in her hands. Jo had explained to her months ago that the Davis families, both Ben's and Frank's, the Stones—Damon's family—the Hughes—the family of Jo's husband, Simon—and the three Williams's families had all been really close. So many of those people were gone now. Including her parents. The only mental image she had of her mother was of her bloody and beaten, tied to a chair, just before she died.

She shuddered again and felt Damon wrap his arm around her shoulder and his heat seep into her.

"You okay?" he whispered into her ear.

"I'm fine." She heard him chuckle and turned to look up at him, her eyebrows raised in question.

"Fine?"

She smiled. "Yes, fine."

"Morgana, can you tell us again about arriving at Copeland's?" Ben asked, breaking her away from Damon's gaze. "Is that where you met Eddie and Rocky?"

"I'm not sure. I don't remember anything before that time, but they were both at Copeland's, although I didn't see them every day."

"We've got descriptions of both men from Simon and a description of Eddie from Jo as well. She spoke to Rocky but never saw his face. We think that was intentional, but haven't figured out why yet. The descriptions don't match the ones you gave us."

"What do you mean?"

Ben reached forward and gently pulled one of her hands

away from its death grip on her mug, giving it a reassuring squeeze. "I don't think it had anything to do with what you saw. We think there was magic at play. Probably on top of the spell that bound you."

Jack leaned back. "I agree. We're just trying to piece things together and figure out who the players are."

Morgana looked over at Jack. When she had first arrived at the Williams's, she'd avoided him as much as possible. Not only was he an intense guy, but he'd been there when she was rescued. Being around him brought back a lot of memories of that time—memories she didn't want to remember.

She blinked, focusing on Jack's words as he continued. "Just before Copeland died, you said there were more children, and later you said you didn't remember. I spoke with the other council leaders, and we think that was the spell masking your memories. Have any of your memories returned since the spell broke?"

"A few." All three men looked at her expectantly and once more she knew she was going to disappoint the people in her life. "Snatches of memories have come to me, but nothing big. I remember baking and being in a small room." She didn't mention the spiders. That wasn't going to help anyone find missing children and they weren't memories she wanted to relive. It was ironic that the few things she did remember were the ones that she wished she didn't and she could only hope that her positive memories returned.

"That's good," Jack said. "Chances are your memories will continue to come back. That's what happened with the W's. Little pieces came a bit at a time, especially when there was something to jar their memory of the event." He paused and then a rare smile spread across his face. "It just occurred to me that you're a W too."

She gave him a small smile in return, but it was bitter-sweet. Being included as a W was nice, but it also meant that there were three other cousins who wouldn't get to be included under that name if she couldn't recover her memories. Rowena believed her brothers were dead, but no one knew what had happened to Jo and Reece's brother, Dylan. It was possible that, like her, he was still alive.

"Do you remember anything else about the healer?" Ben asked, interrupting her thoughts. "Jo didn't see him, but Simon did. He worked with a sketch artist, but so far we haven't gotten any leads."

The day she thought she'd met the healer would be forever etched in her mind.

Morgana shook her head. "Nothing different from what I've already told you. I thought he was dead until Simon mentioned him." Dead because her selfish actions had killed him. The fact that he'd lived didn't negate his suffering. She'd been bored one day and, wanting attention, had claimed to be sick. The healer never let on that she wasn't really sick and healed her anyway, which had drained him. He'd been gaunt and pale by the time he finished and had to be carried away.

Ben and Jack continued to ask her questions for another hour but once more she felt useless. She didn't want Copeland to have been right, but she feared that if she didn't remember more than snatches of memories soon, they might never come.

When they were leaving, Morgana walked by another picture of Ben's daughter. This one was of her with Ben's younger brother, Joel. They had large books spread in front of them, maybe textbooks, and they were both grinning at the camera like they had a secret.

A sudden image of another little girl with a book in front of her sprang into her mind. Burns covered the right side of the girl's face as she smiled at Morgana. She closed her eyes, trying to hold on to the image, but it disappeared as quickly as it had arrived. Opening her eyes, Morgana studied the picture of Julia and her uncle, and a name for the scarred little girl came to her: Sam. Morgana was sure there was a reason this memory was coming to her now. She just had to figure out who Sam was.

12

*D*amon knocked on Morgana's condo door and then walked in without waiting for a response. She stood at the stove with her back to him but looked over her shoulder and smiled.

The sight of her still caught him off guard It'd been a week since the spell broke and he'd sat beside her for hours yesterday, but a part of him was still trying to reconcile that the gray-eyed blond he'd been falling in love with was the beautiful brunette in front of him.

When they'd left Ben's yesterday, he'd asked to take her to dinner, but she'd declined, saying she needed some time alone. It had taken everything in him to respect that and walk away.

Watching her look at the pictures of Julia, he knew she'd been affected more than she'd admitted. He didn't think she'd remembered that she and Julia had been friends. Best friends like only little girls could be after meeting for the first time.

Damon walked over to Morgana and put his hand on her

cheek, drawing her attention his way. "Hello," he whispered as he dipped his head toward hers, capturing her mouth in a kiss. Her hands came up to his biceps and he moved his hand to the back of her neck. Placing his other hand on the small of her back, he tugged her up against his length and deepened the kiss. She tasted like the sweetest ambrosia.

She moaned against his mouth, and he felt himself harden before she pulled away. "I'm just finishing up and then we can take these down to the restaurant."

He looked at the eight dishes on the counter and bent close to one, breathing in the aroma of garlic and chili. "Smells delicious." He turned and winked at her. "We are going to a restaurant, you know."

She elbowed him in the ribs. "Funny."

"I think there are too many to carry, so why don't I just send them down to the restaurant?"

"Is that safe?" A nervous expression crossed her face as she glanced at him, then back at her creations.

"I'm sure it will be but let me check."

He pulled out his phone and typed a message to Meredith.

Damon: Table in SW corner clear?

Meredith: Let me check.

Meredith: Yes, why?

Damon: Incoming

Damon waved his hand in front of the dishes, and one by one, they disappeared off the counter. His phone pinged with an incoming text.

Meredith: Got 8.

Damon: Perfect.

"That's so handy. Sometimes I forget what magics can do."

"You're magic too. It'll come back."

"You seem so sure."

He cupped her cheek and gave her a quick kiss. "I am sure. Have you tried using your magic today?"

She nodded and turned away. Her voice was quiet as she wiped down the counter. "I tried making the bed."

"And?"

"The sheet twitched and then stopped." She whirled around and faced him. "Maybe it will never come back."

"It will. Meredith's came back once the spell was lifted. Hell... Reece's came back after he'd been spellbound twice and almost died. Yours will come back too."

She nodded again but didn't look convinced. "I just have to get my sweater from the bedroom. I'll be right back."

He leaned against the kitchen island as he waited and noticed a laptop sitting open. The obituary on the screen made him do a double-take. It was Julia Davis's.

"I'm ready to—" Morgana's words cut off as she walked into the kitchen. "Oh."

Damon turned around to face her. "She died about six months after you di— after the fire. Did reading this jog any memories?"

She paused and then shook her head. Reaching around him, she shut the laptop. "Ready to go?"

"Morgana, you just learned that someone you knew as a child died... It's okay to be upset."

"Don't patronize me, Damon. I get it. A lot of people died while I was gone."

"I wasn't being patronizing. I just think you've got a lot to digest and it's not all going to be happy-happy. A lot has happened in the time you've been gone."

"Dead. You mean when I might as well have been dead, Damon."

Grasping her arms, he looked her in the eyes. "No,

Morgana, not dead. It doesn't matter what we thought, because you didn't die. You lived a life for over twenty years that has shaped you, whether you remember it or not."

"Just like I don't remember Julia," she whispered.

Damon pulled Morgana into his arms and held her tight. After a few moments, he pulled back and looked down into her hazel eyes, moisture rimming their depths. "Don't put expectations on yourself that all your memories will come back right away now that the spell is broken. Some may never come back. Hell, I don't remember everything from when I was seven. You'll remember when you do, and if you don't, you don't."

"I know," she said and headed for the door.

The defeat in Morgana's words gutted him. "Wait."

When she stopped and turned, he walked over and took her hand, pulling her back toward the kitchen. "Humor me for a moment." He grasped her around the waist and plopped her down on a high stool so the height difference between them wasn't so vast. "I've got something for you. Close your eyes."

He leaned forward and rested his forehead against hers and pulled up a memory. It took little effort for him to float the memory into her mind.

She sucked in her breath as the first images must have become clear. He'd replayed the memory a hundred times in his own mind and knew its length and feel like a trusted friend.

It'd been the summer he and Jack built the swing set that had morphed into an enormous play structure. Molly's face wasn't visible in the memory since he'd stood behind her, pushing her on the swing. Her little girl laughter had been loud and joyful. Contagious even, and he'd caught himself laughing right along with her.

He must have pushed her for more than an hour. By the time she'd had enough, his arms had felt like wet noodles. He would have continued pushing her all night if she'd asked. Her delight had been so pure and innocent, he'd have done whatever he could to make it continue. Being the cause of it was just that much better. There'd been something about the little girl that made him want to make her smile.

"Thank you."

He opened his eyes at Morgana's whispered words and pulled back to see her face. Her eyes were bright with tears, but not even one fell. Leaning forward again, he kissed her forehead before helping her off the stool.

"You're welcome." He took her hand and they walked toward the door again. An image assaulted him and he flung out his hand, catching himself on the small table by the door.

"Damon! What's wrong?"

He straightened and forced a smile onto his face. "Just got a bit dizzy. I haven't eaten all day." The words, not quite a lie, fell from his lips easily. It was true that he'd been so busy since breakfast that he hadn't eaten.

Yet it wasn't the entire truth. His mother had always had visions, although she wasn't as powerful a seer as some. Neither he nor his sister had inherited the magic specialty, though they both had premonitions from time to time.

As they walked to the elevator, he could still picture his vision—Morgana lying on a cement floor, blood on her face and her clothes ripped. Her arm was stretched out in front of her as if reaching for him. Her eyes were closed, and she was covered in dust, mixed with blood, giving her a ghost-like appearance. He had no idea if she was alive. It had seemed so real it'd almost brought him to his knees.

MORGANA PLACED a large tray of Reece's desserts on one of the tables in the restaurant and looked up to see Isaac coming toward her. It was the first time she'd seen him since her final tattoo appointment.

"Hi, I didn't want to approach you during dinner, but since we're having dessert and it's winding down..." Isaac had always come across as a quiet guy, but not insecure. She'd never seen him so nervous before. "Ah... how are you feeling?"

"I'm good. Your tattoo worked," she said with a nervous laugh. God, the guy had touched her skin for hours and had seen her practically naked, they shouldn't be this awkward together.

"The headaches? Are they gone?"

"Haven't had one since the night of the last appointment."

He let out a long breath. "Good." He nodded and turned to go back to the tables.

"Isaac..."

Turning, he looked expectantly at her.

"Thank you."

"You're welcome."

She watched him walk back to the tables and sit a few seats down from Kate, who'd glanced over at Isaac several times, but the man seemed oblivious.

"Okay?"

She jumped at Damon's question and spun to face him. "Shit, Damon, don't sneak up on me. Isaac just wanted to check to see how I was doing."

"He's definitely a talented guy. Come on, I think Jack and Ben have an announcement. They'd mentioned talking to everyone, but wouldn't say about what." Damon put his hand on her back, and she let him guide her back to the table. Every time she allowed it, she wondered if she should stop it, if it was just a subtle way for him to control her. But each time she didn't because she enjoyed his touch.

"Can I have everyone's attention?" Jack asked, standing from his seat next to Meredith's at the end of the line of tables, his voice penetrating through the other voices until a hush fell over the large crowd.

"Consider this me putting on my leader of the North American council hat." Jack paused as nods and agreements passed among those at the tables. "You all know that Jo and Simon retrieved an ancient magic book, but you may not know that it is rumored that there are seven of them in the world. I say rumored because the council leaders only know of the whereabouts of two—the one from Jo that we now have and one held by the council in Eastern Europe."

Jack paused again and Meredith reached out and gripped his hand. "The book in Europe was stolen by Andrew Skalbeck, also known as Snake, and Drew Barnett, a former FBI agent who used the nickname Bullseye."

"You're kidding?" Reece scoffed. "Rather obvious, don't you think?"

Jack gave a humorless laugh. "Yes, Simon and Jo thought so too."

Rowena raised her hand like she was in school and garnered a few chuckles. "I don't get it."

"I didn't either as I've never been much into comics, but apparently Bullseye is the nickname for a character known as Benjamin 'Dex' Poindexter who is an evil FBI agent in the Daredevil comic series," Jack said.

"Jack, dear," Fiona called, getting his attention, "I was under the impression that Drew was still pretending to be on the FBI's side and going undercover with his father, Andrew."

Ben stood and nodded at Jack, indicating he'd take over.

"Once Drew revealed the connection between himself and Andrew… Snake… we knew immediately that Drew had been our mole all along. We were in a bind, needing to rescue Jo and Simon, and because Drew swore up and down that he hadn't been working with his father, we let him think we believed him. In the end, he did help us, but after that, we dropped all pretenses. Drew is evil, end of story."

"Now what?" Reece called out.

"Andrew and Drew killed a powerful magic—"

"No! Not Mary?" Rowena asked.

Morgana held her breath as she waited for Jack's answer. The Emissary had become a friend to them all recently.

"The Emissary—Mary—was injured in the attack but will be okay. I didn't know the person who was killed but it was one of the two magics guarding the ancient book. They both mentally reached out to Mary when they were attacked. She flashed there just in time to save one of them, but Skalbeck and Drew got away. Now Skalbeck has the knowledge to find the magic box." Ben gestured to Jack to pick up the mantel again.

Jack stood beside his mentor and looked at everyone seated around the tables—it was a large group and Morgana noticed that none of the restaurant magic staff were included. Besides those closely associated with the Williams family, the FBI agents who worked with Jack and came to most of the family dinners were also present. "All of you here today have in one way or another been affected by the search for the magic box that started with my father more than twenty years ago. Whether it be because of family you lost or through the FBI, we're all connected and have all suffered."

There were murmurs and heads nodding up and down at each of the tables.

"After Jo and Simon found the ancient book, we—Meredith, myself, and some leaders from other councils—were able to identify the spell that would locate the map to find the magic box. We found the map, but not the box. Everything we've tried with the map has been a dead end. By now, Snake and Drew will have a map too."

Copeland had never revealed much to Morgana, but she'd overheard him rant a few times about a magic box. It was always after he'd siphoned her magic and thrown her on the ground. Thinking she was unconscious, he'd spout off to one of his minions in her presence.

Her heart rate picked up just thinking about her prior hopelessness. She sucked in a breath and blew it out slowly to calm herself.

"You okay?" Damon whispered in her ear. The feel of his shoulder pressed against hers as he leaned close had its own calming effect.

She nodded at him before returning her attention to Jack and raised her voice above the din. "I've heard about the magic box, but I'm not sure what it does."

Jack turned her way. "It's believed that when it's opened, evil unlike anything we've ever seen before will be released, and it will take a strong magic council of fourteen members to contain the evil and close the box."

"How many council members do you have now?" Javier, one of the FBI agents, asked.

"Four. Myself, Meredith, Jo, and Simon. And as much as I'd like to initiate more members into the council, it doesn't work that way. When it's time, members are revealed to us. For now, all we can do is look for the box and hope to find it before Skalbeck does."

Morgana let the chatter carry on around her as another memory flashed before her eyes. Two men were arguing with Copeland as she lay on the floor, weak and drained. One of the men was Snake—who she now knew was

Skalbeck—and the other one went by Maverick. They'd been talking about transporting drugs.

She tried to hold onto the memory, force her mind to see the details, but the image left as quickly as it came.

Flashes of memories were coming faster now. But some, like the memory of Copeland and Maverick, faded before she could fully grasp onto them. Others stayed with her like she'd always had the memory.

Her first true image of Sam was like that. She and Sam had been huddled in a bed, the covers up over their heads. "You're going to leave here one day and then you'll come back," Sam whispered. Morgana had asked her how she knew, but the memory cut off abruptly. The girl had been important to Morgana—she'd loved her. With so few memories, Morgana didn't understand how she knew the friendship had been so precious to her, but it was. She'd do anything to help Sam.

The second memory was just as clear and came to her later that night. Morgana sat straight up in bed and looked around the room expecting to see Sam. In the dream, Morgana had been strapped to a chair in a small room. Rivulets of sweat ran down from her hairline, stinging her eyes. The ceiling fan did nothing to alleviate the oppressive heat.

Sam, maybe ten years old, stood in front of Morgana. The mottled and red burn scar on Sam's face stood out on her pale skin. A terrified look flashed across her face before she flattened her back to the wall. "One day he's going to kill us," Sam whispered.

Raised voices pervaded the room, and Morgana sensed—or perhaps remembered Snake—was coming to punish her for her earlier behavior when Morgana woke from the dream.

She flopped back onto her pillow and turned only her

head to stare out the window. The streetlights illuminated the darkened night, casting an eerie glow into the room. It jarred another memory that lay in her mind, just out of reach. She didn't know the significance, but it didn't matter because she had something far more important to focus on.

Sam was out there somewhere, expecting Morgana to come back for her. And she wouldn't let her down.

13

*D*amon sat in his car outside the Williams's buildings and watched Morgana step onto the sidewalk and look both ways. Stealth wasn't her forte, luckily for him.

He'd been sitting in his car waiting for her to show. She was up to something; he'd known it last night when she was vague about her plans for today. Stopping by Reece's bakery as soon as he opened that morning, he'd casually asked if Morgana was coming in to work today.

His questions hadn't fooled Reece, but Damon didn't care. It wasn't like his feelings for the woman were a secret. Reece told him that Morgana had talked about doing some shopping today. The last time she'd said she was going shopping, she'd been holed up in her apartment all day in pain.

Turning on the car, he checked the street and slowly pulled out, coming alongside Morgana. Pressing the button to lower the window on the passenger side, he leaned toward it. "Need a lift?"

She jumped at his voice and spun toward the car. "What are you doing here?"

"I was at the bakery and saw you. Thought you might need a lift somewhere." It wasn't a complete lie.

Morgana glanced up the street and then back at him. "Ah, no. I'm fine."

"Where are you going, Morgana?"

"Shopping?"

"Are you asking me?" She bit her bottom lip and hesitated. Leaning over further, he pushed open the passenger door. "I know you're not going shopping. Get in and I'll take you wherever you need to go." When she looked down the street again, he pressed her. "Please. Wherever you want to go. Really."

He saw the moment he'd won. Her shoulders dropped and she gave one last look at the street as a city bus drove by.

"Okay."

When she'd buckled up, he turned toward her. "Where to?"

"Copeland's."

He felt his eyebrows hit his hairline, but he shouldn't have been surprised. Once the Molly he knew as a child decided on something, no matter how crazy, she wouldn't let it go. People didn't change that much as they grew older, spell or no spell.

"Okay." He checked traffic and pulled onto the road. He'd never been to the building, but he knew the address because he'd handled the paperwork for Jack to buy it Jack hadn't given much of an explanation as to why he'd wanted it, just that he knew he had to buy it. Jack had visions, like Damon's mother, and sometimes it was best not to ask too many questions.

Whatever the reason, it was a good investment—a newer building at a decent price and located in a great part of town.

Morgana didn't say anything on the short drive. He found

a parking spot and parked, but she stared at the building and didn't move.

"Angel, are you sure this is what you want?"

She nodded and stepped out of the car. He followed and guided her to the building's large double doors and held one open for her. The door attendant greeted them as they walked in and asked for their names.

He smiled at the young man and said, "Damon Stone." The door attendant was non-magic and none the wiser when Damon magically manipulated the visitor list to include his name.

"Thank you, Mr. Stone. Enjoy your visit."

An elevator arrived quickly and Damon followed Morgana inside. She raised her hand to press a button but stopped. "I don't know which floor."

"Sixteen."

She pressed the button and stood staring at the panel. "I was here for a year and didn't know the floor," she said to the wall, her voice barely above a whisper.

Taking her arm, he gently turned her to face him. "You couldn't know. You were never allowed to leave. And you need to stop blaming yourself for what others did to you. Don't be so hard on yourself."

She nodded, but she didn't look convinced, and before he could press, the elevator signaled they had arrived at their destination. They stepped out into a long, lightly lit hallway. There were only a couple doors on the entire floor and he led Morgana to the one marked 1605.

Her steps slowed as they reached the door. She stared at it but didn't move to grasp the handle. "In the entire year I was here, the only time I ever stepped into the hallway was the night Meredith came."

Morgana's voice was quiet, like she'd forgotten he was here and she was reliving a memory.

"Copeland told me to greet a guest at the elevator. I thought it was a trick, but I didn't have a choice, and I guess it kind of was—a trick, that is." Morgana glanced over at the elevator before turning to face him. "Meredith got off the elevator and I told her... I told her to go."

Damon rubbed his knuckles along her cheek. "Angel, you didn't know who she was, but you tried to protect her anyway by telling her to go."

Morgana gripped his wrist like it was a lifeline. "I told her to leave. I said that the woman was as good as dead. I told her to leave our mother!" Morgana's final words came out as a wail, a look of devastation on her face. "I was going to let her die!"

She repeated the words again and again, like a mantra, her guilt more than any person should have to bear. Damon wanted to gather her in his arms and hold her tight. He resisted the urge as he saw her struggle to compose herself.

Morgana was stuck in a hell of someone else's making—one he couldn't truly comprehend. Slowly, she got herself under control and he admired her inner strength.

He leaned over and kissed her forehead, careful their bodies didn't touch. She needed space and he'd give it to her. "You didn't know she was your mother, and you were protecting Meredith. Even without knowing who she was, you still tried to protect your sister," he said, repeating his earlier words, hoping she'd eventually accept that she'd been selfless and had tried to protect someone she thought was a stranger.

Morgana nodded, but he knew she was still too deep in her self-loathing to listen to reason. "You don't have to go in, you know. It's in the past."

She turned back to face the door, but he had a feeling she wasn't seeing it, only the memories that lay behind it. "Yes, I do, and it's because of the past. I need to know if anything will jog my memory from before he brought me here."

"I'll get the door." The door lock was simple and released with little magic. He pushed it open and waited for Morgana to precede him.

The drapes from the large floor-to-ceiling windows were pulled back and the morning sun bathed the room in warm light. The room was empty, and a lingering scent of detergent peppered the air.

Morgana ran her hand along the wall as she walked slowly into the room. He couldn't imagine what was going through her mind.

Jack and Meredith had filled him in on some of what happened the day Morgana was rescued, but he didn't know all the details. Only that Copeland had flung Morgana against a wall and tortured her before it all finally ended in a violent and deadly showdown.

Copeland had held both Morgana and Meredith at knifepoint. Jack couldn't save them without their mother's help, which had led to her death.

"Do you think she knew I was her daughter?" Morgana asked softly, staring out the window. He expected she wasn't seeing what was in front of her, but whatever had gone on that day.

"I don't know, but she was willing to die for both you and Meredith."

Morgana nodded, but he didn't know if she was acknowledging his statement or that Elise had died for her.

She walked down the hall and went into one of the rooms. He followed at a short distance. Looking into the room, he noticed marks on the wooden floor where a bed must have sat against the wall, but the room held nothing else. No shelves to hold knickknacks or holes in the walls where pictures had hung.

The room was small, but something about it wasn't right. There weren't any windows or a closet and it seemed too narrow for a bedroom in a modern condo.

Walking into the room, he placed his hand on a wall and pulled on his magic. Controlling its trajectory, he pushed it slowly into the wall. A piece of drywall, in the shape of a perfectly formed circle about two feet in diameter, fell into the space on the other side of the wall.

Morgana rushed to his side. "What'd you do?"

"Something seemed wrong. The room was too narrow, so I took out a piece of drywall to see if it led into the next room as it should have. It didn't."

She came closer and peered through the large hole. "An empty space? Why would someone want a blocked-off space between the two rooms?"

"I don't think the space was the point. I think Copeland, or whoever designed the room, wanted you isolated. Blocking off half the room and giving you only a small area was one more way to control you and your environment."

"Oh." Morgana peered into the opening between the rooms once more and then turned her back to it. "I was hoping coming here would make me remember more of my past." She walked out of the room and trailed her hand along the wall again, then stopped.

Morgana backed up before moving forward again, dragging her hand along the wall. She said something, but he missed her whispered words. He walked around in front of her and waited for her to repeat herself.

After a few minutes, she spoke again without looking up. "I used to count the ridges in the wall paneling and the tiles on the floor. Sam taught me to do that. It helped center me when I was bored out of my mind or in pain."

"Who is Sam?"

Morgana dropped her hand and met his gaze. "She was

one of the kids with me. I think she was a year or two younger than me. I'd forgotten about her, like I had everyone else." She lifted her hand to the wall again. "I think maybe looking at pictures of Julia Davis and being here must have stirred a memory."

"More memories will come to you."

Morgana looked at her fingers on the wall, not meeting his eyes. "But what if they don't? What if Sam is somewhere waiting for someone to rescue her? Waiting for me to remember her?"

Damon wanted to tell her he'd fix everything, but no amount of money or magic could fix her memories or guarantee that Sam was safe, or even still alive.

"Angel, do you want to talk about what you do remember of Sam?"

"No, it's fine."

Damon hated the word *fine*. Not only was everything not alright, but he also suspected Morgana was up to something. A memory of when she'd been little suddenly came to him. They'd been at the lake celebrating someone's birthday and Morgana—Molly—was sitting under a large maple tree, running her hand back and forth over the grass. When he knelt beside her, he could see tear stains streaked through the dirt on her face, and she wouldn't look up at him. When he'd asked her what was wrong, she'd said she was fine. He'd had to hold in his laughter, amused that a five-year-old would use the word to dismiss his question, but she'd likely heard an adult say it in the same way. He'd learned later that she'd had a fight with Jo over some dolls. The next morning, the hair on two of the dolls' heads had been hacked off. Jo had stood there, her little face pinched in anger, when Molly had finally admitted what she'd done. She'd told all the adults that she'd do it again because Jo shouldn't have taken her dolls and she had to learn a lesson.

Damon was looking at the grown-up version of that little girl and she was going to try to fix what she saw as a problem —by saving Sam.

Damon didn't know where or who Sam was, but he could keep Morgana safe. He'd promised himself he wouldn't use his persuasion on her, but that was before he'd had the vision, and before he knew she was planning on going after her friend Sam.

He couldn't let her do that.

MORGANA FELT A MAGIC PUSH.

Damon used his fingers to lift her chin so she was looking into his eyes. "I think you should let Jack and Ben look into Sam for you."

She felt the push again and knew it was coming from Damon. "Really?" She bit the inside of her cheek to stop the smile that threatened to spread across her face. Holy shit— she could feel his magic. The realization made her almost giddy with relief.

"Yes, it's dangerous and better left to the FBI and the magic council."

The push was stronger this time as it attempted to flow into her very being. She didn't know how, but something in her not only detected the persuasion, it repelled it.

Morgana turned her head and looked down, forcing Damon's fingers to fall away. She bit her cheek again in her losing battle to control her smile as her joy threatened to burst from her. Her magic was coming back, and she had a magic specialty. She just knew it—she could detect and resist persuasion.

She felt a small sting cross over her ribs and then it was gone before she could think much of it.

Walking into the living room, she looked around and memories of Copeland controlling her pummeled through her thoughts. He'd had to spellbind her because she'd been able to resist his efforts at manipulating her. The explanation made so much sense.

She held out her hand and pulled on her magic from deep inside. Closing her eyes, she focused her very essence on her palm to conjure a tissue. After five tries with no success, she let out a huge breath and let her shoulders drop. Still no magic.

Copeland may have been right when he said her magic was weak. That she was only good for siphoning magic that others could use.

"Morgana? Are you alright?"

For a moment, she'd forgotten that Damon was even there, she'd been so lost in her pity. "I'm fine."

"There's that word again." His eyes held laughter as he walked around to fully face her. "You sure?"

"Yeah, I'm good. Let's go."

"Want to make a good memory here?"

She stopped and looked up at him. "What do you mean?"

"This." Grasping her hand in his, he tugged her close. His body was strong and muscled against her curves. Damon lowered his head and kissed her. It wasn't a light meeting of lips; it was a possession. She opened her mouth and allowed him access.

Every nerve in her body felt tuned to him as he lit her up. Her hands moved of their own accord, her fingers running through his thick hair, holding his head close as his mouth devoured hers.

She moaned into his mouth, and he lightly bit her lip and then soothed it with his tongue. His hands roamed down her back and cupped her ass, lifting her up. She felt his hard cock at her core as he dragged her up his body before she wrapped her legs around him.

He turned around, putting her back against the wall as he supported her. "We should slow down," he said against her skin as his mouth moved down her neck, firing up her nerves even more. His words were in direct opposition to his actions.

She much preferred his movements. "No, I want you."

He lifted his head and looked her in the eyes. "I want you too, but not here."

She nipped at his neck and licked where she'd made her small bite. "I thought we were making new memories."

"Yes, and we have, but let's go somewhere more comfortable." She felt his magic push into her again. He was determined to use his persuasion to get what he wanted. She'd been right all along—he'd be kind and loving, but as soon as she didn't do things his way, his controlling nature would come out.

Dropping her legs from around his waist, she pulled back as he let her go. "You're right." Mustering a smile, she took his proffered hand and let him lead her out of the apartment.

Looking at their joined hands, the irony sank deep into her consciousness. She was walking away from a place where she'd been controlled to the point that she'd lost herself and was now holding onto a man who wanted to do the same. Damon had better intentions than Copeland, but did that really matter?

Damon wasn't going to change any more than she could. Morgana needed to be free and not allow herself to be controlled, but that wouldn't be possible with Damon.

14

*M*organa added her wallet to the already full backpack and took one last look around the apartment to make sure she had everything she needed.

A memory of her packing a small purple suitcase flashed into her mind. The memories were coming faster now, and she'd had a long sleepless night of practicing letting them come and go as her mind willed.

After locking the apartment door, she took the back stairs down to street level and exited out into a deserted alley. Thankfully no one was around at five in the morning as she headed for the street corner she'd plugged into the rideshare app. Even at the early hour, she risked someone seeing her if she'd asked the car to pick her up in front of the Williams's buildings instead.

The car ride to the bus station wasn't long and then it was only a short wait before Morgana was on a bus headed south. Thanks to a free apartment and working for the restaurant and bakery, she had a healthy amount in her bank account and didn't have to worry about the costs to get to Mexico.

Mexico. She shivered at the thought of going back there,

but she knew in her heart that Sam was there. Two more memories of Sam had come to Morgana during the night. The first had been of the woman who'd taught her to bake taking Morgana and Sam to a market and then back to a compound. Ana—that had been the woman's name; it'd finally come to her. Morgana didn't know what had become of the woman, and would probably never find out, but in her mind, she thanked Ana for helping her find the compound. The second memory had been of Sam telling her to come back. Morgana now had a destination and a purpose.

Pulling her feet up onto the bus seat, she wrapped her arms around her legs and watched as the world passed by out the window. She wondered how long it would take before someone figured out she was gone. She'd left a note on her kitchen counter saying she was taking a short vacation, but hadn't mentioned where.

Damon would look for her, she just didn't know how soon he'd start his search. Touching her lips with her finger-tips, she closed her eyes and pictured Damon as he'd looked yesterday after he'd kissed her.

The images outside faded as her new memories swamped her thoughts. She remembered when she'd moved with the kids from an apartment in New York to Ciudad Victoria, Mexico. Not that she'd known where she was at the time, she'd only just remembered it thanks to the two new memories.

Morgana read her book or looked out the window as the time passed slowly, and when the bus stopped for a short break, she'd get off and stretch her legs. Back on the bus, she'd go back to reading her book or looking out the window. It was the same routine over and over again for over twenty hours. According to her itinerary, she still had about another eighteen hours to go.

The time crawling by reminded her of being locked in the

room at Copeland's. She shivered as she remembered what her selfishness had done to the healer. No matter how bored she became on the bus, she knew that life could always be worse. Sticking to her book, looking out the window, and taking short naps between stops, she let the hours pass.

The frequent bus stops had blended into one another hours ago and she no longer even looked to see where they were. Hiking her backpack onto her shoulder, she exited the bus at the next brief stop and walked into the terminal, looking for the restroom.

At four in the morning, the place was quiet and weary travelers littered benches and the floor. She stepped over and around people and bags as she made her way to a short hallway at the back of the building.

The restroom was deserted as she used the toilet and washed her hands. She peered at herself in the old, foggy mirror on the wall and a tired, long-haired, hazel-eyed brunette stared back. Hopefully, someday her reflection would no longer catch her by surprise. She gave herself one more glance and pulled the door open.

Three men leaned against the wall opposite the restroom. Two of the men wore checkered long-sleeved shirts buttoned up to their necks. One sported a sideways baseball cap and the other had hair cropped close to his head. Both were taller than Morgana's five foot seven by several inches, but the third man was even taller.

He stepped forward and leered at her. "Where you goin', little girl?"

It wasn't his size that had all the hairs on the back of Morgana's neck standing up—it was his eyes. His pupils were black pinpoints, making them seem lifeless. Tattooed words surrounded his left eye and snaked down his cheek onto his neck.

Morgana felt her magic stir and it told her that all three

men were non-magic. She wanted to shout for joy that her magic was moving and hopefully coming back, but she kept her expression neutral as she faced the tattooed man as he took another step toward her.

She pointed down the hall toward the front of the building. "I need to catch my bus."

"No, we'll give you a ride to wherever you'd like to go."

Baseball cap man moved closer. "Oh, I'll give her a ride."

Morgana slipped her arm through the backpack strap that dangled around her waist so the bag hung securely on her back and left her arms free. Dropping her hands by her sides, she kept them loose and concentrated on pulling her magic from deep within her core. Her fingers tingled and once more she wanted to jump up and down with glee.

Tattoo man reached for Morgana's arm and she spun to the right and held out her hand. A ball of magic glowed in her palm like a beacon.

"The fuck!" Tattoo man lunged for her as baseball cap man did the same.

Whipping her other hand in front of her, Morgana conjured another orb and took aim. Both balls of light sailed across the short distance and connected with their targets. The men fell back, their screams silent as they hit the ground.

Close-cropped man shouted a vicious obscenity and pounced at Morgana. Feeling her magic at the surface, she put on a burst of speed and side-stepped the man, his momentum taking him forward into the wall.

He recovered quickly and pulled out a gun. "Nuh uh, bitch. Stay there. What'd you do to my friends? You some kind of alien?"

"Yes, I am. You better stay away." They'd already seen her magic so it couldn't get any worse. No one would believe them about seeing aliens anyway.

"Yeah? Well, I don't wanna stay away. How 'bout I let you git up close and personal with my Glock here?"

She stared at the gun—maybe things could get worse.

DAMON KNOCKED on Morgana's door and waited. A sense of déjà vu washed over him. She should be home this early. Her headaches had stopped when the spell broke, but what if they were back? He wanted to kick himself for not even asking. When they got back from Copeland's condo yesterday, he'd wanted to talk to her about her plans but hadn't even considered she might not be feeling well or was overwhelmed by what she'd remembered at the condo. He just couldn't let go of the feeling in his gut that was telling him something was up.

An emergency call from work had kiboshed their evening, but it was only seven in the morning now, so unless she was at the bakery, she should be here.

Using his magic, he scanned the apartment and didn't sense anyone. He flashed to the back of Reece's bakery where he'd be out of sight. Large hedges hid him from anyone who might be around at the early hour.

He knew the bakery's layout and would have preferred to flash inside. Unfortunately, Reece had some non-magic employees who could be working inside and Damon didn't want to have to wipe any memories.

The bakery must have just opened as there was a line of customers when he walked around to the front. He directed some persuasion at the people waiting in line, pushing the thought into their minds that he was someone important and they needed to let him pass.

Damon waved at the two staff members he'd seen before,

both magic, as he skirted the counter and headed to the door that led to the kitchen. "Reece in the back?"

The older staff member smiled and nodded before she turned back to serve a customer.

The heat from the ovens hit him as soon as he walked into the back. He took a deep breath and breathed in the scent of fresh bread and the sweetness of cupcakes. He'd have to pick up a few before he left.

"Hey Damon, need a job?"

Damon laughed at the long-standing joke between the two of them and stuffed his hands in his pockets so he didn't accidentally touch any of the clean surfaces. Reece's hands were covered in flour and rolling out what looked like pastry dough.

"Morning. Have you seen Morgana today? I wanted to talk to her and thought she might be working with you this morning."

"No, I actually haven't seen her since the day before yesterday."

Damon's Spidey sense started tingling low in his gut. Never a good thing. It was likely his magical essence stirring, but the thought of him having comic-type superhero powers would have been amusing if he wasn't so worried about Morgana.

The cupcakes could wait. He needed to find her, especially if he was right about her trying to find Sam on her own. "I'm going to flash from here since I didn't see any non-magic staff here today. Alright?"

"Sure. Let me know if you find her."

Damon nodded and flashed back to Morgana's. At her door, he scanned the interior of the apartment and still felt no signs of life. The door lock was easy to bypass, and as he entered the apartment, he got the immediate sense that Morgana hadn't just stepped out for a moment, but was gone. The place was spotless, not even her eReader or a glass laying around, and the drapes were drawn.

A piece of paper on the kitchen island caught his attention. He couldn't remember seeing Morgana's handwriting before. Such a common thing and yet he wouldn't have been able to place it. Instead of cursive writing, she'd written in neat block lettering.

DEAR EVERYBODY,
I NEED TO GET AWAY FOR A WHILE TO THINK.
I'LL CALL IN A FEW DAYS.
LOVE,
MORGANA

Damon knew the getting-away-to-think thing was similar to the claims to go shopping. If all she'd needed was time to think, she wouldn't have kept it a secret. He placed the paper back on the counter and walked to her bedroom. The room was just as spotless as the rest of the apartment.

He opened the door to her walk-in closet. She didn't have a large wardrobe and had even told him once that she didn't need a lot of clothing. There were clothes still hanging from the rod, a few sweaters neatly folded on shelves, and shoes lined up in cubbies. Letting out a breath he hadn't known he'd been holding, he left the apartment and locked the door behind him.

When he'd walked into her closet, a part of him had feared she'd packed up everything she'd owned and left for good.

He flashed up one floor to Meredith and Jack's apartment and knocked on the door.

Jack answered and waved him in. "Morning. Want some coffee?"

"Sure." Damon looked around the apartment that was almost identical to Morgana's. "Where's Meredith?"

"She had an early meeting at the office."

"So no running this morning?"

"Oh yes," Jack said, dragging out the s. "We went out really early." Jack passed Damon a mug and held up his own. "Thus, the coffee. My second cup."

Damon chuckled and lifted his coffee in thanks before taking a sip. "Have you seen Morgana this morning?"

The corner of Jack's lip twitched. "I knew you hadn't come just to catch up. And no, I haven't seen her in a couple of days. I can check with Meredith." Jack's face lost all expression and Damon figured he was mentally talking to his wife. "No, Meredith hasn't seen her either," Jack said, confirming Damon's guess.

"I didn't realize you could communicate over such long distances... Anyway..." Damon perched on a stool and wrapped his hands around his mug. "I think Morgana left."

"Left? As in packed up all her shit and isn't coming back?"

"I don't know. Most of her stuff looks like it's still in her apartment, but she left a note that said she had to get away for a few days to think."

"You don't believe her?"

Damon let out a large sigh. "I don't know. She's lied a couple of times, saying she had to go shopping when she was really doing something else. I got the sense yesterday that she's up to something now too."

"Like what?"

"I think she left to find a woman named Sam."

Jack looked off into the distance for a few moments and then turned back to Damon. "I just asked Meredith and she doesn't know anyone named Sam."

"I think Morgana's memories are coming back and something she saw at Copeland's yesterday may have triggered a memory about her. The girl was someone who was in captivity with her."

"The fuck? I'm guessing Morgana dragged you to Copeland's?"

"I caught her sneaking off and gave her a lift. I didn't want her to have to go to Copeland's place alone."

Jack topped off both their coffee mugs before he spoke again. "The door attendant let you in with no problems?"

Damon smirked. "Not once he saw my name on the visitor list."

"Anything else happen?"

"You might say that. There's a two-foot hole in the drywall of the small bedroom."

"Annnnd, why is that?"

"It was the room Morgana had been kept in. Something just seemed off—the room's size was wrong and there wasn't a window or closet."

"I'd noticed that, but since the place is sitting empty for now, I haven't gotten around to checking it out further. What did you find?"

"There's a false wall. Nothing's in the empty space and there's no way to get out of it. I'm guessing Copeland put it up just to make the room smaller and it was one more way to control Morgana."

Jack's curse blistered the air. "He always was a mean, controlling bastard."

Damon finished his coffee and used his magic to clean the mug. "I should get going. Thanks for the coffee."

"What are you going to do about Morgana?"

"I'm not sure. I'd like to go after her, but I don't know where she is."

Jack gave one of his rare smiles. "I can help you out with that, my friend."

Damon recognized the devious look on his best friend's face and raised an eyebrow.

"We gave Morgana a Williams Company phone—which means we can track it. Meredith was so worried about Morgana's headaches that she feared she'd end up stranded somewhere too sick to reach out, so Meredith put one of those find-my-phone apps on the phone. I'll check with her and let you know."

"Sounds good."

They said their goodbyes and Damon flashed to the parking garage in the basement since he'd driven to the Williams's. He'd go to the office to handle any urgent items and make sure he'd be clear for a couple of days.

By then Jack should have gotten back to him with Morgana's location and he'd find her and bring her home. Then he'd think about why his persuasion hadn't worked on her and find a way to remedy that for her own safety.

15

*M*organa kept her eyes on the gun, not willing to risk glancing away. She hadn't noticed any security cameras, but then, she hadn't been looking for them. The bus terminal was old and small but hopefully in the twentieth century when it came to technology.

Her magic was back, but how much of it? She didn't even know if she could flash. Raising her hands in front of her in the universal sign for surrender, she looked at close-cropped guy. "Okay, don't hurt me."

He waved his gun toward his comrades on the floor. "See if they're breathin'."

She took a tentative step toward the men where they lay sprawled several feet apart on the grungy tile floor. Closing her eyes, she took a deep breath to calm herself. Flashing somewhere sight unseen was never a good idea, but she didn't have much to lose.

She'd seen an alley at the side of the building and didn't know what was in it, but it was probably safer than here. Focusing her entire concentration on her magic, she pulled it forth to flash.

Nothing happened. Opening her eyes, she looked down at the unconscious men on the floor.

"Stop fuckin' stallin'! See if they're breathin'."

Morgana reached forward with one hand and lightly pressed her fingers to tattoo man's neck. His pulse beat strong against her fingers. Repeating the process with base-ball cap man, she found he was alive as well. At least she hadn't killed anyone.

She looked over her shoulder at close-cropped guy. "They're alive."

"Wake 'em up."

A gun pointed at her was bad enough; she wasn't going to ask to be raped. She knew that's what would happen if she faced all three of them while they were conscious because of the sickening vibe they'd given off earlier.

An image of Damon rubbing his knuckles along her cheek, telling her how strong she was, flashed in her mind's eye. She hadn't felt strong, but maybe he'd been right. For two years, she'd felt weak and had let others control her.

Damon had been right—she was strong, and whether she could flash or not, she needed to stand on her own two feet. Clenching her hands into fists at her sides, she closed her eyes and concentrated on her magic.

"Bitch! I told you to wake them."

Morgana ignored the taunt and focused on her hands. The feeling of sand slipping through her fingers felt glorious.

Jumping to her feet, she flung the sand in close-cropped guy's face. Without waiting, she conjured some more and aimed at his eyes. As soon as his weapon hit the floor, she threw out her arm and sent her magic toward the gun. It whipped down the hallway like it was being chased.

Morgana didn't take the time to watch where it landed. Spinning around, she landed a kick to the man's groin with all her magic's force behind her. Momentum carried him backward at a speed so fast he landed halfway in the drywall behind him.

Morgana turned and ran, heading for the bus.

The bus loading area was more crowded now, with several buses lined up and passengers departing.

Side-stepping tired passengers and walking along the sidewalk, she checked the number on each bus.

She found hers just as it was pulling out. Waving her arms, she ran to the door. The bus stopped and the door opened. The driver gave her a tired look when she climbed the stairs.

"Sorry." She gave him her most heartfelt smile then walked back to an open seat and flopped down.

Luck had been on her side when she'd faced those guys. Maybe Damon was right and going after Sam on her own was too dangerous. She looked out the window as the scenery flashed by and wondered if she was making a mistake.

MORGANA RAN her hand through the gravel and pieces of grass where she leaned against a tree to watch the compound. Shifting her position, she tried to relieve some of the numbness in her butt from sitting on the hard ground for so long.

She'd arrived in the city yesterday afternoon and found a hotel, hoping a plan would come to her. Without conscious thought, she'd spoken to the hotel clerk in Spanish and she knew her accent had been flawless. It seemed strange that she hadn't figured out she knew Spanish in the last two years, but then maybe her brain hadn't needed to.

A few months ago, she'd watched the original Jason Bourne movie with Reece; she could be like the movie's main character and not know she could do something until she tried. Maybe she should have tried to use some martial arts on the bad guys in the bus terminal. She giggled at her own joke before she remembered the seriousness of where she was.

During the night, another memory of the had floated into her consciousness, as clear as day, waking her from sleep. Between the memory of Ana taking them to the market and this new one, she knew where to go.

After that, sleep had been elusive and though she'd lain awake, her ever-important plan still eluded her. Hours later, all she'd decided upon was going to the compound to see if she'd get another idea.

The compound was just on the edge of the city. A large gate and fence surrounded the buildings with a guard house flanking the entrance. Two guards manned the small building and others patrolled the area. A few cars had gone in and out, but there'd been no movement in the yard in front of the main building.

Morgana remembered being in that yard, sitting with Sam as they daydreamed about a future away from the compound. Sam had been in love with someone since she was a little girl. The guy's name was on the tip of Morgana's tongue, just out of reach. So many things seemed that way.

Sure, she'd made it out of the compound, but her life wasn't what she'd dreamed it would be. No husband and kids with the white picket fence. Maybe that was all just a child's dream. Or maybe not. She and Damon hadn't spoken about a future but they were more than just attracted to each other.

Fear was holding her back. She knew it, but she didn't know what to do about it. If she let herself love Damon and be with him, would it be enough? What would happen when he tried to tell her what to do? He'd already tried to use his persuasion on her and there would be nothing to stop him from trying again. Well... she could resist it, but what would that do to them as a couple? One of them always trying to persuade and the other always resisting? Eventually, they'd resent each other.

When he'd stopped her on the street on her way to Copeland's, she'd been sure he'd try to talk her out of going. He hadn't; he'd been supportive. Until he wasn't. The thought that she'd detected his push of persuasion had been in the forefront of her mind for days. It had been the first sign her magic was coming back. Why she could sense his persuasion but couldn't even do simple magic like make a bed was a mystery. But it wasn't the only unusual thing that happened the day they'd gone to Copeland's.

When she'd been getting ready for bed that same day, she'd examined her tattoo in her full-length mirror. Another sunflower had changed. That was when she knew that the sting she'd felt was the tattoo changing. She hadn't noticed when the first sunflower had transformed into the butterfly, but after all the pain she had been through and the fear that she was going to die, the slight sting was negligible.

The butterfly had made sense—she'd been transformed. But this new serpent was a bit of a mystery. It wasn't until she Googled serpents that it became apparent. Serpents symbolized cunningness and manipulation. When she'd read that, she'd laughed out loud in her empty bedroom. She'd resisted Damon's persuasion in Copeland's condo, and he hadn't even known. Now she had a visual reminder that she could resist manipulation.

Rubbing her shirt where the tattoo was, she stared out at the compound without focusing on the details. There were four sunflowers left—could there be four more pieces of magic in her future? Four more changes? Her lips twitched at the thought.

The night before in her hotel room, she'd tried to flash again but she hadn't moved even an inch. So she couldn't flash, but she could conjure almost anything she wanted now. She'd conjured an entire outfit piece by piece, and although she'd been so drained afterward that she'd needed a nap, she'd still done it. It could have been just too much, too soon.

Movement caught her eye as she stared at the compound. Three people exited the large building, heading for the parking lot that sat off to the side. There were two large men and a smaller woman, wearing a long billowy skirt, her hair in a braid flowing down her back.

Morgana stood and walked close to the fence line but stayed off to the side, hoping not to bring attention to herself. The woman looked up and Morgana sucked in her breath. It was Sam. Her hair was longer than Morgana remembered, falling in waves over the right side of her face, obscuring her burn.

Closing her eyes, Morgana tried to throw a thought into Sam's mind, but felt a barrier, like the thought had bounced back. Morgana huffed out a breath, angry at herself for not thinking this plan through further. She couldn't follow Sam without a vehicle. Morgana had taken a rideshare to the compound and Sam would be long gone before Morgana could get another one.

One of the men with Sam walked to the driver's door of a large SUV and waited while the other led Sam to the back passenger side. Sam looked up and caught Morgana's gaze once more.

Market. Tomorrow. Eight a.m.

Sam got into the vehicle, and they'd pulled up to the gate to exit before Morgana registered what had happened. She'd found Dam! Holy Shit! And Sam had recognized Morgana and thrown a thought at her. Double holy shit!

"Hello, Morgana."

She swung around and came face to face with Damon.

"How'd you find me?"

He raised one eyebrow. "That's your biggest concern? Meredith was worried about you collapsing from a headache and not being able to reach anyone, so she put a tracking app on your phone."

"But I turned the phone off." As soon as she called the rideshare, she'd turned the phone off. Oh... and she'd turned it back on both times she'd called another rideshare—from the bus terminal to the hotel and then from the hotel to the compound. She wanted to smack herself in the forehead. Duh! She'd read enough romantic suspense novels; she knew she should have bought a throw-away phone, but she hadn't anticipated anyone would actually track her that way.

"What are you doing, Morgana?"

"I—" She gaped for a moment, deciding what to say, then spit out the truth. "I came looking for Sam and I found her."

"You thought coming down to Ciudad Victoria, Mexico, almost 1,400 miles from home, all alone, without any magic to protect yourself was a great idea?" His eyebrows rose further into his hairline with each word, but his voice remained calm. Maybe too calm.

"Well... maybe not a great idea. But I knew if I told anyone, they'd try to stop me."

Damon frowned. "You think so little of me?"

Morgana took a step forward and poked her finger into Damon's chest. "You tried to use your persuasion on me. You told me not to look for Sam. Let someone else handle it, you said." Unlike Damon's, her voice had risen by the time she'd finished, and the end of her finger was sore from poking it into his hard, muscular chest.

"I care about you, Morgana." He put his hand over hers and flattened it to his chest. The heat from his hand and chest had a calming effect, breaking through her anger.

"I know."

Gently grasping her arms, he pulled her back to look into her eyes. "Do you?"

"Yes, but you tried to use your persuasion on me. You wanted to control me."

He closed his eyes for a moment before meeting her gaze. "I know, angel. I didn't know what else to do. I was worried you'd do something like this." He waved his hand toward the compound. "You're a young, beautiful woman on her own. Someone could have attacked you or taken you."

"I know."

"You keep saying that. Do you actually believe it, or are you just saying what you think I want to hear?"

She dropped her head to his chest and rolled his question around in her mind. She did know coming down here on her own wasn't safe; any logical person would know that. But did she really internalize it and think about it? No. Meredith had told Morgana that she'd been impulsive when she was little, but for so long that had been beaten and spellbound out of her. Maybe she really was embracing her old self, whether it was a good thing or not.

Damon lifted her chin with his fingers. "Morgana?"

"I'm sorry for worrying you."

He let out a big breath and dropped his forehead to hers. "Okay."

Cars honking on the nearby street brought them both back to the present and she stepped back.

He took her hand. "Will you come with me so we can plan the next steps?"

She nodded and let him lead her away from the compound. The big question was if she'd let him lead her anywhere else. He was starting to take over her life. First it had been pleasuring her with phone sex, even though she'd enjoyed it, then letting him guide her, and now she was leaving the compound when she wanted to stay and wait for Sam to return. What would she let him dictate next?

*D*amon shut the door to his suite at the Hilton and watched Morgana walk around the room, trailing her hand over the furniture. He'd flashed from Blue Mountain to General Pedro José Méndez International Airport with a carry-on bag and rented an SUV. Keeping up appearances was second nature to him. As a global businessman, he could run into people he knew anywhere he went and had to be prepared. He always got a suite when he traveled for business because he often entertained clients, so he stuck with his routine.

For all the magics there were in the world, their numbers were still small compared to non-magics, which necessitated a lot of business with both sides. That meant keeping up his usual habits and always being prepared for whatever or whoever he came across.

Tossing his keys on a side table, he walked to the bedroom with his bag and Morgana's backpack and placed them on the bed. She hadn't said much on the drive. He felt the anger radiating off her. They'd gone to her hotel to grab her backpack and check her out, then proceeded to the Hilton.

She was standing at the sliding glass doors looking out, but he had no idea what was going on in her mind. He wasn't sure if any magics could read minds, but it wasn't out of the realm of possibility. He wished he had the skill right at that moment. She thought he wanted to control her but that wasn't true. He just wanted to keep her safe.

Devastation wasn't a strong enough word to explain how he'd felt when he'd lost his father, but it would do. Not knowing what had happened to him was the worst. He'd wondered for years if his father was still alive until his mother told him she'd had a vision of his father's death. He couldn't say for sure he'd believed even then.

Morgana could have come down here and disappeared without a trace. She'd been alone in his bloody vision of her, just her reaching her arm out, so he didn't even know if he'd been there. As soon as he'd discovered she left, his vision of her was front and center in his mind, driving him to find and protect her.

He'd thought about telling her about the vision, but then changed his mind. She didn't need to worry about that on top of everything else she'd been through, especially since it might not come true. But if something did happen to her, he didn't know if he'd survive. She meant so much to him. Was he in love with her? Probably. And if it wasn't one hundred percent love yet, it was pretty damn close. Seeing her smile brightened his day and all day, every day, he wanted to know what she was doing. If there was anything he could do for her.

Damon walked up behind Morgana and pulled her back against his front. He hadn't realized until he'd pulled her back to him that he'd started holding her this way so she was close but wouldn't feel smothered. "I don't want to control you. I just want you to be safe."

She turned in his arms and tilted her head to look up at him. "Really? What about the persuasion?"

"I told you—it's for your safety, angel." He was starting to feel like a broken record. Why couldn't she understand? Fuck, he hated this circular argument. "I was worried you'd do something stupid, like come down to Mexico by yourself!"

Morgana pulled back, putting distance between them. He shoved his hands into his pants pockets so he wouldn't pull her back into his arms like he desperately wanted to.

She put her hands on her hips, and he knew the feisty person he'd remembered from their childhood was back. "That's bullshit, Damon. You could have talked to me. We could have figured out a plan. But you didn't and you wonder why I didn't tell you what I was doing?"

Her question was rhetorical and he watched her take a quick breath without waiting for him to respond. "I knew you wouldn't let me make decisions on my own. That you wouldn't support me. Instead, you'd just be the big, sexy, alpha CEO and do whatever you wanted."

He kept his expression neutral and didn't respond to the *big, sexy, alpha* part, but he so wanted to. "I know, and I was wrong."

"Do you actually believe that or are you just saying what you think I want to hear?" she asked, throwing his words from earlier back in his face. Touché.

He circled the back of her neck with a large hand and leaned forward, placing a soft kiss on her lips. "Yes, I know it. But knowing I was wrong and forcing myself not to make the same mistake again are two different things."

"I need to do things on my own." She took a step back.

"Why?"

A look of skepticism crossed her face. "What do you mean why? I need to be independent and not feel weak. Other people controlled me for years. You told me I'm strong... well, I need to find out for myself if I really am."

He held in the sigh he wanted to release, knowing she'd read too much into it. "You are strong, and there's a difference between being controlled and asking for help." Was he not waiting for her to ask for help? But would she if she was in trouble?

"Right, and there's a difference between knowing when to step back and when to take control."

He lifted the corner of his mouth as he looked down at her. "Right. I guess we both have a lot to learn, angel." He leaned forward and gave her another kiss. What he'd meant as a quick touch of the lips turned into so much more. She grasped his biceps and pulled him toward her.

Anger still vibrated off her. Her kiss was heated, but he got a sense it was outrage and her needing to release pent-up tension more than passion. He should pull back, but he wanted her as much as she did him. His magic essence didn't care anymore than his cock did if it was just angry sex—they both wanted her.

"Remove my clothes," she said against his lips.

His cock twitched in his pants at her comment. They were going too fast, and his dick would be pissed at him for pulling back, but they needed to. He'd made love to her with his lips and hands, but this would be the first time their bodies truly came together. "We need to slow down." He told himself that they should wait, but he was quickly losing his logic as to how long or even why.

She carded her fingers through his hair and then grabbed a handful of strands and pulled his mouth back to hers. "No. Fuck me, Damon," she said against his lips.

He needed to be honest with himself—he didn't want to wait and he had to trust that Morgana knew what she was doing. He called on his magic and dispensed with their clothing, the items landing in a pile on the floor. The first touch of her naked body flush against his sent sparks of desire straight to his cock.

Her hand worked between them and gripped his cock in a firm fist then stroked him. He groaned against her mouth. Gritting his teeth, he forced words out. "Stop, or I'm going to come too soon. I want to worship you, angel."

She gripped him tighter. "No. You don't get to do that. You don't get to come down here and tell me what to do and then say you want to worship me. You either want to tell me what to do or you don't. You can't have it both ways, Damon. You want to tell me what to do? Fine. Take me, control me. Fuck me."

This wasn't how he thought their first time together would go, but unless she told him to back off, he wouldn't stop. He snaked his hand between their bodies where she still gripped him and split her sex with two fingers. She was soaking wet and ready for him. He rubbed her clit and she sank deeper onto his hand.

"No. Not sweet and you only pleasuring me. If we're going to do this, then we're doing it together." She spun away from him and faced the back of the couch, putting her hands on the back ledge and thrusting her ass into the air. What a gorgeous ass it was.

She pushed her ass back into him. "Fuck me."

He ran his hands along her back and kneaded the globes of her ass. Then he held one hand out, palm up, and called for a condom that had been in his wallet. He let go of her just long enough to rip open the packet and sheath himself.

She had turned away from him so he couldn't see her face. She was trying to convince herself that this was just fucking and not making love. But she was wrong. No matter how fast or hard it was, he was making love to her. He gave the head of his cock one more squeeze to stave off his orgasm, then ran his hands up her back and then down along the tattoo on her sides.

Running his fingers along the sunflowers, he stopped and focused more closely on them, then counted. There were now only four sunflowers when there had been five. The first of the six, as he remembered, had transformed into a butter-fly. The second was now a coiled serpent with its head in the air.

"A serpent?"

She looked over her shoulder at him. "It happened after you tried to control me with your persuasion." She pushed back against him again, and his cock rubbed along her folds, covering him with her juices. Glaring at him as if to dare him to stop, she pushed back again. "Are we going to have sex?"

She was still trying to convince herself that it was just sex, but he was going to make love to her, regardless of how rough it was. He positioned himself at her entrance and pushed the head of his cock into her heat. They both groaned at the delicious sensation and he knew he wouldn't last. He pushed in a bit farther, then stopped. She was so tight, she was like a vise on his dick. An amazing, hot vise.

The thought stopped him. She'd been held in the compound almost her entire life and then she'd been Copeland's captive. "Angel?"

"I'm not a virgin," she said, as if reading his thoughts. "I knew I wasn't, but now I have a vague memory of a guard."

"Did he force you?"

She hung her head. "I don't remember much, but there was consent."

Even though she wasn't a virgin, it had obviously been a long time for her. He bent over her and wrapped his arm around to her front and fingered her clit. Her breath hitched and she rubbed against his hand. Slowly, he pushed the rest of the way into her hot sheath.

When his fingers were drenched, he pulled his hand away and gripped her hips with both hands. "Rub your clit."

She did as he said and let out a soft moan before pushing back into him. He pulled out and thrust back in, picking up speed as she met him thrust for thrust. Lifting her hips to change the angle, he knew he'd hit just the right spot when she tightened around him and screamed his name. He let go and gave a soundless shout as he released into her.

Their heavy breathing was the only sound in the room. He pulled out of her and disappeared the condom before flipping her around to face him. She looked down at the floor. He couldn't tell if she was embarrassed or ashamed, but he wouldn't have her feeling either one. He picked her up in his arms, ignoring the way she cried out in surprise, and cradled her against his naked chest.

It was time to execute step four and show her they could be good together... and that he could keep her safe.

MORGANA WOKE UP SLOWLY, taking in her surroundings. She was in a bed with a large, warm arm draped over her waist. Damon. They'd made love last night. She'd tried to tell herself that it had been just sex, and maybe the first time was, but not the others. They'd worshipped each other's bodies, no matter what she'd told him earlier. After the first time, Damon conjured them some robes and they'd sat on the couch and ate food delivered by room service.

When they'd finished dinner, she couldn't resist him, and they'd showered together and made love in the warmth and wet. They toweled each other off and crawled into bed sated, and she fell asleep in his arms. Sometime in the middle of the night, he'd woken and reached for her, making love to her again like she was the most precious thing in the world. It was everything she'd dreamed of.

Now, with the morning's sunlight streaming in through the window and the weight of Damon's arm across her body, she wondered if she'd made a mistake. Would he now expect her to act like a docile little woman who would do his bidding? She'd told him she wouldn't make love to him, but she'd folded and done it anyway. No matter what she'd said, he'd still gotten his way.

Damon tugged her tighter to his side. "You're thinking too hard over there."

She needed to get on solid footing again and not live in her white-picket-fence fantasy. Pushing his arm off her, she sat up and swung her legs over the side of the bed. "We need to get up and get going." According to the clock on the dresser, she had less than an hour before she needed to be at the market.

Morgana stepped over the robes they'd tossed on the floor and her skin warmed from the image of Damon taking it off her the night before. Giving her head a shake, she grabbed her bag and hurried to the bathroom.

"Morgana, what's wrong?"

"Nothing. I just need to get ready." She locked the bathroom door and leaned against it, letting out a slow breath. Damon wasn't going to buy that, but she would have the time in the shower to fortify her walls. She needed to stand on her own two feet.

As she took her shower she wondered if her plan had any holes. She used her fingernails to thoroughly scrub the shampoo into her hair, using the slightly painful sting to calm her anxiety. Damon had said it was stupid to come down here. Rescuing Sam wasn't stupid, but not having a solid plan likely was. Sam had recognized her yesterday and reached out, but it had been a couple years since she'd seen Sam—was she even the same woman anymore? Morgana hadn't stopped to consider any of this, she'd just acted without thinking, like Copeland had always accused her of doing. Sam might even resent her for leaving and not coming sooner. Or Morgana could be walking into a trap.

She rinsed her hair, washed, and got out of the shower. Deep down, Morgana knew that no matter what happened, she couldn't *not* meet Sam.

Twenty minutes after she entered the bathroom, she exited, clean, dressed, and with her damp hair hanging down her back in a high ponytail. She was ready to face whatever was waiting for her.

Damon was sitting on the bed, propped up against the headboard, doing something on his phone. His gaze swung her way when she walked into the bedroom. "You ready to tell me what's wrong?" He pushed back the covers and got out of bed, walking toward her in all his naked glory. The man was magnificent.

Forcing her eyes to meet his, she plastered on a smile and consciously avoided the word *fine*. "I'm good."

He leaned down and kissed her, his breath minty fresh from magic, and her mouth had a mind of its own, opening to him. By the time he pulled away, her lips were swollen from his kisses, and she was breathless.

"I'll take a quick shower and be out in a few minutes. I ordered coffee and huevos rancheros for breakfast."

Morgana worried that if she wasn't careful, Damon would wear her down with kindness and sex. Then he'd be able to walk all over her even without using his magic of persuasion on her.

After a quick, delicious breakfast and an infusion of

caffeine, they were on their way to the market. They talked about the weather and where they were going, but neither mentioned what had happened the night before. She wasn't ready to admit what was growing between them.

Damon parked the car and placed a hand on her arm as she reached for the door handle. "Morgana. What's wrong?"

She couldn't tell him she was falling for him and was worried he'd take her independence away because he'd just tell her he wouldn't. Words were meaningless—life had taught her that. "Nothing."

"Do you regret last night?"

"No. It was great sex between two friends."

Morgana could see a muscle pulse as Damon clenched his jaw and she feared he wasn't buying her story.

He rubbed the back of his knuckles against her cheek, like he'd done before, and she wanted to melt into his touch. But every time she melted into him, it would become harder to pull away. "Angel, it was more than sex and we are more than friends. You can lie to me, but don't lie to yourself."

His gaze was so intense, but she forced herself not to look away. "Yes, it was fantastic sex, but that's all it was."

"It wasn't, but we can table that discussion for later. Now, let's talk about what's next—how I can protect you."

"I can protect myself, but speaking of that… I need you to stay back and let me talk to Sam on my own."

He gave a single nod. "I can do that, and if necessary, I can distract Sam's guards, if she has any."

Morgana reached for the door handle again and threw her next comment over her shoulder. "Oh, she will." Talking about Sam got them off the topic of what they'd done together, but Morgana wasn't naïve enough to think that Damon wouldn't circle back around to it eventually.

The market was crowded for so early in the morning. They stepped around people stopping at stalls and Morgana kept an eye out for Sam. Not looking where she was going, she bumped into a woman.

Instinctively, Morgana threw her hand out and touched the woman's arm. *"Perdón, no te había visto."* She hadn't seen the woman, and the apology in Spanish flew out of her mouth without thought. The woman was shorter than Morgana and striking with long, straight dark hair, an olive complexion, and the deepest, brownest eyes she'd ever seen.

"Perdón, no quise decir eso," the woman responded and nodded at Morgana before stepping around her.

Morgana watched the woman depart but turned back around as she felt Damon touch her arm. "You okay?"

"Yes, just not watching where I was going." They'd strolled around the market for a few more minutes when Morgana spotted a woman up ahead at a vendor. She tilted her head, causing her hair to fall over the right side of her face. A memory popped into Morgana's mind of Sam doing that and a man pushing the hair out of her face, telling her not to hide. Morgana couldn't clearly picture the man, but that didn't matter at the moment. "That's Sam," she said to Damon, lifting her chin in Sam's direction. "Let me approach her alone."

"Okay, but if I think you're in trouble, I won't stand back."

"I know." Him staying back to start was enough of a compromise for now. Morgana walked over to the vendor stall and stood beside Sam, picking up a bag of tomatoes for sale. "Sam," she whispered, but didn't look up.

Sam inhaled sharply. "Morgana, it is you."

Morgana handed money to the vendor. "I was worried you wouldn't recognize me."

Sam hesitated before she spoke. "This is what you looked like most of the time I knew you. And I was there the day Maverick had you spellbound and changed your appearance."

Sucking in her breath, it took everything Morgana had not to turn to Sam with surprise. "Until the spell was broken recently, my past was a blank canvas. I'm sorry. I came for you as soon as I remembered."

Sam paid the vendor for her fruit purchases and strolled to the next vendor. Morgana walked around the stall from the other side, looking down at the colorful fruits and vegetables. "I came here to get you."

"Go home, Morgana. It's not safe for you here."

"No, I can't leave you. Don't you want to go home too?"

Morgana caught Sam's reflection in the mirror hanging on the beam of the vendor's cart. Her eyes looked tired and far older than her years.

"I can't leave. I need to stay for Mirek."

"Mirek? I've heard that name... my cousin?"

Sam glanced down and her curtain of hair obscured the burned half of her face. "You don't remember him?"

"I was told he was my cousin and thought to have died over twenty years ago with me, along with Dylan and Taren. I don't remember them—my memories are coming back in pieces, but I'm still missing so much."

Sam nodded again and glanced over her shoulder before walking to the next vendor. Morgana followed her gaze and saw Damon talking to one of Sam's bodyguards.

"You need to leave. The guards with me are new so they won't know who you are, but if they describe you to Snake or Maverick, they'll send someone looking for you and you'll be in danger." Sam looked up from the vegetables she was studying and met Morgana's gaze. "Thank you for coming for me."

A man walked up behind Sam and gripped her shoulder, eliciting a flinch. "Sam, who is this woman?" the man asked in Spanish.

Sam turned her back on Morgana and answered in flawless Spanish. "Just a woman shopping."

The man leered at Morgana, causing the writing tattooed on his upper lip to distort grotesquely as his other hand snaked out toward Morgana. He gripped her wrist and squeezed painfully before she could flee. "I don't think so."

17

*D*amon kept his eyes and magic focused on the thug watching Sam. He'd approached the man from behind, careful not to let the thug see his face, and spoke softly in his ear. Damon's high school Spanish was barely passable, but magic was a great equalizer—his persuasion didn't need many words.

Another man, with indecipherable writing tattooed on his upper lip, loitered at the edge of the stalls, leaning against a wall. The man's gaze alternated between the thug and Sam, but Damon saw the exact moment lip-tattoo man caught on to Damon's presence. He stared straight at Damon for several long seconds before pushing away from the wall.

Damon glanced over at Morgana and Sam and saw they'd moved two vendors away. Lip-tattoo man was heading directly for them. If Damon headed toward Morgana, he'd break his persuasion connection with the thug. Fending off two thugs, especially magic ones, might be more than he could handle, but he didn't see another choice.

Turning away from Thug One, he headed in Morgana's direction. Lip-tattoo man had almost reached Sam and

Morgana. Damon increased his pace, dodging around shoppers.

His connection to Thug One snapped and the man yelled for Damon to stop. Ignoring the thug, he continued to stride toward Morgana and was less than twenty feet away when a woman walked in front of him. She was the same woman Morgana had bumped into earlier. "I'll stop the other guy," she muttered in English as she walked past him.

Damon didn't have time to wonder why the woman was willing to help. When he turned away from her, lip-tattoo man had his hand on Sam's shoulder. Damon dropped all pretense of stealth and ran toward Morgana.

"Let me go, asshole!" Morgana shouted, drawing the attention of shoppers all around them. Instead of stopping to help, people started to scatter. By the time Damon had covered the final few feet to get to Morgana, the area around the vendor was almost deserted. People scampered away like mice amidst a herd of cats.

A glint of metal caught Damon's eye and he pushed Morgana behind him. She grabbed onto his arm but didn't try to get around him.

A woman's high-pitched voice yelled in Spanish and all heads turned in her direction. The woman who said she'd help was cursing the thug and blocking him from getting closer to lip-tattoo man and Sam.

Damon was on the other side of the stall with Morgana when lip-tattoo man lifted his hand holding the gun and jerked Sam with his other. He dragged her toward the thug and the woman. Sam didn't fight, a look of resignation as clear as day stamped across her face.

"No! Let her go!" Morgana yelled, dropping Damon's arm. She pushed past Damon, rushing to Sam as he reached for her.

The woman grabbed Thug One by the arm and Damon

thought he saw the air move as the man knocked the woman to the ground. Thug One flashed the short distance to Sam and lip-tattoo guy, blocking Morgana's path.

Damon felt like his heart stopped as Thug One raised his hand and aimed his gun at Morgana's head. Damon flashed in front of Morgana. His aim had been off when he flashed, so he landed at an angle, not fully in front of Morgana as he'd intended. Thug One still had a clear enough shot at Morgana. Damon pushed Morgana to the ground just as Thug One fired.

The bullet hit Damon in the arm and spun him around, the continued momentum propelling him backward. He lost all sense of time and space as he fell. In his mind, he was back in the alley with Meredith when Copeland lodged a poison dagger in his shoulder. Helpless once again. One more person he'd failed to help, one more situation he couldn't control in order to protect the ones he loved.

He closed his eyes and ran his magic through his body, checking for injuries. Unlike the poison that had quickly spread through his blood stream when he'd been with Meredith—heading to all parts of his body—only his arm was injured. Sending magic to the wound, he cooled it to slow the bleeding.

"Damon!"

He opened his eyes as Morgana's hair hit his face. She was bent over him, her eyes wide with fear.

"I'm okay." Lifting his good arm, he guided her off him and sat up. "Sam?"

"They took her."

He turned his head to look around and a wave of nausea hit him. Closing his eyes for a moment, he took in a slow, steadying breath and sent more magic to his arm to control the pain. When he opened his eyes, he looked around again.

The woman who had helped them stood just off to the side talking to some of the bystanders.

Using the vendor stand as a crutch, he hauled himself to his feet. "That woman," he whispered, "she's the same one who bumped into you earlier. She did something to Sam's guard."

Morgana leaned closer to him. "What?"

"I'm not sure, and usually magic isn't visible, but I swear I saw something. Let's find out who she is."

"We need to get you to a doctor."

Damon placed his hand on the small of Morgana's back and walked toward the woman. Seeing a doctor about a gunshot wound in a foreign country wasn't at the top of his list of things to do. "I'll be okay. I think the bleeding has already stopped, and I'll heal the rest when we get back to the hotel."

"I'm Isabella," the woman said in English when she sees them approaching. "There were only a few people who witnessed you being shot, and I wiped their memories."

"I'm Morgana and this is Damon. Thank you for your help."

"You know the woman you talked to?"

Damon's Spidey senses tingled and he'd learned to always trust his gut. "Why do you want to know?"

Isabella looked Damon in the eyes. "I am not the enemy. I think we're after the same thing. I will meet you at your room in the Hilton."

The fact that she knew where they were staying didn't sit well with Damon. If she'd been following Sam, it was possible that Isabella had seen them yesterday and followed them too. "We'll meet you in the lobby."

Isabella nodded and Damon watched her walk around a building until she was out of sight. "Let's get to the vehicle."

The market was filling up with people again now that the

commotion was over. It was as if there'd been an announcement that the cats were gone and the mice could come back to play.

Morgana wrapped her arm around his back as they walked to the vehicle. At the passenger side, he unlocked the vehicle and opened the door for her.

She trapped her bottom lip between her teeth and worry marked her eyes as she looked up at him. "Are you sure you can drive?"

Lifting his lips in what he hoped was a smile and not a grimace, he leaned down and placed a soft kiss on her forehead. "Yes, angel, it's my left arm. I should be fine."

The ride back to the hotel was a lot quieter than the one to the market. He parked the vehicle and stepped out as he conjured a new shirt, disappearing the old one. A blood-stained shirt was never a good thing to wear in public.

He spotted Isabella as soon as they walked into the lobby. She was standing by the elevators, looking up at the numbers displayed above it, as if waiting. When it arrived, all three of them stepped into the empty elevator at the same time and Morgana pressed the number for their floor.

Once the elevator doors opened, Morgana led the way to their hotel suite. Inside, Morgana grabbed his right hand and tugged. He let her lead him over to the couch, but he didn't sit down.

Damon turned to Isabella. "Empty your pockets."

Morgana tugged on his arm. "Damon, that's rude."

"Her cargo pants' pockets are bulging. I want to know what's in them. The fact that she's magic is bad enough, I don't need her whipping out a gun or a poisoned dagger." He'd been there and done that already. If her magic was strong enough, she could retrieve a weapon in the air. But for now, he'd deal with the threats he could see.

Isabella walked to the low table in the sitting area and

pulled items out of her pockets—money, keys, a small length of rope, a pocketknife, a phone, an energy bar, a charging cable, and a few other odds and ends. He was almost at the point where he wouldn't have been surprised if she'd pulled out a kitchen sink or a tent. It was strange how much she carried considering she could conjure anything she needed. Perhaps it was for appearances.

When she was finished, she pulled out the pocket linings to show him there was nothing else. "Satisfied?"

Damon walked to the table and picked up the rope. He'd recognized it for what it was instantly. Place it around a person's wrist and their magic would be rendered useless. It was also very difficult to conjure and most pieces in existence had been passed down through generations or came from someone very powerful. "I'll take this." He slipped the rope into his pocket to lock up later. "Now your backpack."

Isabella picked up the backpack she'd taken off when she'd emptied her pockets and pulled out one item at a time. She had some clothes; bottles and a toothbrush in a clear bag that looked like it was for toiletries; a small towel; two old, worn paperbacks; a journal; two pens; and several protein bars. She looked at him and shrugged. "I only carry enough not to raise suspicion. I conjure whatever else I need."

He tilted his head toward a chair, indicating for her to sit. "Are you from here?"

"I'm originally from San Diego. I'm just down here for a few days and checked out of my hotel this morning." She waved her hand at the backpack she'd just restuffed as if she'd stated the obvious but didn't offer anything more.

Morgana tugged on his arm again, and this time he lowered himself to the couch beside her. "Damon, Isabella is fine. She helped us and I trust her. I'm worried about you. I don't know how to heal, but we need to look at your arm."

167

Isabella stood and walked over to him; their eyes were level while he was seated. "I'm a pretty decent healer."

He sat back and disappeared his shirt, sending the particles back into the ether. It was lazy but easy, and now that his adrenaline from the market had worn off, he felt wiped. Having Isabella help him wasn't his first choice, but his instincts were telling him he could trust her, and needing to be healthy to protect Morgana overrode everything else.

Morgana kneeled on his right side and grasped his hand. He leaned toward her and looked into her eyes. "I'm okay," he whispered.

Tears welled in her eyes; she blinked and nodded.

"This may hurt a bit," Isabella said, pulling his attention back to her. He squeezed Morgana's hand and turned his head to watch Isabella heal him. A slight sting sang through the wound, like a hand dragging across a sunburn.

"That's it. I think you're good." Isabella stood and shook her hands, her magic cleaning them before their eyes.

"Thank you." Damon took in all of Isabella for the first time since they'd bumped into her. She was petite and had long, straight dark hair, almost black. She appeared Latina with her dark features, and she was beautiful, but he didn't trust her one hundred percent. "Now, who are you?"

"My name is Isabella Garcia Flores."

Damon wasn't sure if she was being cagey or not. "Let's try this again, Isabella Garcia Flores... who are you and why did you help us?"

18

*M*organa understood Damon's need to question Isabella. She just didn't think it was best for him to do it right after being healed. She rubbed his good arm. Her feelings were so conflicted when it came to him. One minute she craved him deep inside her, like last night, and the next she wanted him to let her be. Her feelings for him were contradictory—she wanted him, at the same time, she thought he wouldn't be good for her. "Damon, why don't we get some lunch and then you can rest? We can talk about this later."

He must have seen the worried look on her face because his lips curved into an almost smile. "Sure, we can do that. Angel, why don't you call for some lunch? We'll talk over dinner tonight." He turned toward Isabella. "But first..." He pulled Isabella's magic rope out of his pocket and grabbed her arm. She didn't resist while he wrapped the rope around her wrist, just above her watch. He circled it with his fingers and held her for a moment before letting go. "I've spelled the rope, so I wouldn't try to take it off if I were you. You could do some nasty damage."

Isabella just shrugged.

Morgana called for room service and Damon pulled out his wallet to tip the server when it arrived. He tossed his wallet to Morgana and brought the food to the coffee table. Isabella said she wanted some time alone and took her meal and retreated to the second bedroom, throwing a "bye" over her shoulder. Morgana had thought Damon's habit of booking a suite was a bit ostentatious, but it had come in handy now that Isabella was with them.

She sat on the corner of the couch and crossed her legs, balancing her plate on a pillow laid over her lap. "You didn't have to treat Isabella that way, you know. She helped us."

"She's got a great meal and is sleeping in a nice hotel; I'd say she's not hard up. Until we know what she's doing, I won't trust her completely."

Morgana felt Isabella was trustworthy, but Damon was right; she had a meal and a bed and she hadn't complained. Just then, Morgana's stomach rumbled, and she put all thoughts of Isabella aside for the moment.

Her enchiladas were cooked to perfection. She took a bite and let out a small groan when the flavors burst on her tongue. She felt her cheeks flush as she looked up at Damon.

The corner of his lips twitched when he looked at her. "Yup, it's good."

"Mmm hmm." They kept the conversation light over lunch, talking about the market and what Morgana had remembered about the area. When she'd had enough of her meal, she leaned over to put her plate on the table next to Damon's wallet, accidentally knocking it to the floor, the contents falling out. She didn't have the energy to get up— the morning's events had emotionally drained her.

"Sorry. I dropped your wallet and stuff fell out." Putting one foot on the ground so she could reach the wallet while still being lazy, she swiped the items closer to her so she could stuff them back in. A picture caught her eye. She held it up and felt the blood drain from her face. "Damon?"

"Hmm? What's wrong?" He leaned over to see what she was holding. "That's the last picture I had of my dad. He'd been telling me and Jack a story..." Damon chuckled as if remembering. "I'm sure he embellished it a bit, but we were all laughing and my mom snapped that shot. Do you remember him? He'd be older in that picture than when you knew him."

Morgana shook her head and continued to stare at the photo. The last time she'd seen Curtis Stone hadn't been in Colorado. She lifted her eyes to Damon. "No, he looked just like this."

"Well, this picture was taken years after you last saw him, so he had more gray hair here."

"No, Damon. Your dad was this age when I last saw him. I saw him here."

Morgana watched Damon as the meaning of her words sunk in. "My dad was here? At the compound?" Damon stood and paced in front of the table before turning back to face her. He grabbed his hair with both hands before running his fingers through the strands, then started pacing again. "No, my dad would never have been involved with the assholes who took you and killed the Williams brothers."

"He wasn't. I think he found out what was happening here and came to save us."

Damon stopped. "What did he do?"

"I don't know... I mean, maybe I did and those memories haven't come back yet. Or maybe I never knew. But I do remember him and I know he said he was going to get us out of there. Then Snake found out—or I'm not sure... it could have been Maverick. But one of them killed him. After that was..." She let her voice trail off. This was about his dad, not her; she didn't need to say any more.

"What?"

"It doesn't matter."

Damon came back around to the couch and sat down with one knee drawn up, touching hers. "Angel, it does. Tell me."

"After that—" Morgana took a big breath and looked Damon in the eyes. "That's when they started to use spiders." Over the last two years, she'd had flashbacks, but nothing truly concrete until the day on the patio when the spider had crawled across her shoe. So many of her memories were still missing, but not those—they were as clear as if they'd happened yesterday. Morgana told Damon what they did with the spiders in as few words as possible. She shuddered and looked down at her arm, almost expecting to see a spider walking along it.

Damon picked up her hand and rubbed it between his own. His warmth seeped into her. Until then, she hadn't known she was cold. A warming sensation moved up her arm. "Are you doing that?"

"Yes. You're cold." He picked up her other hand and warmed them both, the heat settling through her body like a comforting blanket. "Were you punished because of my dad?"

"No, I don't think it had anything to do with him. The timing was probably a coincidence. I was outspoken and they wanted to control me."

"I don't, you know."

She met his gaze. "It sure seems like you do. Even this morning in the market, you came over when you said you'd stay back."

"No, I said I'd stay back if you weren't in danger, but the guy had you by the wrist."

"And you didn't let me handle it."

"For Christ's sake, Morgana! Do you think he would have just let you go? And there were two of them. They weren't even afraid of using magic or shooting someone in a public market."

Morgana pulled her hands out of Damon's and stood up. It always came back to this—he wanted to control her to keep her safe and she needed to be independent so she'd never be weak again.

She faced him, her hands on her hips like a superhero—she needed to channel all the strength she could to have this conversation. "Damon, we're like hamsters on a wheel, doing the same thing over and over again. I'm an adult. You can't control me."

Damon let out a long sigh and ran his hand through his hair again. "I'm not trying to control you, angel. I care about you. I can't protect those around me unless I'm strong and can take control of the situation." He waved his hand toward his dad's picture on the coffee table. "I couldn't do it with my dad. Is it too much to want to protect you so something bad doesn't happen to you too?"

She dropped her hands to her sides. The pleading look in his eyes was enough to break through even Wonder Woman's defenses. "No." She walked back to the couch and sat in the corner. "I get it, but I need to be strong for myself and make my own decisions."

"I know." Damon rubbed his knuckles along her cheek. "We'll figure it out."

She turned into his touch; she'd started to crave the familiar gesture. "Okay." She looked around the hotel suite. "What should we do now? I could get Isabella or maybe you should rest…"

"Why don't we just relax this afternoon?" Damon held out his hands and his eReader and her tablet landed on his palms. He passed her tablet to her. "Want to read for a bit?"

"Good idea." She turned on her tablet and as it booted up, she glanced over at Damon. "Are you reading a paranormal?"

"No, a romantic suspense this time. You?"

"Same." They settled into reading their books and Morgana got caught up in the story. It was the third in a series about Navy Seals and the women were all strong, and yet trouble seemed to find each one of them. All the men were super alpha, but they loved their women to death. She knew it was fiction, but the love between the characters always made her wish for that for herself.

She dropped the tablet in her lap as a realization struck her. Was Damon being just like the alpha guys in the book? Was he loving her? Well… he hadn't said that word yet—but he did care for her. And yet, was he trying to protect her too? Morgana didn't think the women in the books were weak just because the men helped them. But then, there wasn't magic involved in their stories and the men didn't try to use persuasion on the women.

"What's wrong?"

Morgana looked up at Damon. "Ah… nothing. Just thinking about the book. How's yours?"

"Good."

Damon had hesitated and a blush moved up his neck. Oh wow, he was embarrassed. She flung herself across the cushions between them and grabbed his eReader before he could protest. She flipped open the device and looked down at the page he'd been reading. "Oh."

Now it was Damon's turn to chuckle. He'd been in the middle of reading a sex scene.

She looked up at him, a devious grin spreading across her face. "This looks interesting."

He raised one eyebrow. "You want me to read it out loud?"

"No."

"Okay." He looked disappointed as he reached to take the device back.

"I want us to act it out." She dropped her tablet on the coffee table and went to her knees in front of Damon. Pushing his legs apart, she moved in between them and put her hands on his thighs, loving the feel of his hard muscles underneath her palms.

She looked up through her lashes and met his intense gaze. Reading about the Navy Seals and how they loved their women made her realize she'd been fighting Damon their entire relationship and only taking what he gave It was time to give a little.

Reaching for the zipper of his pants, she wondered if he'd be quiet when he came or if she could get him to yell her name. He'd been quiet when he'd come during phone sex. She wiggled her brows at him in fun. "I want to see if I can get you to be loud."

"You do, do you? We'll have to see." The glint in his eyes was a challenge she gladly accepted. He waved his hand toward the second bedroom. "I put a protection spell on Isabella's door so she won't walk in on us, and it also muffles sound."

Good thing one of them was paying attention—she'd totally forgotten about Isabella. Morgana reached for Damon's zipper and stopped. He'd taken control to protect them both from Isabella seeing or hearing them, and she hadn't minded. Maybe it was okay to give up control sometimes, but she wasn't going to think too deeply about the subject just yet. She wanted to see Daman lose control.

Damon ran his hand through her hair. "You change your mind, angel? It's okay if you did."

She pulled down his zipper and grinned at him. "Oh, no. I'm just savoring the moment, big boy."

"Big boy, huh? That's a new one." He chuckled, but stopped abruptly and sucked in his breath as her hand reached under his briefs and gripped his hard cock.

Oh yes, now she was in control. She stroked his length and tightened her grip at the top before loosening her fingers and teasing him on the down stroke. She raised her gaze to see him as she lowered her mouth to his cock. "Take your clothes off."

Sticking her tongue out, she laved around the head of his cock and had only licked him once before his clothes were magically gone. She used her tongue to swirl the head before taking just the tip into her mouth. Teasing him, she took him further before pulling back and then doing it all over again.

Both his hands wound in her hair, and she relished the slight sting as he tugged at the roots. Not once did he try to guide her, letting her go at her own pace. She felt powerful as she licked up and down his length, alternating between licking and sucking him into her mouth.

Damon's breathing sped up, and as his fingers dragged through her hair, she felt herself get wetter. She tingled deep in her core, and he hadn't even touched her most sensitive parts.

She looked at him through her lashes again, wanting to see his reaction as she took him deeper into her mouth. The tip hit the back of her throat and she swallowed to avoid gagging.

"Oh fuck, angel. Yes!" He gripped her hair harder, the tug sending ripples of desire straight to her core, but he still didn't push her head. He was truly letting her lead.

She pulled up, swirling her tongue around the head before taking him deep into her throat again.

"Stop, angel." He grasped her by the arms and gently pulled her off his cock. "I don't want to come in your mouth. I want to be in you." He lifted her up onto his thighs and her clothing magically disappeared as his had. His thighs were thick and warm beneath her, the hair on his legs a sensuous feeling. The length of his cock rested in the v of her thighs and enticed her even further.

He held out his hand like he had to retrieve their books and a condom appeared. He had himself sheathed in no time and for a brief second, she wondered if she should be upset that he was taking over. No… she shouldn't. They were both allowed to chase their own pleasure. She gripped his shoulders for leverage and leaned forward, kissing him while his cock nestled in her wet folds. Without breaking their kiss, he lifted her over his cock. "Guide me into you," he said against her lips, his voice husky with desire.

Reaching down, she centered him on her core and sank down an inch at a time until she was gloriously full. She broke their kiss for only the time it took her to plant her feet beside his thighs before she lifted and lowered herself on him, tightening her muscles around his shaft. Putting his hands on her hips, he helped her lift, but didn't thrust up, letting her drive the show. She drank him in as they kissed and she rode him, chasing her climax.

As her body tightened and pleasure tore through her, she flung her head back. "Ye—" Damon swallowed her scream as he pulled her mouth down to his with one hand behind her neck and then used his other to help slam their bodies together. More pleasure rippled through her as her orgasm seemed to go on forever. Her body tightened around his, and with one last pulse, she felt him erupt within her.

When their breathing finally slowed, she opened her eyes. "That was better than fine."

He laughed and gave her a quick kiss. "Yes, it was." He paused and his expression became serious. "Thank you." He kissed her again before pulling back. "Let's get cleaned up." Damon used his magic to get rid of the condom and clean them both before they redressed, and he released the spell on Isabella's door.

She settled back into the corner of the couch with her tablet when he got his. "Not close enough," he said. She looked up to ask him what he meant when he pulled her legs onto his lap, one hand draped over her, and opened the flap on his device.

Maybe they could both learn to give a little.

19

*D*amon couldn't remember the last time he'd enjoyed an afternoon so much. It wasn't just the sex either. Having Morgana beside him, her legs in his lap while they both read, had felt right.

While he'd been reading, he'd rubbed his hand over Morgana's legs and also let his mind wander.

Everything about Isabella had just been too convenient—from her being in the market to helping out and her willingness to come back to the hotel with them. Something wasn't as it seemed and he wanted answers. He'd had enough of being nice and pussyfooting around the issue. Isabella had known who they were, and she'd done something to Sam's guard.

In the early evening, Isabella had joined them in the main room and they'd ordered from room service. As soon as they'd finished, Damon had directed Isabella on where to sit and was ready for some answers.

He looked Isabella in the eyes. "Are you ready to tell us who you are?"

"I told you. I'm Isabella Garcia Flores."

He admired her for looking him in the eye, and even with the enormous difference in their sizes, she wasn't intimidated. At least not that he could see. "Your name doesn't tell me who you are. You purposely bumped into Morgana. Did you do the same thing to her that you did to Sam's guard?"

Isabella glanced at Morgana. It could mean nothing, or it could be a tell. He'd bet his company's next acquisition it was the latter and that she had done something to Morgana.

Damon stood with his back to the window and faced Isabella, still seated in the chair he'd directed her to. Putting her squinting into the sun was a dick move, but he wasn't a tried interrogator and he needed every advantage he could get. Making her uncomfortable could play in his favor.

"I'm a private detective and I'm here looking for someone."

She hadn't answered his question. "Who are—"

Morgana cut him off before he could go any further. She was practically bouncing in her seat. "Really? That's so cool."

Damon didn't think it was cool. It was suspicious. "Who are you looking for?"

"My brother."

If he was going to have to pull more words out of this woman one or two at a time, he was going to lose his temper soon. "Why do you think your brother is in Ciudad Victoria?"

"He disappeared years ago, so I look for him everywhere I can. I came for a job and decided to look for him since I was already here. I'd heard of magics doing some drug running in the area and thought my brother could be with them."

Damon's senses were on high alert now. Everything still just seemed too convenient. "What kind of a job?"

"I had to pick up an item at the market for a client."

"You came all the way down here to go to the market? Bullshit. I'm not buying it. And why would someone hire a private detective to go to a market?" Her story also didn't explain why she had helped him and Morgana. There were just too many things that weren't adding up.

"It's what the client wanted. I don't ask my clients questions; I just do what I'm paid to do."

"How did the client know to contact you?" Damon watched her carefully guarded face and wondered if it was time to call in the big guns. He figured he had two good options. One, call in Jack, who knew how to properly interrogate people, or two, use his persuasion to get her to talk.

Option two was faster, and since he didn't know how much time they had, it was the better choice. Sam's bodyguards had seen them so it probably wouldn't be too difficult to find what hotel he and Morgana were staying in. The right amount of money could get you practically anything you wanted. He'd try option two and keep option one in his back pocket just in case.

Pulling on his magic, he let his persuasion float into Isabella. "What did you do to Sam's guard and Morgana?" She seemed unaware of his magic. Morgana was the only person who'd ever been able to detect his gift, although he'd never tried it on someone powerful, like Jack.

The thug this morning had been easy to manipulate, but Isabella had strong defenses. He gave his magic another push and then waited a few moments until he felt it settle into her.

Damon moved away from the center of the window so he wasn't directly in front of Isabella. The window faced west, and the low evening sun hit her directly in the eyes.

"I put a tag on them."

"What do you mean? What's a tag?"

"It's a magic locator that allows me to track a person or object." Her eyes widened. "What did you do to me?"

He shrugged. "Let's just say I got tired of you not answering my questions. Is the tag harmful?"

"No, and it dissipates after a few hours. Which means the tag I put on the guard has probably already worn off."

Damon shrugged again. The guard wasn't his concern and he'd likely gone back to the compound. "What led you to the city?"

"I told you, a client asked me to pick something up at the market."

"How did you know to go to the market?"

"I know where certain items are located. I can find things." She winced. "Stop forcing me to tell you things. It could be dangerous for me if I reveal too much."

Damon leaned back against the edge of the window and crossed his legs at the ankles. "On the contrary, I think it's very enlightening and until you tell me more, I won't know if it is dangerous or not. How can you find things?"

She furrowed her brows as she glared at him. "The same way you can make me tell you things I don't want to. It's my specialty… Look, I'm telling the truth. I came here to pick up a lost family heirloom for a client and while I was here, I decided to look for my brother. As soon as I bumped into Morgana in the market, I knew she was important."

Morgana leaned forward in her chair. "Important in what way?"

Isabella stood and looked at Morgana before turning back to Damon. "I've had enough of this bullshit interrogation and staring into the sun. I only went along with it to show you I'm not the enemy. I want us to collaborate because I think we have a common goal. That's why she's important."

"Fair enough." Damon's respect for the woman climbed another notch. He snapped the persuasion connection between them. She walked over to the couch and sat beside Morgana. "I can find people and objects. I can't tell you exactly how my magic works, but I get a feeling. Sometimes I know exactly where to look for someone or something and other times I just get an inkling that I'm on the right path."

Morgana's eyes widened. "You felt that with me? That I was leading you on a path?"

"Yes." She glanced over her shoulder at Damon and then returned her gaze to Morgana. "It was why I put a tag on you. I didn't mean any harm. Then when I saw the men walking toward you, I tried to help by distracting the first guy."

"Thank you," Morgana said quietly.

Isabella gave her a single nod. "I saw you at the compound yesterday and I recognized the woman you were talking to at the market. I'd checked out the compound because I'd heard about it, but I didn't know if it was truly linked to my search until I saw you again at the market with the other woman. I've been back here several times in the last few years. I don't know why, but something in me keeps telling me to come back, even though I never find him."

Morgana leaned forward. "What's your brother's name? I don't remember everything from when I used to live here, but maybe I can help."

"Mateo." Isabella held out her hand and the backpack she'd left on the floor by the corner floated over to her. The strap landed on her outstretched fingers. She rooted around in the bag for a moment, then pulled out a journal. Flipping it open, she turned the pages until she came to a section with photos taped to several pages. She held it up for Morgana to see.

Morgana sucked in her breath and looked over at Damon. "It's Eddie."

He walked over and sat beside Morgana, placing an arm around her shoulders. "You're sure?" The man in the picture wasn't a man at all; he was a young boy, around twelve to fourteen years old.

"May I?" Morgana took the album from Isabella when she handed it over. "Yes, I'm sure. He's older now and I still don't remember him from before, but this is definitely one of Copeland's guys who came in and out while I was in the condo."

Isabella accepted the album back from Morgana. "Where is the condo?"

"It's in Blue Mountain, Colorado, but it's empty now. I was held there for a year but I was rescued almost a year ago now. A few months ago, Eddie, er, Mateo was with one of my cousins in a different apartment building in Blue Mountain, but he left."

Isabella pursed her lips. "Eddie... hmmm."

Damon wanted answers, but at the moment, all he had was more questions. "Why did you say his name like that?"

"For years, I've been asking about Mateo. It never once occurred to me that he could be going by a different name. Eddie Guerrero—considered the best Mexican wrestler in WWE history—was Mateo's idol. Since you were with him, it explains why my magic was pulled to you."

Isabella looked back at Damon. He didn't trust her magic specialty, but he knew she would help them again. Now he just had to figure out a way to ensure Morgana didn't do something reckless like go into the compound all alone to get Sam.

MORGANA SAT with her back against the tree and watched the compound, her eyes shifting from side to side, looking for movement. She couldn't believe it'd only been two days since she'd sat in this exact same position and watched Sam come out of the compound. Only two days since Damon found her and they'd made love.

Now here she was, back against the same tree.

By the time they'd finished talking to Isabella yesterday, it had been late, and they were all emotionally drained. Isabella went back to the second bedroom and Damon had taken Morgana to their bedroom. They'd taken a shower together, washing away the dirt and emotions from the day.

He'd taken her to bed and kissed her, once more making her feel like she was the most precious person in the world. They hadn't made love, but she'd fallen asleep wrapped in his arms.

She wanted to feel that feeling every night, but she was terrified it would come at a cost—the cost of her freedom. Damon had taken control of the situation with Isabella yesterday and Morgana had felt him use his persuasion on the other woman. It might have been the right thing to do, or maybe Isabella would have eventually opened up to them all on her own once they'd gotten to know each other. Now they'd never know.

It had all worked out and the three of them were working together, but what would happen when Damon wanted to persuade her and it wasn't what she wanted?

Morgana stood to shake out some of the stiffness from sitting for so long. She scanned the fence along the front of the compound until she could see the guard house. Damon leaned against the shack with a casual air, talking to the guard on duty. Damon would be using his persuasion, and since they needed information, she didn't have a problem with it. But should she? The guard had no idea he was being manipulated, so did that mean Morgana had a double standard? She was okay with someone she didn't know being manipulated, just not herself or someone she cared about? Or was it that she only agreed when it benefitted her? Damon would probably say that he always had her best interests at heart. Should that be enough? And besides, she reasoned with herself, the guard wasn't a good guy. If the tables were turned, he probably wouldn't hesitate to use magic on them. Sometimes it was too easy to rationalize decisions.

She let out a big sigh and scanned the grouping of buildings that made up the compound. The plan they'd devised was for Morgana to look for movement and see if she recognized anyone coming or going. Damon was to see what information he could get out of the guard and anyone else he came across. And Isabella was to look for access points and see if she could detect her brother's or Sam's presence.

"See anything?"

Morgana spun around, her hand to her heart. "Holy shit, Isabella, you scared the crap out of me."

"Sorry." She shrugged, not looking sorry. "Did you see anything?"

"No. No one came or left the compound the entire time I was here. You find anything?"

"I didn't sense Mateo, but Sam was there, and I identified all the exits. It looks like Damon is finished. We should head to where we left the vehicle. You want to try flashing again?"

Morgana knew it was useless but tried anyway. "Nope, nothing. We need to walk."

Isabella nodded and they fell into step with each other. They'd been walking for a few minutes when Isabella turned around and walked backward, facing Morgana. "I saw a picture on the coffee table yesterday. Damon's dad?" She looked over her shoulder and then turned around, walking beside Morgana.

"Yes. I hadn't remembered Curtis Stone from when I was a kid, but…"

"But you remembered him from somewhere?"

"Yes, here. He came here to help, and Snake killed him."
She gave Isabella the CliffsNotes version of what had
happened. "I think that's why Damon tries to control everything in his life now. He wants to be able to make decisions
and do things his way to prevent someone else he cares
about from being hurt or killed."

Isabella looked at her sideways. "You don't agree?"

"I'm an adult. I should get to make my own decisions."

"Even if someone you care about disagrees with that
decision?"

Morgana didn't respond because she didn't have a good
answer. Ever since Damon told her about his dad, she'd ques-
tioned her own decisions. She couldn't let him control her,
could she? Someone making decisions for her could mean
she'd be traveling a slippery slope—and there might not be
an end in sight.

By the time they'd hiked the mile back to the vehicle,
Damon was waiting for them. He'd flashed to the car, just
like Isabella could have if it wasn't for her. Morgana wasn't
sure if her magic would eventually come into its full
strength, or if she'd remain weak and what she had now
would be the extent of it.

Her throat tightened at the thought that she might never
have what her sister and cousins had.

20

*D*amon paced across the suite before turning and looking back at Morgana and Isabella. "I don't like it. It's not safe."

Morgana slammed her hands on her thighs and leaned toward him. "Then what would you have us do, Damon? We've been brainstorming for hours and you've rejected everything we've come up with. We need to get into the compound to see if we can talk Sam into going with us and to see if there is any information about Mateo. I refuse to leave Sam again!"

Isabella conjured a beer and raised an eyebrow while she tilted the bottle toward Morgana. Morgana shook her head and conjured herself a glass of soda.

Morgana's magic seemed like it was as strong and full as it was going to get and she still couldn't flash. That meant she couldn't flash out of a situation if something went wrong. Since Jack, Meredith, and the other council leaders were the only magics Damon knew of who had enough power to flash with someone, there'd be no way to flash Morgana out of somewhere dangerous if she couldn't do it herself.

"Oh shit!" Morgana sprang up, looking like she forgot about the soda in her hand. Isabella reached out, rescuing the soda before Damon could reach it.

He followed Morgana as she rushed over to the table at the side of the room. They'd drawn a rudimentary map of the compound and marked all the exits. "Did you remember something?"

Morgana picked up a pencil and pulled the map toward her. "I think so. See the fence on the back side of the compound?" Using her pencil, she pointed to an area at the top of the paper where they'd drawn a line to represent the back of the compound. "I think there's a gate in the fence, but it must be under a spell."

Isabella walked to the other side of the table, facing them. "I couldn't get really close to the fence for fear of being seen, but I didn't see a break in the fence or a gate anywhere. It would have been pretty noticeable."

Morgana erased part of the drawing and drew in a gate. "Not if it was covered up by a spell. I remember that the guards used to come in and out of it all the time when they weren't transporting drugs, so it couldn't have been a spell that only worked with one person. It had to be something common.... Oh my god, drugs. I just remembered that's what they used the compound for."

Damon was thankful that Morgana's memories were coming back, but not if it was going to make her do something risky. "Good to know, but we won't worry about the drugs. That's more than we can handle—let's just focus on rescuing Sam. As for the spells... there are some common to all magics, used just to keep non-magics out, but it raises more questions."

Morgana straightened and looked up at him. "Like what?"

"If a common spell was used, why didn't any of you children know it?"

Isabella picked up another pencil and absently tapped it on the table. "If the children were taken when they were young, they might not have known the spell and those at the compound probably never taught them."

Damon considered that. Morgana had been seven when she'd been taken and Taren a year younger. Mirek and Dylan had been ten, but even at that age, their magic would have been fledgling and their knowledge of spells limited.

He looked at both Morgana and Isabella. "Okay, it's possible none of them knew it. But what good will it do us if there is a gate there? That's a big if, plus the spell could have been changed years ago."

Morgana dropped her pencil and put her hands on her hips. Oh boy, she was going to let him have it.

"I didn't say we'd have to storm in there, Damon. I was just remembering something that might be helpful. To answer your first point—if the gate was there years ago, then it's likely still there. And point two—most people tend to take the easy route. So, if the spell was enough to keep the children out, even when they grew, then they likely wouldn't have changed it. And lastly, the gate is in the back in an area that isn't watched very often. We could use it to get inside and look for Sam."

Damon met Morgana's gaze. "No."

"What? No? Just like that?" Morgana's hands seemed cemented to her hips as she glared at him.

Morgana was being naïve and too quick to jump into the unknown, but Damon wasn't about to voice that opinion and open that can of worms. He also didn't care; he wasn't backing down. "It's not safe. We don't know what we'd be walking into, and you couldn't flash out if there was a problem."

"I thought we were a team." Morgana's face was flushed,

the color having crept up from her neck. "You're not the CEO of me, Damon."

"Morgana, be reasonable." The moment the words were out of his mouth, Damon knew he'd made a grave tactical error.

Isabella's muttered "Uh oh" only confirmed it.

"You think I'm not—"

He cut Morgana off. "That's not what I meant. I just think we should think about the plan carefully. And make sure that we go about it as safely as we can." He wrapped his hand around the back of her neck and looked down into her eyes. "I wouldn't survive if something happened to you."

"Okay," she said, her voice barely above a whisper.

Damon reluctantly pulled away from Morgana, remembering Isabella was in the room.

"Morgana, I think Damon has a point." Isabella raised her hand to stop any protest Morgana might have had. "It might be the only plan we've come up with so far, but it is a bit risky."

"Fine." Morgana walked over to the couch and flopped into the corner. "What now?"

Damon didn't dare comment on Morgana's 'fine' as he perched on the edge of the coffee table and faced her. "I think we need to call in backup. There's only three of us and we might be in over our heads."

Isabella sat on the opposite end of the couch. "Who's your backup?"

"My best friend, Jack, is the leader of the new North American council that is being set up and his wife, Meredith, is co-leader and Morgana's sister. Jack is also on the FBI's magic task force. He should be able to round up enough people to help, especially when he learns that we're here to rescue two people who are here against their wills."

Damon watched an emotion play across Isabella's face, not able to read her, before she looked away.

"Isabella? Do you need to tell us something?"

She turned back to them, but her gaze wasn't as direct as it'd been all day. "Mateo isn't there against his will. At least I don't think so."

Morgana reached forward and placed her hand on Isabella's knee. "What do you mean?"

"I think my brother may have been recruited, but he was just a kid. Only fourteen."

Damon felt for the woman. "Recruited or not, maybe he needs help to get out." From what Simon and Jo had reported about their time with Snake, Damon very much doubted Eddie was innocent. He'd come across as a thug and had willingly hurt both Jo and Simon, from what Damon had heard.

"Let's call in the cavalry." Damon grabbed his phone and pressed Jack's contact info.

"Hey, Damon, did you find her?" Jack asked in way of greeting.

"I did. We also found some other people and need backup."

Damon heard Jack pause. "You want to tell me or wait until we get to you?"

"Let's wait."

"Are you talking about just me and Meredith or agents?"

"Since having FBI agents here could land you in a pot of hot water, let's keep it legal and just have you and Meredith."

"Can you wait a couple of days—maybe the day after tomorrow? Rowena is in the middle of something right now and needs our help."

"Is she alright?"

Jack's sigh came through clearly over the phone. "She will be. I'll explain everything over a drink when you get back."

"Sounds good, and sure, another day won't hurt."

"Text me your hotel info and we'll meet you in the late afternoon."

"Will do." They both said a hasty goodbye and hung up.

Morgana looked at him expectantly. "They're coming?"

"They are. We just need to wait a day." It would give him a chance to spend more time with Morgana and let her know that he'd realized over the last two days that she was it for him. He just had to convince her he was the right one for her.

Morgana was back at her tree keeping watch while Damon and Isabella approached the guard manning the front gate. They'd come after dinner hoping there'd been a shift change and they'd be able to talk to someone different who might have new information. It looked like that had worked since it was a different guard than the one Damon had spoken to yesterday morning.

They weren't sure what they'd learn but since they had time to kill, Damon figured it wouldn't hurt. They wanted to have as much information about the comings and goings of those at the compound as they could get.

Freeing Sam was Morgana's priority and yet, she hadn't rushed to the door to come back to the compound tonight. Guilt ate at her because she'd wanted to stay in the cocoon she and Damon had created. They'd spent the entire day in the hotel together and he'd taken the opportunity to pamper her.

The night before, after Damon had spoken with Jack, Isabella had made herself scarce, saying they probably wouldn't see her until dinner tonight. She'd been true to her word and had left them alone.

As soon as Isabella's door had closed, Damon picked Morgana up and carried her to their bedroom. She'd practically swooned that he had the strength to carry her and gently lay her down on the bed. A small part of her brain had worried that him picking her up and depositing her where he wanted was a caveman act, and what would be next... him telling her where to be and what to do?

Morgana had pushed the annoying little thought to the back of her mind, shoving it in a mental box and throwing away the key. She'd preferred to look at the gesture as something out of the romance books they both liked.

He'd proceeded to undress her and make love to her. She could still feel the roughness of his whiskers between her legs. She rubbed her thighs together and felt herself blush.

Grinning to herself, she glanced over at the front gate. It was dark now and difficult to see, but she could make out Damon's large shape and Isabella's much smaller one next to a third figure.

Damon and Isabella moved away from the gate and headed toward their rental as they'd planned. Damon had explained earlier that although he could persuade a guard to tell him what they wanted to know, wiping his memories was a bit trickier because he was magic. If they did anything suspicious, like flash to where Morgana was, it could trigger the man's memories.

Having the guard watch them head to their car and drive away would cement the lies they'd implanted in his thoughts. Once they were a safe distance away, Damon and Isabella would flash to Morgana's position.

Morgana was waiting for them when their feet touched down beside her about ten minutes later. "Hey, did you find out anything?"

Damon gave her a quick kiss and grasped her hand. "Yes." He paused and looked over at Isabella.

Morgana became anxious. "What?"

"The guard told me that there's a rumor going around in the compound that Snake found something."

Morgana sucked in a breath. "The magic box?'

"He didn't know, but he says the compound is closing and almost everything that wasn't staying has already been packed and moved."

"Why would they close the compound? I thought they used it to make drugs. I think that's why they keep Sam around—as a chemist? I still can't remember all the details." Morgana looked between Damon and Isabella for answers.

Isabella shrugged. "I don't know, but if they close the compound, they'll take Sam with them and any evidence that could lead me to Mateo."

"Then we need to break in tonight."

21

*D*amon shook his head before Morgana even finished her sentence. The moon was behind him, a halo highlighting him like a god sent to save her. But he wasn't. He was just a man, and she needed to remember that. "You can't stop me, Damon."

He wrapped one large, strong hand around the back of her neck and bent down so he could see in her eyes. She loved it when he cradled her neck in his hand. It had become his go-to move and usually she wanted to melt into him, but not now.

"I don't want to stop you, angel. I want to keep you safe. We don't know what will happen if we go into that compound. That was the reason we agreed to wait for Jack."

She kissed his lips, the quickest and lightest of kisses, before moving sideways out of his hold. He dropped his hand. "I have to get to Sam," she pleaded, hoping he would understand that she couldn't walk away. "I had forgotten about Sam. Not a single memory left of her for years. What kind of friend does that? What will I be if I walk away from her now? How could I face Ben and Stella? How could you?"

Even in the darkness, she could see the puzzlement on his face. "Ben and Stella?" He frowned. "Wait… You're telling me that Sam is their daughter Julia? That's why you were looking at her obituary?"

Morgana nodded. "I thought you knew." She twisted her fingers together as she waited for Damon to process the information.

Damon scrubbed his face with his hands. "Maybe I was in denial. In my mind, she was just your friend Sam. If anyone else told me that we needed to rescue a friend thought to have died over twenty years ago, I would walk away, thinking they were crazy. But you're living proof of the atrocities that have happened."

"I know." Morgana choked on the two words.

"Sam told you at the market that she didn't want to leave Mirek. How will we convince her to leave now?" Damon's voice sounded curious, not accusatory.

Morgana had pushed down her hope that Damon would help until he told her himself. For almost two years, she'd had no idea who she was or where she belonged. Now she had a family and the opportunity to reunite someone else with theirs.

But now, no matter how much she told herself it was too early to hope, it started to build within her. Damon was going to help her rescue Sam. Morgana was going to prove that she wasn't weak and useless, and she would do something good. "You can ask the guards about Mirek, and if he's not here, we'll convince Sam to come with us so we can find him." Morgana looked over at Isabella. "When we find Ed—Mateo—he can help us find Mirek."

The Eddie that Morgana knew wasn't the loving brother that Isabella spoke of, but perhaps his sister's love could convince Eddie to help. If not, they'd find Mirek on their own.

Damon turned to Isabella. "What do you think about going in now?"

Isabella looked between the two of them before answering. "I think the guard was speaking the truth. They're going to close the compound. Whether it's tonight or tomorrow, or even the day after, the guard wasn't sure, but it will definitely be soon. If we wait for your backup, we risk losing Sam and any evidence that's inside about Mateo. I have nothing to lose. I say we try."

Sadness cloaked Isabella's statement, but it wasn't the time or the place to dig deeper. Morgana looked up at Damon hopefully. "Damon?" He didn't have the stakes in the game like she and Isabella had. Now that he knew Sam was Ben's daughter, it probably changed things for him, but he didn't have anything to prove—unlike Morgana.

He let out a large breath and his huge shoulders deflated. "Okay. We'll go in tonight, but Morgana, you need to listen to me. If I think it's not safe, we have to leave."

She nodded in agreement, but her mind was already working on her argument to convince Sam to leave with them.

For several minutes, they brainstormed the best way to approach the compound and what they'd do once they got inside. They decided they would all stick together and make their way to the back of the compound where the invisible gate was located.

Morgana planted each foot carefully, toes first. She tested the ground with the toe of her shoe, feeling for anything loose, before fully planting her foot. That's what a hero from one of her favorite books told the heroine to do. It was working. Her steps were quiet as she followed Isabella, with Damon bringing up the rear.

She'd wanted to go first but finally acquiesced to the others as Isabella was smaller and less likely to be seen. Plus, she'd be able to stop them if needed by speaking into their minds, something Morgana still couldn't do. She clenched and unclenched her fingers as adrenaline poured through her. She shook her hands and tried to keep her muscles loose as tension crept up her arms and into her shoulders. Excitement at rescuing Sam competed with the adrenaline and something else—she was scared shitless.

There.

Isabella threw the single word into Morgana's mind, and she turned her head, searching for what Isabella saw. About twenty feet ahead, there was a man leaning against the fence with a rifle hanging off one shoulder while he played on his phone.

The area around the compound was sprinkled with trees, but not enough to provide cover, and none near the fence line. A cloaking spell covered them, courtesy of Damon, similar to what he'd used to block Isabella's door at the hotel. It helped, but it wasn't perfect. It only muffled sound, not blocked it, and if any one of them stepped even a fraction outside the cloak's edges, they'd be seen.

Morgana caught movement out of the corner of her eye and turned to see Damon step out in the moonlight. The cloak shimmered but didn't collapse. He'd only made it a few feet before the guard yelled to stop while swinging his weapon up into his hands, aiming dead center at Damon's chest.

Unless Morgana and Isabella revealed themselves and distracted the guard, there would be nothing to deflect his bullet. Damon would be hit right in the heart.

When they were putting together a plan, Damon had explained that he usually had to be within ten feet of someone for his persuasion to work. Morgana held her breath as Damon walked closer, the guard yelling at him again to stop.

Damon held up his hands in surrender. Less than ten seconds later the guard lowered his gun and Damon walked closer to the man.

The cloak around them dissolved and Morgana walked the short distance to Damon with Isabella. Isabella jumped in to interpret as the guard didn't know English and Damon's Spanish was so bad the questions weren't going well.

Isabella pulled out the picture of Mateo and showed it to the guard. He told them that he'd seen Mateo before, but not in weeks. They didn't have a picture of Mirek, but the guard knew Sam by the scar on her face and confirmed that she was inside.

The guard didn't move from his post, having been persuaded by Damon not to alert anyone to their presence. Morgana followed Damon and Isabella into the back of the compound.

She walked through the door and ran her hand along the wall—dents and holes in the plaster rubbed against her fingers and... she remembered. The door to her right was used for storage. The next two rooms were classrooms.

"Wait," Morgana whispered as loudly as she dared. Damon and Isabella turned on silent feet and faced her.

"Bedrooms," she mouthed, hoping they understood.

A loud noise echoed down the hall. Curses followed as they heard men arguing.

Damon gestured to one of the empty classrooms and ushered them in. He left the door ajar as all the rest were, and they rushed to the back of the room and crouched behind a desk.

Isabella leaned into them. "They were packing and dropped something," she whispered. "That's what the shouting was about."

"It's too dangerous. I didn't cloak us because they could have bumped right into us and they would have known. It was better to get out of the hall, but we need to leave. Now." Damon's intense gaze focused solely on Morgana.

She didn't want to leave. This could be their only chance to find Sam. Morgana couldn't imagine facing Ben and Stella, knowing she hadn't tried everything she could to save Sam. Morgana had seen firsthand what it did to her family when they found out someone they loved had been alive for years when they'd believed them dead. "No, we just have to wait until they leave."

Morgana felt the magical push and she swung her eyes to Damon. "Don't you dare," she hissed at him, keeping her voice low. "Your persuasion won't work on me."

"Angel, we could all get caught and then we'll be useless for helping Sam. Be reasonable about this."

"Here we go again," Isabella muttered under her breath.

Morgana ignored her and faced Damon. "They could be gone by the time Jack arrives. Can't you use your persuasion so we can find which bedroom Sam is in?"

"And where Mateo normally stays," Isabella added.

Damon opened his mouth and then shut it. He pushed his head back and took in a large breath. When he met Morgana's gaze, he looked resigned. "I'll do it, but you need to stay here."

"No!" Morgana whipped her head around to make sure no one had heard her. She hadn't meant to be so loud, but she wouldn't be left behind. "I need to be the one to talk to Sam."

"It's not safe."

"You just don't trust me, Damon."

"You can't flash out of here if something goes wrong."

"I can run."

"For fuck's sake, Morgana, you can't outrun a bullet."

They threw their whispered words back and forth until

Isabella shoved her hands between them. "Stop it! We're getting nowhere and we don't have time for this."

Morgana laid her hand on Damon's forearm where it rested on his crouched legs. "I couldn't live with myself if I didn't try to save Sam."

"I get that, but we won't be any good to Sam if we're all killed." The frustration in Damon's voice was as evident as his words were true. "We need to leave before someone does a magical scan and senses us in here."

Isabella frowned. "Why would someone do that?"

"I do it at night when I'm leaving my offices, just to make sure the spaces are clear. They could do it here."

Isabella nodded then whipped her chin up. "I hadn't thought of that, but you might be right. They have a lot to hide, so they're probably paranoid assholes… I have an idea. I didn't get a good look at Sam at the market, but if you send me a clear memory of her, I might be able to locate her in the building."

Morgana turned to Isabella. "What? How?"

"I need something to locate a person—an object or a picture. A memory works the same as a picture."

Footsteps and arguing clamored in the hall right before the door of their classroom crashed open, banging into the wall behind it.

Morgana stayed rock still; only her eyes moved, darting to Damon. A man yelled to another in Spanish that there wasn't anything worth saving in the room. Another door banged against a wall, and then a third before the sound of the man's footsteps receded.

Time seemed to stand still as they waited to make sure no one else came by. Morgana's legs cramped in her crouched position and she clenched her teeth to prevent from calling out. Closing her eyes, she focused on her magic. She pushed some to her lower limbs to increase the blood flow and clamped her hand over her mouth to stop her shout of glee. Every day she could do more magic. Hopefully, she'd soon be able to flash.

"Send me the memory," Isabella said, disrupting Morgana's happy thoughts.

Morgana called up a memory of Sam from the market but didn't know how to send it. She looked from Damon to Isabella, unsure of what to do.

Isabella lifted her hands and gently cupped the sides of Morgana's head. "Touch my forehead with yours, then push the memory."

Morgana did as instructed and felt the memory split, like it'd made a copy, and pushed it into Isabella.

Letting go of Morgana's head, Isabella pulled back. "I've got it." She closed her eyes and then opened them a moment later and smiled. "This hallway turns left and Sam is in the last room on the right."

They moved with Isabella leading the way. Checking the hallway, she then looked back, motioning for them to follow. Damon put his hand on Morgana's arm, halting her.

Stay here. We'll bring Sam.

Morgana shook her head and yanked her arm out of his grasp. She had to be the one to get Sam because she wouldn't even remember Damon. She'd been too little when she'd been taken.

They were at the bend in the hallway when Morgana heard more voices. They crouched down and plastered themselves against the wall.

Cloak.

Damon shouted the word into her mind.

Nothing happened. She couldn't feel the barriers of the cloaking spell.

"Welcome home, Morgana. And don't bother, Mr. Stone. Cloaking spells won't work in my hallways."

Morgana looked up. Snake stood only a few feet away with one hand wrapped around Sam's upper arm.

Morgana felt Damon's hand on her arm, and he helped her to her feet. Isabella stood as well. The three of them faced Snake—Andrew Skalbeck. She'd learned his real name after she'd been rescued.

Snake had been a frequent visitor of Copeland's while she'd been held in the condo. His mustache had gotten bushier in the last year, giving him a sinister look, as if the enormous snake tattoo on his arm wasn't enough. Due to his short-sleeved shirt, the enormous snake was on full display and looked like it was slithering toward Sam. Morgana shivered at the thought and returned her gaze to Snake's.

Snake smiled like someone welcoming home a long-lost relative. "We'll have to get you back to the old lady Maverick had spellbind you. After she bound you, it was so nice to have you quiet and docile for once. You always were such a horrible, impulsive child."

Long-forgotten memories came pouring back and all her hatred for the man bubbled up inside her. She had to push them aside as she struggled to focus on the asshole facing her. "Fuck you."

Morgana felt Damon's hand wrap around her waist, pulling her back against his body. *Don't antagonize him.* She could feel Damon pleading from the thought he'd thrown into her mind.

Snake made tsking sounds like a disapproving grandmother. "We'll beat that out of you soon enough." He turned toward his men and instructed them in English to lock them up.

Three men walked toward them, each with a strand of rope in their hands. Morgana was intimately familiar with that type of rope, even before she'd seen Damon use it on Isabella. Since Morgana's magic had never been very strong, it had never been a big issue, and it wasn't even now, since she couldn't flash. But it would incapacitate Damon and Isabella.

Run. Get Jack.

Damon threw the thoughts into her head as he grabbed her around the waist with both his hands and hauled her up. She had only a second to react, thrusting her hands in front of her as he threw her toward the wall.

Before her hands hit the plaster, an enormous hole appeared. The plaster and concrete from the outside wall of the building made a thunderous sound as it hit the ground. Wind whipped at her hair as she sailed through the air.

22

*D*amon divided his attention. He'd used all his strength with a bit of magic behind it to heave Morgana at the wall. At the same time, he'd wielded an enormous amount of power to blast a hole in the building's thick outside wall just in time for Morgana to sail through it.

Without waiting to see how she landed, he called on the last of his waning power and filled in the wall. A patch of plaster and concrete that resembled something a child might craft with paper mâché stood where the wall once had. But it was solid enough to stop anyone from following her through the hole.

Damon bent over, his hands resting on his thighs as he sucked in air. He felt like he'd just sprinted a marathon and hoped it had been enough. If there were still guards outside, they might have stopped Morgana, but he'd only seen the one. When he'd interrogated the man, he'd implanted the thought to leave Isabella, Morgana, and Sam alone if he encountered them. The embedded thought wouldn't have worn off yet, so she should be safe.

"That was very creative, Mr. Stone."

Damon lifted his head and looked at Snake. He vaguely remembered the man from when he'd been a council member alongside his father. With the hideous snake tattoo and overgrown mustache, Damon wouldn't have recognized him if they'd passed on the street.

With his breathing finally under control, he straightened just as one of Snake's thugs grabbed his wrist. Damon didn't have the strength to fight, and it wouldn't have done any good if he had. It would take some rest before his magic regenerated enough to be of any use. Perhaps an hour or two. Eating always helped too, and even if he did have access to his magic, he had no energy to conjure any food.

"Isabella, I presume?" Snake asked after one of his men slipped a magic rope on Isabella's wrist.

Damon watched Isabella out of the corner of his eye. Even without magic, he wasn't willing to completely let Snake out of his sight. He still had a firm grip on Sam as he addressed Isabella.

"Eddie—I believe he went by Mateo when you knew him —he's been such a good employee. He made loyal contacts in the U.S. to distribute our product and he's always good for a right hook."

Isabella's entire body stiffened, but she didn't take the bait.

"He had to escort some of my other assets back to Colorado. It's too bad that you just missed him," Snake continued. "If only you'd been able to see him again before you die."

The man was like a bad TV villain monologuing. Too bad Damon wasn't the hero who could flash in and rescue them during the man's long-winded soliloquy.

"My men will escort you to your quarters." He laughed at his own joke and yanked on Sam's arm. She let out a small whimper as he took her down another hallway and out of Damon's sight.

The guards pushed him and Isabella into a nearby empty room. He would have fallen if the guard hadn't had such a strong grip on Damon's arm when he shoved him into a metal chair.

Two guards focused their rifles on them while two more zip-tied their arms and legs to the chairs.

Damon yanked his arms, but the straps didn't budge. The guards had tied them between his wrist and the magic rope, making it impossible to slip the rope off.

He looked over at Isabella just as he saw the butt end of a rifle coming at his head.

As the ground came at Morgana, she wrapped her hands around her head and rolled. She tumbled head over feet four times and as soon as she slowed, she jumped up and took off like a sprinter hearing the starting gun.

Chancing a glance over her shoulder to see if anyone was after her, she caught sight of the wall she'd just come through. It was intact.

She rounded the side of the fence and stopped dead in her tracks. Sucking in a breath to calm herself, she concentrated on her magic and attempted to flash. Nothing.

A shout sounded behind Morgana, and she took off again, running as fast as she could. She used her magic to cast a cloaking spell. She wasn't as good as Damon, but it would blur her image.

With the cloak in place, she slowed her run to catch her breath. She'd been sucking in air and wouldn't be able to continue at the pace she'd set. Meredith had asked her to run with her in the mornings when Jack was busy so they could spend time together. If any of them made it out of this alive, she just might take Meredith up on her offer.

Alive. Damon and Isabella were still inside. Morgana knew what a sadistic bastard Snake was. He'd think nothing of torturing them just for fun.

Morgana dropped the cloaking spell as she reached the street and slowed to a walk, not wanting to bring attention to herself. She looked up and down the street wondering what to do next. Damon and Isabella had helped her find answers. They'd become a team. And because she wanted to do it her way and not listen, they could be dead.

She fished her phone out of her pocket and turned it on, calling up the rideshare app. After she'd ordered a vehicle to pick her up at the corner she'd been dropped off at the other day, she started walking again. The glow from the street-lights guided her feet, but her mind was elsewhere.

For the last year she'd been so worried about someone telling her what to do, she'd let it affect how she viewed people. It'd become such a trigger that she'd wanted to do the opposite, just because she could. When they'd been in the classroom and Damon had wanted to stay back, she'd bristled.

Had Maverick been right to spellbind her? Was Snake right? *You always were such a horrible, impulsive child.* His words floated into her mind. Had her impulsiveness put Damon and Isabella in harm's way? If it wasn't for her, could they have flashed out? Why didn't they flash out without her?

As soon as the question entered her mind, Morgana knew the answer. Damon and Isabella staying meant Snake had someone to focus on. He wouldn't bother to come after Morgana. She was weak, after all.

She was such an idiot. Coming down here to get Sam hadn't shown anyone she was strong and independent.

Instead, she'd endangered several lives. *Useless.* That's what Copeland had always called her. She stopped when she got to her corner. Oh god, what had she done?

Her ride arrived. On the way back to the hotel, her thoughts spiraled further downward. She hadn't been useful, she wasn't truly independent, and not only had she not rescued Sam, but now Damon and Isabella were being held captive.

As the car sped toward the hotel, she thought about the memories that being inside the compound had evoked. All the times that Copeland and Snake had drummed it into her that she was useless. The humiliation and pain from their torture sessions.

By the time she'd made it to the suite, she felt lower than she'd ever felt before.

She walked further into the room and flopped back on the couch. She closed her eyes as a new memory floated into her thoughts.

In her mind, she could see herself holding her hands in front of her, sparkling water below as she stood on the edge of a large swimming pool. It had been the last summer she remembered in Colorado. She'd been seven.

Damon stood in the water. He'd been taller than most adults, even at twelve. She'd been so afraid to jump in the water. Not even her dad could get her to do it. She'd stood at the edge of that pool and cried.

After a few days of trying to coax her to jump, her father said she didn't have to do anything she didn't want to. She'd played with her toys while her sister and cousins splashed around in the pool. Her chest ached while she watched them have fun. She'd wanted to jump in the pool, but she was terrified.

The next day Damon had taken her hand and told her all she had to do was stand at the edge of the pool. She didn't have to jump. Every day she'd stood with the ends of her toes inches from the edge of the pool while Damon talked to her.

The first day he winked at her and said she'd jump when she was ready. She couldn't remember how many days he'd talked to her while standing chest-deep in the water.

"You've got this, Mol."

"I'm scared."

"I know."

"Dylan said I'm a baby. A weakling. Even Jo can jump in."

Damon scoffed. "Don't listen to Dylan. You're not a baby, Mol. Sometimes we need help to do things."

In the memory she could feel her younger self's confusion. *"What do you mean?"*

"Some things are hard, and when we're ready, we can get some help to do them. Asking for help doesn't mean someone is weak. We all need help sometimes, no matter how strong we are. I'll catch you. I believe in you."

The following day, she'd jumped. Damon had caught her just like he'd said he would. Her fear hadn't evaporated with that first jump, but each day he'd been there to catch her, and each day it got a bit easier. By the end of the summer, she could jump in the pool on her own.

Morgana opened her eyes as the image of twelve-year-old Damon faded. He'd always been there for her—when she'd been Molly, when she'd been blond Morgana, and now.

Holy shit—she was such a fool. She'd looked at his caring for her and need to keep her safe as controlling. Yes, Damon was commanding and liked to control his environment, but he wasn't controlling her. He wasn't Copeland, Snake, or Maverick.

She pulled out her phone and made a call.

23

*D*amon heard his name as if called from a great distance. His eyes felt sealed shut and his head hurt like a motherfucker. Lifting his head, he groaned.

"Damon!"

Recognizing Isabella's voice, Damon pried his eyes open and immediately shut them. "Fuck." The light felt like it was searing right into his brain. He tried again, slowly opening one eye and then the other until he could handle the light.

Isabella was blurry. He blinked several times until she came into focus.

"Thank god! You've been out of it for almost two hours. I thought the guy had given you brain damage, he rifle-butted you so hard."

"T—T—" Talking was difficult. He drew in a long, slow breath. "Two? How?"

"How did I know?" Isabella tilted her head toward her wrist strapped to the chair. "I'm obsessed with counting steps. I absolutely hate working out, so I walk everywhere. I'll even walk instead of flash somewhere so I can get in steps. Walking is also a better way to look for Mateo than driving or flashing. I never go out without my watch slash pedometer."

"Phone too?" He took a deep breath and let it out slowly. Some of the pain in his head receded. "Can you text from it?" He didn't know how they'd manage to type, but he'd find a way if they needed to.

She shook her head. "Unfortunately, no. I didn't think I'd need to text, so I didn't bother with that model. When we get out of here, I'm upgrading."

He spoke slowly, focusing on enunciating each word. "What about the things in your pockets? Pocketknife?"

Isabella looked defeated. "I emptied my pockets before we went out. I didn't want anything that could make noise." She let out a huff. "I won't ever do that again."

Damon looked around the room and didn't see anything that would be useful, even if he could manage to move.

Isabella looked nervous. "Do you think Morgana made it out?"

He couldn't stop the corner of his mouth from lifting into a smirk. "Oh yeah." His speech was coming back as long he spoke slowly, but his head still pounded like his brain was trying to escape. "She made it. She's the toughest person I know."

"I thought you guys were going to go head-to-head a few times in the past couple of days."

"True. She's only just learning who she is and testing the waters. She did that when she was little too."

"Funny. I got the feeling that Morgana lived here for a long time. And I thought you were from Colorado."

"Both true. Morgana was taken from Colorado when she was seven. We thought she'd died in a fire along with her father, two uncles, and three cousins. Her father and uncles are dead for sure, but we don't know about her cousins."

"Could they be here?"

Damon shrugged and immediately regretted the movement. "Fuck, that hurt. I doubt they're here, but I don't really know." Taking in slow breaths, he tried to ease the throbbing pain in his head. He couldn't even begin to imagine what Morgana must have suffered for months if her migraines felt anything like what he was feeling now.

"Tell me about your brother." He'd already heard about Eddie from Jo and Simon, but he needed something to take his mind off the pain.

Isabella sucked in a breath and blew it out slowly. "Mateo is younger than me by ten years. I had finished college, was working, and wasn't home much when he was fourteen. Mateo was an oops baby so my parents were pretty absent by the time Mateo was a teenager. I'm the reason he got caught up with a gang."

Damon snorted. "Doubt it."

Isabella's eyes grew wide. "How can you say that? You don't even know us."

"I know you're a good person and you've put your life on hold for years to look for your brother."

"Weren't you listening? That's because I'm the reason he disappeared."

"He hasn't disappeared. Morgana has seen him. So has her cousin. That means he could have contacted you if he'd wanted to."

She sucked in her breath at his harsh words. The Eddie he knew wasn't a good guy and Damon's head hurt so much he didn't feel like pretending he was. "I get you want to find him, but maybe he doesn't want to be found."

"That's because of the people he's mixed up with."

"Maybe. Or... giving him the benefit of the doubt... maybe he was spellbound like Morgana and doesn't remember his past. Either way... tell me why you think you're responsible for his fate."

"My parents weren't around much, so I looked—"

"Stop. Listen to yourself. Your parents weren't around. They're the ones responsible for their kid, not you. They could have intervened with Ed—Mateo."

"Probably, but they didn't. They relied on me to look after him. I practically raised him and then I got so busy in high school and then college that I just wasn't there for him, and by the time I started working, I was almost never around. I knew my parents weren't doing much in the way of parenting. I should have stepped up."

Damon lifted his shoulders and slowly brought them down, trying to ease some of the strain in his neck and head. "You're allowed a life too, but I get it, you love him. So, that's why you feel you failed him?"

"Mostly."

"You can't control what other people do."

She laughed at him. "Well, that's rich coming from you. When we get out of here, I think you need to look in a mirror."

He felt insulted. "The fuck?"

"Do you not listen to *yourself*?" She threw his own words back at him.

"Explain it to me."

"Okay, let's start with Morgana. I get that you want to keep her safe and she's a bit reckless?"

"A bit?... Ow, fuck." His head throbbed, reminding him not to be so forceful in his answers.

"Right. More than a bit, but you get what I mean. She's an adult and she has the right to make her own decisions. And by the sounds of it, she didn't get to make them for a long time, so maybe she's just going a bit overboard right now. Her pendulum will eventually settle in the middle."

Damon felt like a child being chastised for getting caught with his hand in the cookie jar. To go with the analogy, he'd been trying to get the cookie for a friend, not himself. He'd do anything for Morgana.

Isabella raised both her brows and her eyes widened. "Now, let's talk about your father."

"What the fuck has my father got to do with this? And how do you even know about him?"

She shrugged as much as the bindings would allow. "I saw your dad's picture on the table and Morgana told me a bit. She said that your father going missing defined so much of who you are. I get that. I really do. But it sounds like you blame him for it."

He got an uncomfortable feeling, like his tie was too tight, but he wasn't wearing one. "I didn't know what had happened to him. For years, I wondered if he was even alive."

"But your mom knew he'd died."

"Yes, but I couldn't bring myself to believe it." He winced at the volume of his own voice.

"Look, it's not my place to judge, and I'm not. I just think you need to see that you don't know what decisions your dad made. You don't even know if his decisions led to his death and you can't control that. Just like you need to let Morgana make her own decisions."

Damon knew Isabella was right. He'd just spent his entire adult life making sure that everyone around him was safe. Letting it go wouldn't be easy.

"Damon," Isabella said quietly, nodding to the front of the room behind him.

Snake walked into the room and stood so both Damon and Isabella could see him.

If Damon had met the man on the street, he wouldn't have thought much of him. Maybe that his mustache needed a good trim, but besides that, he seemed to be aging well. It just showed that you never knew what was on the inside.

"I hope you're both comfortable," Snake said, laughing at

his own joke. "But it doesn't matter, you won't be around much longer."

STAND *to the side of the room.*

Morgana heard Jack's instructions in her head and rushed to stand by the wall.

A moment later, Jack, Meredith, and Ben flashed into the middle of the room.

"Ben, you good?" Jack asked.

Morgana looked between Ben and Jack. "What's wrong?"

Meredith rushed to Morgana and crushed her in a hug. "Oh my god, you're okay." Morgana hugged her back. "Nothing, we just gave Ben a boost."

Morgana frowned and turned to Ben. "I thought you could flash."

"Yes, but unlike these two," Ben said, gesturing toward Meredith and Jack, "I can only flash normal distances like most magics."

Meredith let Morgana go and gave Ben a wink.

It was still weird having a sister, but the memories that had come back to her over the past few days were helping Morgana become more comfortable around her.

Morgana faced Jack and Ben. "Thanks for coming."

Jack nodded once. "Of course. That's what family does."

"What about Rowena? You weren't going to come until tomorrow because of her. Is she okay?"

"She'll be fine. She's got some other help. Now, fill us in on what's happened," Jack said.

Morgana swallowed and wondered how the hell to say what she had to. She'd spent the hour since her phone call to Jack practicing what she needed to tell him, but the words still didn't sound right in her mind. She decided to just jump right in. "I need to tell you something first. Let's sit down."

Meredith and Jack took the couch and Ben and Morgana took the seats facing them on the other side of the coffee table.

"My memories have started to come back. Not everything but a lot." She looked at her sister and felt like she should apologize. "I still don't remember our cousins."

Meredith smiled and it gave Morgana the courage to continue. "I remember a young girl who was with me. Her name is Sam. That's why I came down here. I knew she was here and still being held captive. At least I thought she was, so that's why I came."

Jack and Ben exchanged a glance before Jack frowned. "I don't remember a file on a missing child named Sam, but then I wouldn't have recognized a Morgana either. Did you find her?"

"Yes, but then a bunch of shit happened... we were at the market... Shit, that's not important now. She's in a compound and that's why Damon asked you to come and help. We found out that everyone in the compound was going to be moved and we couldn't wait. We had to go in tonight, before we lost track of her. But I screwed up and Damon and Isabella were taken." She'd vomited her words out and had to take a big breath when she finished.

"Who is Isabella?" Jack asked.

"I'll explain, but first I have to tell you one more thing."

Morgana took another big breath and turned to Ben. "When I was at your house, the picture of your daughter triggered my memory of Sam. Sam is Julia."

"That's not possible, sweetheart. We buried Julia."

Not once when she was practicing what to say did she imagine this reaction. She was prepared for anger and surprise, but not disbelief. She didn't know why that hadn't occurred to her; she'd just figured he'd believe her.

Morgana didn't know what to do. She looked over at Meredith and Jack. Meredith nodded.

"It's true, Morgana," Jack said, like he was trying to break bad news to a child. "Julia's funeral wasn't long after you di— were taken."

Shit. If she didn't prove Julia was alive, Ben could be blindsided, and she'd already learned tonight that that wasn't a good idea.

She turned back to Ben. "Can I give you a memory? I've only done it once, but it worked."

"Sure."

Morgana leaned toward Ben and then sat back and coughed an awkward laugh. "I need to touch your forehead with mine. It's the only way I know how to do it."

Ben patted her knee, and the corner of his lips turned up in a smile. "Go ahead."

Morgana called up the image of Sam at the market. Sam standing beside Snake as the first image of his daughter he'd seen in twenty years might not be the best plan. With the image of the market firmly in her mind, Morgana touched her forehead to Ben's and pushed the image into him.

She heard Ben's indrawn breath and felt him pull away. When she opened her eyes, Ben was standing several feet away, his hands covering his face.

"Morgana?" She hadn't noticed that Jack had moved to her side and sat on the coffee table in front of her. "Can I see?"

"Yes." She leaned toward Jack, but he held up his hand.

"You don't need to do that." He moved his hand closer to her and closed his eyes. "Fuck." Jack turned and held his hand in front of Meredith.

"It's her," Meredith said quietly.

"I thought she was dead. We buried her." Ben's whisper-thin response was filled with anguish. "I never looked… For over twenty years… Oh my god… she's been alive, and I didn't know." He put his hands back on his face and his shoulders shook.

Jack walked up to his mentor and pulled the older man into his arms.

Ben's image blurred and Morgana blinked to clear her tears. If she'd remembered when Copeland first brought her to Blue Mountain, Ben could have had his daughter two years earlier. Or even last year when she'd been rescued, she could have told someone about Sam then.

Logically, she knew her loss of memory wasn't her fault, but it didn't stop the guilt.

Jack and Ben separated, and Morgana couldn't hear the words between them, but Ben straightened his shoulders and came back to his chair. His eyes were dry. "Tell us everything you know."

"Start with Isabella," Jack said. "Who is she?"

24

*S*nake had mentioned twice that they were going to die. Isabella looked resigned to it, but he wasn't.

He had to crane his neck to look up at Snake and it made his head throb harder. "Are you going to leave us here when you move?"

"You heard about that, did you?" Snake grinned and the sides of his mustache slipped into this mouth.

"Yes, one of your guards had loose lips." It seemed like a million thoughts rushed through his mind in a micro-second. He hoped that Morgana wouldn't be reckless and decide she could save them before help arrived. Had Isabella been right? Was Morgana more reckless than she would be normally because he'd pushed her? Had him protecting her backfired and instead made her think she had to prove to him that she wasn't weak?

He shook his head to clear it and regretted the movement. He must have been hit in the head harder than he thought.

Snake sneered and his brows furrowed. "Make all the jokes you want, Mr. Stone, but you won't be laughing in the end. Just like your father wasn't."

Damon kept a neutral expression on his face, but only because of years of training. He wanted to scream at Snake and then kill the man. He'd never wanted to kill someone before. "What do you know about my father's death?" Damon was almost surprised he'd managed to keep his voice so calm.

"Curtis came sniffing around after Jack Knight killed his father." Snake laughed again, this time sounding like he actually found the situation funny. "How ironic. The almighty Daniel Knight killed by the teenage son he thought was too weak to lead."

"My father was here?" Damon already knew the answer because of Morgana, but he wanted to hear Snake say it. All those years Damon had wondered what had happened to his dad—and the answers had been here all along.

Snake eyed Damon for a moment. "You look like your dad. He thought he was so tough because he was a big fucker. He wasn't any better than the Williams brothers. They all thought they were better than us."

Damon schooled his features and kept his gaze on Snake. Telling Snake he was wrong would be like throwing a basketball against a brick wall—it would just bounce off. His dad had been physically big and strong, but he'd been a gentle soul. He'd also been humble, like all three of the Williams brothers. Damon knew that deep in his own soul.

The realization hit him like a punch to the solar plexus.

He'd always known his father had the kindest of hearts... so why had he ever thought his dad would have left his family by choice? He wouldn't have. Damon watched Snake, but for a moment, the man's image blurred in his vision.

A memory of his dad and mom cuddling in front of the fireplace popped into his mind. Then one of his dad teaching him to ride a bike. Next, an image of his dad showing off his brightly colored fingernails and fingers, because he'd let four-year-old Kate paint them. Curtis Stone had been a family man, through and through.

Damon had been an idiot to blame his father for leaving and a double-idiot to think that he could control his world and everyone in it so nothing bad would ever happen again. Shit happened. It didn't matter how much you controlled or loved someone.

His dad had died because he'd been doing what he thought he should. Isabella was right. Damon had to let people make their own decisions. A picture of Morgana glaring at him with her hands on her hips appeared in his mind, and he had to hold back a smile. Yes, she would always make her own decisions, but that didn't mean he couldn't offer advice and protect her if she allowed it. And be there to help her pick up the pieces if she needed him to. He couldn't focus on Snake as Morgana filled his thoughts.

Magic pummeled the left side of his face, like the force from a truck hitting his cheekbone, sending him careening through the air, chair and all. His right shoulder hit the concrete floor first, followed by his head. Stars shot across his vision as his body's momentum continued along the floor, creating the perfect belt sander for his face

His entire body came to a stop against the wall a fraction of a second before the chair righted itself. He floated with the chair back over to his original position across from Isabella. With Damon's strength drained and pain radiating from his head, face, and shoulder, his head fell forward. The headache he'd had since being hit intensified and he could picture his brain exploding like a pumpkin being dropped from the balcony of a twenty-story building.

Snake grabbed Damon by the hair, his hand fisted in a thick clump of strands, and he hauled Damon's head backward. "Do I have your attention now? You're just like your father. Think you're too good to listen to me."

Damon's jaw pounded as badly as his head, a throbbing that matched his heart beat-for-beat. He wet his lips with his tongue, tasting blood, and felt more dripping down his cheek. A film covered his vision and he thought he was going to pass out. Taking in a deep breath, he let it out slowly, like he'd done before, and hoped he'd be able to speak. "I—I'm lis'ning." His words were slurred and barely audible to his own ears.

Damon's head dropped forward, his chin bouncing off his chest when Snake released him. It took what felt like an enormous amount of strength to lift his head.

"Good. Your father didn't listen when I told him to go back home. He'd be alive today if he'd just listened."

That was a lie. Neither Snake nor Maverick would have let his father live once he'd discovered what they were doing.

Damon's eyes were almost swollen shut. Snake's image blurred as the man paced back and forth. There wasn't much room in front of the chairs Damon and Isabella were tied to, but Snake's restless energy ate up the short distance as he paced. Damon wanted to close his eyes since Snake's movement made his headache and dizziness worse, but Damon didn't dare.

He'd learned through the years that many people liked to stand and look at their audience while they were extolling their own virtues. He hoped Snake was no different—if he could get the man to stand still. It would get Snake to cease his movements and give them more time for help to arrive.

Morgana would bring help. He just had to buy her enough time.

Clenching his hands into fists to distract himself from the pain, Damon looked through the slits of his swollen eyes at Snake. "How'd my dad die?"

Snake spun around and stopped pacing. Damon let out a small breath of relief.

"How?" Snake smiled and the edges of his mustache disappeared into his mouth. "Slowly. You know the tale of the death of a thousand cuts? Well... he bled to death."

The thought of his father going through such torture ate at Damon's soul. No one should have to suffer like that, and especially not someone with a kind soul like his father.

Snake had no idea the kind of pain his words had inflicted on Damon.

"So, you think you're a big man because you tortured a kind-hearted soul? My father was a hundred times the man you'll ever be." Damon knew he was taunting Snake, but hearing him talk casually about his dad's death made it like his dad had died all over again—the grief fresh.

Snake's face became red as he sputtered. "You... you think you know everything! You know nothing! He tried to take Morgana and the other kids with him. Thought he could just waltz in here and tell us what to do. Curtis wanted to shut us down. He didn't understand why we needed the kids and the drugs."

Damon didn't understand either and at risk of being thrown across the room again, he decided to ask anyway. "Why did you?"

"Daniel Knight was the one responsible for killing the Williams brothers and he took their kids so he could siphon their power." Snake shrugged. "He could have siphoned magic from anyone, so I think taking the kids was just a 'big fuck' you to the Williams family."

That didn't make sense to Damon. "But they were dead."

"It was either take the kids or let them die in the fire with the Williams brothers. Knight had just lost one of his sons. I don't know... maybe the bastard was sentimental. Anyway, once Knight was dead and Copeland brought the kids here, they became useful. Each had their own talents we could benefit from."

Bile rose in Damon's throat from the constant pounding in his head. He swallowed it back and masked his disgust from Snake. He was talking about exploiting human beings—children—not using the talents of people he'd hired.

Morgana could resist persuasion, but that would have been the exact opposite of what they'd needed. They would have wanted mindless minions. No wonder they'd had to spellbind her. His angel was so strong. "What talents?"

Snake made a tsking sound again. "It doesn't matter. They helped us build the cartel and our empire. We have enough money to do whatever we want, and with the extra magic we'll obtain, we'll be able to control all non-magics."

"Why? Why do you need that?"

Snake whipped his head toward Isabella at her question, as if he'd forgotten she sat less than ten feet from them. "Why? How can you ask such a thing? Because non-magics want to oppress all magics. That's why!" Snake shouted. Spittle hung from his lips as he glared at her. "We have to hide from non-magics and can't be our true selves! We can't perform magic in public! They don't even know about us and yet they control us! Non-magics would kill us if they knew what we could do, but not if we control them first."

Damon didn't disagree with some of what Snake said, but controlling non-magics wasn't the answer. He watched Isabella take in Snake's words, a look of pity on her face. "Who hurt you?" she asked quietly.

"Hurt me?" Snake yelled, leaning over Isabella, bracing his arms on her chair. She shrunk back as far as the chair would allow, but her gaze didn't waver. "My parents tried to brainwash me and then they did the same thing to my son!" Spittle hit Isabella on her cheek, and she lifted her shoulder, wiping it away.

"How are you going to control non-magics?" Damon

asked, hoping to get Snake's attention back on him and away from Isabella.

Snake straightened and faced him, his face red, his lips wet with spit. He waved a hand in front of his face and magically dried himself, returning his color to normal. "With the magic box. It wasn't a myth and I have it. I'll use the power within it to control all non-magics and then we will be free to do whatever we wish."

Damon let out a derisive laugh. "No one knows where the magic box is."

Snake's eyebrows lifted into his hairline as a bizarre expression twisted his face into an imitation of the Joker's. "Ah, not true. I have the box."

"You mean you found it with the book you stole by killing people?" The more Snake nattered on, the more Damon wanted to push the man and see what he knew.

Snake waved his hand. "Semantics. Drew found the box and is holding it for me in Blue Mountain. When I leave here tonight, I'll have everything I need to put my plan in place."

"Thank you," Maverick said, interrupting Snake.

Damon twisted as much as he could and watched Snake turn toward Maverick, a look of puzzlement on his face. "What?"

Maverick lifted his right hand and a gun magically appeared. He pointed it at Snake. "I was saying thank you to Mr. Stone for pulling the information out of you that I needed."

The gun's retort was deafening in the small room.

25

*S*urprise registered on Snake's face a split second before the bullet pierced the front of his skull. Brains and blood shot out the back of his head, splattering the wall behind him as he toppled face forward.

Damon heard Isabella's gasp, a mirror image of his own. A sudden coldness swept over him that had nothing to do with magic or his head injury. He'd wanted Snake dead but hadn't expected his death to come so violently or at the hand of the man's partner.

Maverick walked over and waved his hand at Snake. The man's body flew to the side, slamming against the wall like a ragdoll. Maverick looked away from Snake and met Damon's gaze. "Snake has always been in my way, even in death."

Damon hadn't known Maverick—Forest Sharpe—well, but he'd seen him around when he'd been a magic council leader with his dad more than twenty years ago. Maverick looked the same as Damon remembered, just older. His hair was as thick as it had been years earlier but was now sprinkled liberally with gray and his mustache was even bushier than Snake's.

Maverick gave Damon a mock bow. "Thank you. I've been trying to get the location of the box out of Snake for over a week. Now that I have it, I didn't need him anymore."

And I don't need you two either. Maverick didn't say the words, but Damon could tell the man thought them. Damon needed to stall him to give Morgana more time to get help.

Damon focused on his words and enunciated each one with care. "The magic box is a new acquisition... but you've been working with Snake for over twenty years... why kill him now?"

"You look a bit worse for wear. Snake had some fun, I see." Maverick chuckled. "You want to chat, do you? Are you stalling? Well... it won't matter, the plan is already in place. I suppose I can humor you for a few minutes since I'm waiting for something to start." Maverick conjured a wooden chair and turned it around to straddle it, resting his arms on the top of the back.

Damon's Spidey sense tingled and he knew he wasn't going to like what was coming next, but he needed to be prepared for when Morgana brought help. Schooling his features like he'd done with Snake, he looked Maverick in the eyes. "What plan?"

"You're direct, I like that. And just so you know, I had a lot of respect for your father. He was a good man, but I'd worked too hard to let him stop us."

If Maverick thought that comment would endear him to the man, he was gravely mistaken. Whether he'd been the one to kill his dad or not, he was at least partially responsible for his death by not saving him.

Damon needed Maverick to talk and waste time, just like he'd gotten Snake to do. It didn't matter what Maverick talked about as long as he stalled him, but Damon couldn't stomach talking about his dad's death and needed to change the topic. "The plan?"

"You're going to die. Both of you." Maverick gave Isabella a cursory glance before looking back at Damon. "Too bad you won't get a chance to see what we did here. I even impressed myself. Running drugs has been a good way to keep us flush in cash, but I don't need it anymore. This place has become a liability. It needs to go. Charges have been set to blow up this place, and you'll go up with it." Maverick relayed his plans as if talking about a casual day at the office. There wasn't a single note of remorse in his voice.

"You used Snake, and others, like Isabella's brother, to run drugs?"

"Isabella's brother?" Maverick looked over at her. "Who's your br— oh, Eddie. I see the family resemblance. Yes, he's been very helpful and I'll keep him around a while longer. I love it when today's youth are so easily molded."

Heat flared in Isabelle's eyes. "He was a good boy."

Maverick chuckled. "Yes, he's been very good for our business. He's quite personable and over the years he's been able to cultivate a tremendous number of contacts to find peddlers for our product."

Damon shook his head at Isabella, hoping to catch her attention. They couldn't do anything about Eddie at the moment, and riling up Maverick wouldn't do them any good either. She gave him a single nod.

Maverick swiveled his head between the two of them and picked up on the silent exchange. "Ah… you're reasonable and you'll listen to Damon. Good girl."

Thankful that Isabella ignored Maverick's patronizing words, Damon knew the best thing was to bring Maverick's attention back to him. If Morgana was able to get a hold of Jack right away, he would have gotten to the city as quickly as he could. He and Meredith were both powerful enough to flash the long distance from Colorado without needing to rest and regenerate their magic halfway through. But it might be a different story if they brought others with them. That would delay help from arriving.

Damon turned back to Maverick. "Snake said he wanted to rule non-magics. It sounded like he had mommy and daddy issues. Did your mommy neglect you too?"

Maverick's mustache lifted in what might be considered a smirk before he rotated his wrist and looked at his watch. "No, I loved my parents and they doted on me. I was an only child and they loved me until they took their last breaths."

"You kill them too?" Isabella asked, and if the metaphorical lasers she was shooting at Maverick had been real, he'd have dropped dead in a second.

Maverick didn't spare her a glance and focused on Damon. "My parents died in a car accident years ago. Unlike the assholes who raised Snake and his son and who taught them to hate all magics, my parents understood the potential of magic people. They brought me up to believe I could rule the world, and I'm going to. Once I have the contents of the magic box, I will control all magics."

Maverick glanced at his watch again and stood before disappearing his chair, the particles disintegrating back into the ether from where they came. "It's about time for me to say farewell."

Damon sneered at Maverick. "So... you're just going to leave us here? You're not even man enough to untie me and fight?"

Maverick laughed. "I can't tell if you're desperate or stupid. Probably both. You're the ones that managed to get captured."

"I know I don't need the magic box or to play God to get what I want. I'd say that makes you the weak one—having to resort to these measures to get what you want. It proves you're just not strong enough to do things on your own." Damon smiled and knew he was letting his emotions get the better of him. Goading Maverick probably wasn't the best move and he'd completely skipped step one, but then, the man didn't deserve to be comfortable. Step two was easy—Maverick was a power-hungry bastard and Damon wanted himself, Isabella, and Sam to make it out of this alive.

Maverick's composure seemed to fracture before Damon's eyes. "Because you're shortsighted. I know all about you, Mr. CEO. You own a company where you get to decide who gets money and who doesn't. Isn't that playing God? You hold all the strings." Maverick took a step closer and bent down to look directly into Damon's eyes. "That is no different than what I'm going to do—just on a bigger scale. Instead of playing around with some businesses and non-magics, I'm going to control the real power—all magics!"

Maverick's breathing sped up after his impassioned speech and Damon realized for the first time how much more dangerous Maverick was than either Copeland or Snake. Perhaps Maverick had been the real mastermind all along.

"I don't play God. I lay out the rules and let others decide if they want to join me or not." The thought that he may not have let Morgana make that decision because he followed her here, wasn't lost on him. There was the gap... Damon realized that he hadn't always willingly let Morgana make her own decisions, regardless of what he thought of them, and Maverick wouldn't allow others to either.

"That's where you're going wrong. Most people need direction and I'm going to give it to them." He pulled out his phone and glanced at the screen before shoving it back in his pocket. "It's been nice chatting with you," Maverick said almost sincerely. "I can't have this place intact when I leave so the explosives we've rigged will go off at intervals, making it look like there was a gas leak that set off multiple fires and explosions."

Damon feared they were out of time and that there was no getting to step four with a man like Maverick.

JACK RELEASED Morgana when her feet touched the ground near her tree outside the compound and she stepped back. She still couldn't flash and an Uber would have taken too long. Once Jack had pulled an image of the compound's grounds from her mind and passed it to the others, they'd planned where to flash to. The distance from the hotel to the compound was short enough for Ben to flash himself, so Jack took Morgana.

"I'm going to do a quick surveillance of the grounds," Jack said and disappeared.

Ben took a step closer to Morgana. "You said Julia was in the hallway at the back of the building when you last saw her?"

His daughter wasn't Julia anymore, but Morgana kept her mouth shut. They didn't have time for her to explain and she wasn't sure she even could. She'd been taken from her family, just as Sam had, and everything they were before then had been wiped away.

When the spell had broken on Morgana, her family had seen her as Molly, but inside, she wasn't that girl anymore. Ben would eventually figure it out, but it wouldn't be an easy journey and she had no way of knowing how Sam would react. She still had her memories of Morgana, but she didn't know if she remembered Ben and her mom. Sam had been so little when she'd been taken.

They'd have to find their own way, just like Morgana had. Meredith and her cousins had wanted to call her Molly, but she hadn't been that person for decades. Sam would have to explain it to her parents when they got her out of the compound. To people who hadn't lived as someone else, a name would probably seem like such a small thing, but it wasn't.

It was just one of many things that made her who she was, just as it would be with Sam. But all that would come—for now, she had to focus on getting Sam, Damon, and Isabella out of the compound. "Yes, the place is a maze. It's huge and there are hallways that spread in every direction. I still don't remember everything, but I know that much."

Ben took another step closer. "Maybe we can extract the memories from you."

Meredith suddenly stood between Ben and Morgana. Meredith had moved so quickly Morgana hadn't even seen her take a step.

Meredith held up a hand in front of Ben. "No, Ben. We don't know what it will do if we try to force Morgana's memories. They're only just returning. We'll get Julia out no matter what."

Ben nodded and scrubbed his hands over his face before dropping his arms loosely at his sides. "You're right. I'm sorry, Morgana, I'd never do anything to hurt you."

Morgana gently pushed Meredith to the side and wrapped her arms around Ben. He'd been nothing but kind to her in the last year and was the only father figure she had. Morgana couldn't imagine what Ben must be going through. "We'll get her out," she whispered into his neck as his arms tightened reassuringly around her.

Ben let her go. "I know; I think Julia being alive hasn't really sunk in yet. Maybe it won't until I see her."

Jack appeared and he must have taken in the looks on their faces. "What happened?"

Meredith wrapped her arm around her husband's waist. "Nothing, it's just an emotional time."

Jack gave Ben a single nod. "I didn't see any guards outside, which isn't a good sign. It means that they're likely already on the move." He turned to Morgana. 'Since your magic started coming back, have you tried to reach out to someone telepathically yet?"

Morgana nodded. "I've tried a few times, but not in the last couple hours." She closed her eyes and concentrated on sending a message to her sister. When Meredith didn't respond, Morgana opened her eyes and looked at her. "Nothing?"

Meredith's eyes widened. "You tried to send me a message?"

"Yes."

Meredith pulled away from Jack and gave Morgana's hand a quick squeeze. "Sorry. I didn't get it." She turned back to her husband. "You or I can reach out to Damon."

"I will. But I wanted to see if Morgana could reach Julia. I don't think me, you, or Ben should because it's been so long since she's seen us and she might not remember. She could become suspicious and warn the guards."

Jack looked over at Ben and the older man held up his hand as he said, "It's okay. I understand."

Morgana's heart was breaking for Ben, but soon he would have time to get to know his daughter again. What was important right now was getting to Damon and Isabella because they didn't know how much time they had. "Jack, we can get to Sam when we're inside. Can you try Damon?"

Jack looked off into the distance and his eyes unfocused. He was silent for quite a while. Morgana knew that full tele-pathic conversations were difficult for most magics— throwing out one or two words was easier. But Jack wasn't a normal magic person.

Jack ran his hand through his already mussed hair and

focused on the three of them. "Damon couldn't answer me, but I could feel him."

Morgana couldn't hold back her panic. "What do you mean? What happened? Is he okay?"

Morgana glared at Jack when she felt a cooling sensation form through her body. "Don't try to make me calm down, Jack. I'm worried, okay? I'm allowed to be."

A sheepish look ran across Jack's face for a moment, and then it was gone. "Sorry, I was trying to help. Damon is my oldest friend and I've always been able to sense his presence when he's close, and tonight was no different. I think he couldn't respond because his magic is blocked. That doesn't mean he didn't hear me and doesn't know that we're coming."

Morgana wiped her damp hands on her pants. "You'll take me in with you?"

"No. I don't think we should all go in at once. Ben and I will go in first." He turned to Meredith. "Bubbles, will you go with Morgana to the back of the compound and wait for my signal? Since that's where Morgana last saw them, they're probably still in that area."

Meredith went on her tiptoes and gave Jack a quick kiss on the lips. "Be careful." She turned to Morgana and grabbed her hand. "Come on, let's go. I can shield us."

Morgana wanted to argue but her not listening to Damon had gotten them into this mess. She let her sister pull her away but glanced back over her shoulder at Jack. "Get them out."

Jack nodded. "We will."

26

*D*amon heard Isabella's indrawn breath, but either Maverick didn't hear it or didn't care as he continued. "My men are packing up and leaving as we speak. Everyone else who is still useful to me, like Eddie"—he smirked at Isabella before turning back—is already long gone."

Damon turned his head to face Maverick. "We're the only two left in the building?"

"No, Sam is here too, but without a reason to make drugs, I won't need a chemist anymore. She'll be blown up with the two of you. She was believed to have died a long time ago anyway, so it's sweet justice."

Damon felt a pressure on his brain and blew out soft pants to ease the pulsing pain.

We're here.

Jack's voice was crystal clear in Damon's head. He pulled on his magic, hoping he could access enough to respond, but the binding of the rope around his wrist held firm.

Damon?

I feel you.

We're coming.

Jack's second comment pushed into Damon's consciousness and after a short pause, a third and fourth one followed. Damon knew a little silence wouldn't be enough to deter his friend. Jack would come for them. Damon bit the inside of his cheek to prevent the smile that threatened to appear and then groaned. The side of his face felt like he'd gone a couple rounds with a sledgehammer. Or a concrete floor.

Maverick laughed at Damon's pain. "Still feeling the effects from Snake? He always did have a bad temper. No worries, you won't be feeling anything soon."

"Hello, Forest, it's been a long time," a familiar, deep voice said, interrupting them.

Damon whipped his head up and groaned again at the movement. Ben and Jack stood between him and Isabella, across from Maverick. Moving his head from side to side slowly to combat the dizziness, Damon took in everyone. When the dizziness became too much, he kept his eyes only on Maverick.

"Wow, Ben. It has been a long time. A little out of your jurisdiction, aren't you?"

Damon wanted to slap the smug expression off Maverick's face. He couldn't begin to imagine what Ben must be feeling—to face the man who kidnapped his daughter and led him to believe she was dead.

"Where's my daughter?" With Damon's eyes still trained on Maverick, he couldn't see Ben, but the steel in his voice was unmistakable.

Maverick snickered. "It took you long enough to figure out she wasn't dead. What? Over twenty years? Some father you are."

Out of the corner of his eye, Damon saw a flash of magic hurl toward Maverick. The man was fast and sidestepped Ben's blast, throwing one of his own.

A bolt of magic whipped by Damon and he sucked himself back into his chair.

"Fucking stop!"

"Stop!"

Damon and Jack both yelled at the same time, but Ben and Maverick were too busy to pay attention. Damon chanced a glance toward Ben just as a bolt of magic bounced toward him. Damon ducked but braced himself for the pain anyway.

Nothing happened. Damon opened his eyes to see Jack standing in front of him. He'd blocked the shot and pushed Damon's chair back while sending small charges of magic to the straps around Damon's ankles and wrists, freeing him.

"Get the rope off," Jack yelled over the cacophony of breaking objects as magic zinging through the room smashed into walls and broke the classroom desks. The blasts of power bounced off shields and hit the floor and walls, ricocheting through the small space.

Jack flashed over to Isabella. "Put up a shield," he yelled back at Damon.

Once free, Damon shoved the magic rope off his wrist and moaned at the agony the motion caused. A flash of magic flew by his arm, causing him to focus. His magic was weak, but he had enough to throw up a protective shield.

The hours he'd been tied to the chair should have been enough to recharge his magic, but his injuries were too severe. He was lucky to be alive. Flashing out of the building wasn't going to be an option, but nothing would stop him from walking out.

Damon straightened up just as the building shook, a thunderous sound blasting throughout the compound. Grabbing onto the chair for support, he looked over and saw Ben turn to Jack. It was just the distraction Maverick needed. He whipped a ball of magic at Ben, catching him in the chest.

Ben flew back, smashing into the wall behind him, and slid to the floor like a deflated balloon.

"Ben!" Jack screamed his mentor's name as he charged at Maverick, but the next second, the man was gone. He'd flashed away.

Jack laid his hands on Ben's chest. "For fuck's sake, Ben, hold still. I need to heal you."

Another blast rocked the room, sending dust and plaster onto Damon, knocking him to his knees. He grasped his head with his hands to still the pounding in his brain. His vision blurred and he toppled forward, catching himself on his hands.

Jack turned around and glared at him. "What the fuck was that?"

Isabella rushed to Damon and laid her hands on his head. Coolness seeped into him as he heard her answer. "Maverick rigged the building to blow. I don't know how many charges, but he said it was supposed to look like gas leaks."

"Holy fuck." Jack turned back to Ben. "I've got to get you out of here so I can heal you before the whole place blows up."

Ben reached up a hand to grab Jack's shirt, but his hand dropped limp in his lap. "No. Julia."

"You won't be any fucking good to Julia if you're dead. I need to get you out of here before the building collapses on us." Jack stood and grabbed onto Ben's shirt, hauling him into a standing position. "Damon, healing Ben won't be fast, and I have to save him. Can you find Julia?"

Damon coughed from the dust in the air and managed a nod. His head still hurt like a bitch, but the little healing Isabella had done was helping. "We'll find her."

Isabella walked over to Ben and laid a hand on his shoulder. "I can find her. I can't explain how, but I will."

Jack didn't wait for Ben to respond and flashed out of the building with him.

Damon took a tentative step, testing his stability. He would make it. He looked at Isabella just as another blast rocked the building. The ground underneath him crumbled, sending his leg into a crack in the floor.

The lights went out.

He spread his arms out to either side, reaching for purchase, and grasped onto Isabella's hand. "I've got you." She used the strength of her magic to haul him up onto solid ground. A small ball of magic glowed in her open palm, giving him enough light to see her face.

"I saw Sam so I have a picture of her in my mind. I can lead us to her."

Damon stumbled a few steps before he was stable enough to right himself and follow Isabella. The doorframe leaned to the right, forcing Damon to duck to get through the narrowed opening.

Isabella looked over her shoulder at him. "Sam is on the other side of the compound, but it's too dangerous to flash there."

"I agree. We don't know what we'd be flashing into. Lead the way."

The building was eerily quiet. There weren't any alarms or shouts from people trying to escape. Dust floated in the air and pieces of plaster continued to fall as it lost its tenuous grip on the ceiling.

Navigating the hallway was a slow process as they stepped over chunks of ceiling and upheaved flooring. They turned into a second hallway and Damon stopped short to avoid a collision with Isabella. She'd stepped back as fire ate its way up the walls, blocking their path forward.

27

*M*organa watched the back of the building and wished there was a sign that Damon and Isabella had made it out. She turned to Meredith. "Can you reach out—" Morgana's words were cut off as an explosion rocked the quiet night.

Meredith grabbed onto Morgana as a heaviness settled in the pit of her stomach. They both watched dust and debris float up into the night sky. "I can't see what happened. Can you?"

Dropping Morgana's arm, Meredith's eyes became unfocused as she held up a finger to her sister.

Glancing back and forth between the building and her sister, it felt like forever before Meredith turned to her. "Jack said—" Another explosion split the night air. Morgana and Meredith watched as flames went up over a part of the building she knew was near Sam's lab.

Morgana took off at a run around the outside of the building, not waiting for her sister. There were doors all over the building that led to the outside and if they were lucky, they'd be able to get inside and find Sam.

"Morgana, stop!" Meredith yelled behind her, but she kept going.

Morgana smashed into her sister when Meredith flashed in front of her. "What the hell, Meredith! We have to get inside."

"It's too dangerous. Jack said that there are charges set around the compound to blow the place up."

"So we're just going to let Damon, Isabella, and Sam die?" Morgana's words were eaten by the noise of a third explosion as it shook the ground around them.

They watched as more flames rose, mixing with the dust in the air. Meredith gripped Morgana's arm, spinning her around to look in her eyes. "I don't want them to die, but I don't want you to die either."

Morgana heard the anguish in her sister's voice. They'd both lost so many people they loved, but Morgana wasn't about to lose any more. She would find Damon if it was the last thing she ever did. "Remember when you walked off the elevator at Copeland's and I tried to stop you?"

Meredith looked wary but nodded.

"Nothing I could have said would have prevented you from going to your mom—our mom—right?"

Meredith nodded again and her shoulders slumped. Morgana knew she had her.

"Right. You would have done anything to save her, just like Jack faced Copeland for you." Morgana turned enough to point at the burning building. "I need to go in there."

"I get it. But let me reach out to Jack again."

Morgana chewed on the inside of her cheek and bounced on her feet. She didn't want to wait. She wanted to run into the building and find Damon. She'd been such an idiot thinking Damon wanted to control her. In reality, he'd been willing to die just to keep her safe.

"Jack can't leave. Ben is severely hurt and he thinks he'll

die if he doesn't stay with him. He said that Damon and Isabella know where Sam is and they're going to get her."

"I think I know where she is too. Follow me." Morgana led her sister to a side door. Morgana gasped, out of breath from running, and leaned over, trying to slow her breathing down so she could listen. "I don't hear anyone. I think it's safe."

"Except for the building falling down and the fire," Meredith muttered as Morgana pulled open the door.

Morgana coughed as she sucked in a breath full of dust. The hallway was pitch black and, except for the sounds of the building collapsing, it was eerily quiet.

Meredith came up beside her, a small glowing orb in the palm of her hand. "Make a ball of light."

"Right." It had been so long since Morgana had used magic, and it was still coming back to her, that she'd forgotten the simplest of things. Within seconds she had light emanating from her hand, and if the situation had been different, she would have shouted in joy.

They walked forward, winding around chunks of debris. A loud crack in the ceiling rent the air. Morgana looked up to see a piece of the ceiling dangling above them. She yanked Meredith's arm, pulling them both backward just as the roof caved in.

The crash vibrated through the hall and dust rose in the air with a smothering force. Morgana's cough tore through her lungs and her eyes watered, tears streaming in rivers down her face. After a moment, her coughing subsided enough for her to speak. "You okay?"

"Yeah, and now we have another problem." Meredith held up her hand with the light orb and pointed to a section of ceiling that blocked their path. "If we work together, we might be able to move it since it's just plaster. Let's both push from this side."

Morgana disappeared her light as she moved to Meredith's side. Morgana felt the strength of Meredith's magic as the plaster moved a few feet. They were both breathing hard and covered in dust. "Let's—" Morgana stopped to cough and took in a shuddering breath. "Let's try again."

Meredith nodded as her body shook with a cough. When she could suck in a breath, they both raised their hands and tried again.

Morgana focused on her magic essence. The feeling of her power was still foreign as it stirred within her and she called it forth. Their magic slammed into the section of ceiling blocking their path, lifting it with such force, the plaster shattered, sending pieces flying through the air.

Meredith tugged Morgana's arm to her. "Run!" Debris and dust rained down on them as they hauled ass down the hallway. When they were clear, Morgana was sucking wind as she turned back to look at the way they'd come.

Portions of the ceiling hung precariously and the wall on one side of the hallway had collapsed where they had stood moments ago. She straightened and raised a brow at her sister. "I guess we're stronger than we knew."

Meredith chuckled. "I think that was you."

Morgana didn't think so, but just shrugged. They continued down the hall at a slower pace, giving Meredith a chance to recover her breath. "I guess we'll need to find a new way out."

Morgana huffed out a laugh. "Come on, the lab's not far." She rounded a corner when another explosion ripped through the air. The force of the percussion wrenched Morgana and Meredith into the air. They flew several feet and crashed against a wall. The thick dust floated in front of Morgana, obscuring her view of her sister. "Mer? Mer? Can you hear me?"

"Yeah." Meredith's voice came out of the cloud of ashes and then her hand appeared. "How much further?"

"It's the room up on the left."

Morgana winced as she placed her full weight on her right ankle. She held up a hand to her sister as she rushed over. "I'm good, it'll be fine. We need to hurry." Her entire body ached as she pushed forward.

Isabella's quick thinking to conjure baking soda had doused enough of the fire that they were able to get through to the other side.

They'd made it into the last hallway where Sam should be only to find another obstacle blocked their path. Sweat poured off Damon as he used his waning magic to try to push a ceiling beam out of the way. It wasn't enough.

Isabella elbowed him out of the way. "Let me help."

Using the sleeve covering his forearm, he wiped the sweat out of his eyes and smeared dust in them. "You need to save your strength so you can find the way out of here."

"We'll flash out and Morgana's sister can get her out." She put her hands on the beam and grunted. "Let's move it the non-magic way." They leaned into the beam and shifted it enough to create a space for them to crawl under.

The dust hung heavy in the air, and he could feel the heat from the fire behind them that was quickly gaining ground. It had only been a few minutes since they'd left Jack, but it felt like a lifetime.

Damon could just make out Isabella's form. He wasn't sure if it was the dark, the dust, his eyes being almost swollen shut, or the relentless pounding in his head, but seeing ahead of him was becoming harder and harder.

Isabella coughed and waved her hand in front of her face, disappearing some of the dust. "It's around the corner. I can sense Sam, so she didn't escape. I thought maybe with Snake dead and Maverick gone, she might have been able to get out on her own."

Damon.

Damon heard Jack's voice in his head and reached out a hand to Isabella, halting her progress. "It's Jack."

Morgana and Meredith went inside.

Fuck! He should have known Morgana wouldn't stay put. She'd do anything to save Sam.

We'll find them. Damon threw the thought back at Jack.

He turned to Isabella to relay the message. "Morgana and her sister are in the building."

Isabella stood still and closed her eyes. "I can feel Sam and I think Morgana too. They're together." Her eyes sprung open. "There are two more people with them, but I don't know who they are. There's either too much interference or I don't know them."

"One will be Meredith, Morgana's sister." Pain pulsed through every part of Damon. Using his magic to dull the pain would lessen the little power he had left. He couldn't risk it. Pushing forward, they reached the doorway of Sam's lab and Damon feared what they'd find on the other side.

I'll go low. You high.

He nodded at Isabella, acknowledging the thought she threw at him, and called up a ball of magic, ready to strike.

He turned into the room and stopped. Isabella did the same from beside him.

Sam was gagged and tied to a chair with magic rope. Maverick stood beside her with a gun to her head.

A few feet in front of them, Morgana and Meredith faced Maverick with their hands raised, balls of magic swirling in their palms.

28

*M*organa's breath hitched as Damon and Isabella almost fell into the room. The right side of Damon's face looked like a three-day-old hamburger. His eyes were almost swollen shut and he was covered in dust and blood and barely standing upright.

He met her gaze and the left corner of his lip lifted.

It looks worse than it is.

She almost laughed when he threw the thought in her head, but he flicked his chin in Maverick's direction. Maverick's rule had to end. She focused her attention back on the sorry excuse for a human. "Let Sam go, Maverick." Morgana was proud of the strength in her voice. "You don't need Sam. The building is about to fall, and you're out numbered."

Maverick flung his arm forward, changing the aim of his gun—it now pointed directly at Morgana. "Well, well, our tough little Morgana—or should I say Molly?—is back."

Morgana was tired of the shit she'd endured because of this man and his partners. Whatever her name was, he was right about one thing—she was tough. A thought hit her... she was so tough that the only way three grown, powerful men could handle her was to spellbind her. She wasn't weak at all.

"Let Sam go. You don't need us."

Maverick grinned, the corners of his trimmed mustache turning up like a macabre version of himself. "You're right, I don't. But I don't want your little band of do-gooders to hinder my plans. I was going to let Sam here go down with the building, but I think killing her myself just as her daddy shows up to save her would be perfect irony."

Morgana's hand felt heavy and wavered as she continued to hold up the ball of power in her palm. She braced her bent elbow at her waist for support. A little fatigue wasn't going to stand in her way. "Really? What plans? You've just blown up your income stream. Going to be kind of tough to make drugs now." She heard Meredith hiss beside her as she taunted Maverick, but she ignored her sister.

"Such short-sighted thinking, Morgana. I'd let Mr. Stone fill you in, but you're not going to be alive to worry about it." He rotated the gun's muzzle back to Sam's head.

Morgana watched Sam's eyes widen and knew their time was running out. "You can't outrun us all, Maverick. Let Sam go."

Maverick glanced at his watch. "You know what? I think I will and let her father pick the pieces of his daughter out of the rubble. I've got somewhere else to be."

The gun fell to the floor, bouncing twice as Maverick disappeared.

Morgana took a step toward Sam and the entire building shook. Her knees hit the concrete first. The magic ball in her palm rolled off the ends of her fingers and disintegrated as it fell, leaving only a spark to hit the floor before it faded as her momentum propelled her forward, her arm still extended.

Damon shook his head to clear the dust from his eyes as he pushed himself up onto his knees. "Fuck!" He couldn't discern a single point of pain in his body—he hurt everywhere. His ears rang from the explosion and something dripped from his temple. He swiped at the annoyance and his hand came away covered in blood.

He'd been watching Morgana when he saw Maverick check his watch as the gun dropped from his fingers, then he flashed just as another bomb went off. Either that, or he'd been the one to pull the ceiling down on them before he left.

Grabbing onto what was left of the doorframe, he hauled himself to his feet. Isabella had started to stir beside him and he looked down at where she'd fallen to her knees.

She gave him a feeble attempt at a wave to brush him off. "I'm alive. Find the others."

Dust created a layer so thick it hung like a blanket suspended in the air. Plaster and wires dangled from above him. Looking up, he could see stars shining through a crater-sized hole in the roof. The floor in front of him was littered with obstacles where Morgana and Meredith had just stood. His heart rate picked up, and he sucked in a breath against the pain in his head. "Morgana?" he called.

"Here!" The shout came from Meredith.

Isabella came up beside him. Her right arm hung by her side and she cradled a light orb in her left hand. He pushed wreckage out of the way as fast as he could as he maneuvered further into the room. Glass and wires cut his hands as he moved rubble to the side.

Damon saw Morgana's hand first and his breath stopped. He was looking at the vision he'd had when he'd been in her apartment. Pushing forward, he dropped to his knees and, using both hands, ignored the pain as he flung a piece of tile off her.

As in the vision, her eyes were closed, and blood covered one side of her forehead and cheek. Her shirt was ripped at the shoulder, showing abrasions and more blood mixed with dust.

"Morgana?" Damon bent forward, placing his hand on her back and listening for sounds of breathing. He felt her back move first and then her breath on his cheek—it was one of the sweetest things he'd ever known. "Angel? Can you hear me?"

Moving her head first, she looked up and pulled her outstretched arm closer to her body. "Oh fuck. Everything hurts."

"Can you sit up?" He wanted to pull her into his arms but didn't know the extent of her injuries and didn't want to make them worse.

"Let me scan." She closed her eyes and he waited impatiently, wanting to scan her for injuries himself. When she opened her eyes again and lifted just the corner of her mouth in a crooked smile, he knew he wanted to see that every day for the rest of his life.

"Nothing's broken." Grabbing on to him, she hefted herself up and he stood with her. Her eyes became frantic as she moved her head from side to side, clearly searching for her sister. "Meredith?"

"I'm here."

Damon looked in the same direction as Morgana. Meredith and Isabella stood on either side of Sam. They'd removed her gag and untied her, but Sam's face was deathly pale, and lines of pain were etched around her mouth.

He looked down at Morgana. "Can you walk?"

"Yeah."

They made their way to the other women.

He looked from Sam to Meredith. "What's wrong? Can you all flash?"

Meredith shook her head. "Sam can't. Maverick broke her leg and drained her magic. We're—"

An earsplitting crack sounded from above them and they all looked up as more of the ceiling rained down on them.

"The roof is collapsing!" Isabella shouted. "And the fire is spreading!" She pointed behind them.

"Meredith, get out! Take Sam! Damon and I'll follow!" Morgana yelled, Damon just making out her words above the jarring sound of the roof caving in. He could hear the crackle of fire as it burned toward them through the halls.

"No! You can't flash!"

"I can now. My magic is back. We're behind you! Go!" He watched Morgana look from Meredith to Isabella and he knew Morgana had just lied.

"Right behind us!" Meredith yelled again as parts of the roof collapsed behind them, rocking them on their feet and sending more dust into the air.

"Yes! Go!"

Meredith grabbed onto Sam's arm and they were gone. Isabella flashed right after them.

Damon heard another crack above him and lunged for Morgana. He shoved her out of the way using all the force he could muster and lurched after her.

He wasn't fast enough. A piece of concrete beam caught him as he lunged forward. A yell erupted from deep within him.

29

*D*amon's strength propelled Morgana forward. She landed on her outstretched hands but didn't stay down. She jumped up and spun around.

"Damon!" Concrete from the roof let go of its moorings as Damon lunged for her. His scream split the air, and Morgana thought her heart would stop.

She was at his side in a second and knelt in the rubble, sharp ends digging into her knees. "Damon!" She reached out a tentative hand, fearful of touching him, but needing the contact. "Damon? Talk to me!"

He groaned and shifted his weight. "Fuck! My ankle." He pulled on his leg and his face went white underneath all the blood and dust. "I can't move."

Their voices hoarse, they had to yell to be heard over the crackling of the fire. Morgana could feel the heat getting closer. She coughed as smoke started to build and mingled with the dust that already thickened the air. "Can you mentally reach Jack?"

Damon's eyes glazed over before he shook his head. A moan escaped his lips. "Fuck. I need to stop doing that." He panted a few short breaths. "I couldn't reach Jack. I don't know if he's too far away or if my magic is too weak or what. Why don't you try him?"

Morgana didn't have the heart to tell him she'd failed to reach Meredith when she'd tried earlier. She closed her eyes and reached out to her sister. She was met with silence. "No, nothing."

Damon winced as he reached up and cupped the back of her neck, pulling her down to speak into her ear. "You need to get out of here. There's a door at the back that still looks intact. Go."

She blinked away the tears that threatened to spill over. Grasping his biceps, she pulled back to look in his eyes. "I won't leave you." She lifted one hand and gently ran it along his temple and down his neck, not caring about the blood that coated him. She was careful to avoid his injuries. "I love you, Damon." First declarations should be whispered tenderly, not yelled over the sounds of destruction. But she didn't know if they'd make it out alive. She needed Damon to know how she felt.

She would love this man until she took her last breath, even if that day was today. She'd thought she was weak, but anyone could feel tough and strong holding a gun. Or think themselves powerful because they could siphon someone's magic. But Morgana knew where real strength came from—from loving someone. She loved Damon with everything she had. She bent forward and kissed him. It wasn't a kiss of passion or lust; it was one of love and care for the other person.

"I love you too, angel," he said against her lips. Then he pulled back and coughed, the smoke thickening in the room. "I love you so much that I'd die if something happened to you. I know you lied and that you can't flash. Please get the woman I love out of here." His voice rougher now from the smoke as he yelled to be heard.

She shook her head as talking became more difficult. There was no way she'd leave him. She coughed as she stood and realized they were almost out of time. The first explosion had been less than fifteen minutes ago, but the building was coming down around them.

Turning to step around Damon to get to the slab of concrete, she looked over to the doorway. It was consumed in flames. The fire would soon be upon them.

Her skin pinched, right along her tattoo, a familiar feeling now. Another sunflower on her tattoo had changed. She was surprised she could even feel the sting when it had to compete with the other aches and pains and the adrenaline coursing through her body. She didn't have time to look. She had to move Damon.

"Morgana, run!"

She whipped her head up in time to see a wall of fire coming toward them. Without thinking, she threw her hands up and closed her eyes. Calling on her magic, she felt it stir and rise up, shooting from her palms toward the fire.

Opening her eyes, she watched as the fire stopped in its tracks, like it hit an invisible barrier, preventing it from moving forward.

Continuing to pour from her as if there was an endless supply, her magic resisted the fire's forward path. The flames sputtered out a bit at a time until all that remained were glowing embers.

"Holy shit!"

Morgana turned to Damon and dropped back to her knees in front of him, grinning like an idiot. The room was quieter without the sounds of the fire. "I did that!"

"You did!" He laughed with her, disbelief written on his face.

A deafening crack split the air. Morgana jerked her eyes up and saw the remaining part of the roof wobble, tip, and dangle for a moment, as if time had stopped.

"Look out!" She heard Damon's yell over the sound of concrete scraping against concrete as she threw up her hands. Her palms faced the roof as the massive concrete slab let go and thundered toward them. Holding her hands steady, she sent her magic up through her palms.

The roof stopped its downward trajectory and hung suspended in the air.

Leaning in the direction she wanted the roof to move, Morgana dragged her hands forward and down, directing the concrete slab to follow. When it smashed to the ground, the floor shook like a magnitude-ten earthquake had hit, knocking her back into Damon's lap. As dust and debris rained down on them, Morgana once again threw her arms in the air with her palms up, slowly splaying them out to her sides. All the detritus parted and fell down around them, missing their heads.

When the air started to clear, she dropped her shaking arms into her lap as adrenaline continued to race through her system. "Holy shit!" She turned to Damon. "I did that!" She repeated her earlier words, her mind unable to come up with something different.

She laughed and ended up coughing. "We need to get out of here." Gently easing off Damon's lap, she stood and examined the huge slab of cement still crushing his leg. If she tried to push it off him, she could do more damage. She needed to pick it up—have it float away like the piece of roof had.

Turning her palms toward the slab of concrete laying over Damon's leg, she focused on her magic, sending it out through her palms, and hovered her hands near the concrete before she lifted them skyward.

Damon grunted as the concrete shifted and he braced his hands on the floor.

Directing with her hands, like she had before, the slab of concrete floated away from Damon with her hands' movements, but this time Morgana lowered it to the ground slowly.

"Holy shit, I did it!" The words had become her mantra. She flung herself at Damon and as they toppled backward, she put her hands out, slowing their fall to the ground. She kissed him until he moaned, but not the good kind. "Shit! I'm sorry."

Morgana helped Damon stand and looked around at the ruined building. The roof was gone, and the walls were partially destroyed. What used to be the entrance to the hallway was blocked by the remains of the roof.

They turned toward the back of the room, where Damon had said he'd seen a door. Morgana hooked her shoulder under Damon's armpit, and they made their way in that direction.

"Shit! Not again!" A corner of the roof had collapsed, blocking the exit. Her hope crashed. "There's not much holding up the building anymore and if I move this, the rest could collapse on us."

"The door leads outside; we'd only have to move about two feet to be in the clear."

"Yes, but the doorway is blocked."

Damon shook his head and then winced. "Sorry, I'm not being clear. My head hurts, my everything hurts. If you move the piece of roof that's in the way, we'd only have to go two feet to be clear; I can flash us both that distance."

Even flashing someone a few feet was a lot for most magics. Yes, some could do it, but it drained them. "You sure? You're weak, you—sorry, I didn't mean it like that."

"I know what you mean. The last fifteen minutes or so

has been tough and I was already hurt and drained. But, yes, I can do it."

If she wanted him to trust her, then she'd do the same. "Okay. How do you want to do this?"

"We'll get as close to the door as we can, so I only have to flash us a couple of feet." They edged toward the door and Damon pulled Morgana's back flush with his front. "This will leave your hands free and still let me hold onto you. As soon as you move the roof, I'll flash us out."

"Okay, on three." She stuck her palms out toward the slab of roof and called up her magic. "One. Two. Three."

The concrete slab flew to the side and Damon flashed them out.

They landed in a lump on the gravel and turned just as the rest of the building came down in a heap of rubble. The sound reverberated through the night.

Morgana flung her body over Damon's, protecting him from flying debris as the ground shook under them. She felt a sting in her side, sharper than the previous ones, but her tattoo was the least of her worries as she covered Damon. Dust flew up in the darkened sky as pieces of the building rained down around them.

30

*D*amon rubbed his hands along Morgana's back where she lay across his chest. He brushed particles and dust off her, stinging the many abrasions already littering his skin. They were a small annoyance and so worth it to have Morgana with him and safe. "Angel, look at me," he said quietly.

She lifted her head and twisted to lie more fully on him so she could see his face. "Hi."

He rubbed his hand along her hair and pulled out a piece of plaster, tossing it on the ground. "Thank you."

She frowned. "I couldn't let the stuff fall on you."

"I'm not thanking you for that… well, yes, thank you for that… but I meant for saving us inside and for trusting me to flash us out." Taking her hands in his, both of them dirty and bloody, his skin torn, he looked into her eyes. "You just saved us—three times. You are the strongest, most amazing, beautiful woman I have ever met. I love you, Angel."

"I love you, too."

Morgana's eyes widened. "The tattoo!" She jumped up, hiking up her shirt to reveal the sunflower that had been below the serpent. It was now a flame. The fourth sunflower had changed too—now a bright, shiny red apple. "An apple?"

It all made sense now. "Resistance."

She kneeled in front of him, squinting her eyes. "What?"

A grin spread across his face. "Resistance, that's your specialty. When you resisted persuasion, a serpent appeared. When you resisted fire, a flame appeared. And then an apple because you resisted gravity."

"Morgana! Damon!" They turned their heads in sync as Isabella ran up to them. "Are you hurt?"

Morgana stood and offered her hand to help him up. He shoved his ego aside and accepted her help. Holding in a groan, he managed to straighten and held her hand. Doing anything more would hurt too much.

Isabella ignored him and wrapped her arms around Morgana. He was close enough to hear her whispered words. "I'm so glad you're okay."

Morgana didn't let go of his hand and gave Isabella a one-armed hug. "Me too."

Isabella fell into step with them as they walked. "Meredith knew you couldn't flash and that you'd sacrifice yourself to get Sam out of the building. It almost killed her to do as you asked."

Morgana turned her head to look behind them. "Where is Meredith? Is she okay?"

"She's fine. She said to tell you she loves you and she'll be right back. She had to go get something." Her expression sobered. "Want to talk to Sam?"

"Oh shit, right." Morgana tugged Damon's hand as they followed Isabella to the front of the compound. The door they'd blasted out of had been on the corner, so luckily they didn't have far to go. He was feeling the effects of the last hour, and not in a good way.

As they got closer to the others, he noticed Sam sitting on

the ground not far from them. Since Jack had to flash Ben out of the building and stay to heal him, Damon didn't even know if Sam had been reunited with her father yet. He looked over at Isabella. "How's Sam's leg?"

"We were able to heal it with no problems, and Sam might have been able to help herself if her magic hadn't been drained." Isabella scrunched up her face. "I hear there's been a lot of that going around."

"Agreed."

Isabella turned to face them as she walked. "Meredith took off a few minutes ago, after she helped me fix Sam's leg."

Morgana squeezed Damon's hand and met his gaze. "It felt far longer than a few minutes ago that you flashed out."

"True." He huffed out a dry laugh and then coughed. "Shit, the dust."

"Let me help." Isabella rested her hand on his back, forcing him to stand still.

He felt her magic pour into him, easing the tightness in his chest. He took a deep breath, filling his lungs, and didn't cough. "Thanks. Can you help Morgana too please?"

"It's okay, I'm—"

"Please let her help you. I thought we realized earlier that we can accept help."

"True." Morgana parroted Damon with a laugh, then started to cough. Isabella rushed to her friend and healed her as she had Damon. Morgana kissed Isabella's dirty cheek and Damon saw raw emotion pass across the other woman's face before she returned Morgana's smile.

"Thanks," Morgana said. "Now, can you fix Damon's ankle?"

Isabella sighed. "Sure, but instead of doing it standing, why don't we all sit down and fix everything?"

A hushed awkwardness hung in the air when they reached the others. Sam sat in the dirt with her arms wrapped tightly around her knees, and Jack was bent over Ben's prone form.

Morgana let go of his hand and rushed to Sam, dropping to her knees in front of her. "Sam, I'm so glad you're safe."

Sam's face was dirty and pale, but it was the expression of grief stamped on her features that tore at Damon. "You should have let me go with Maverick."

Morgana's eyes widened. "What? No! He would have killed you."

Sam shrugged. "Maybe, but now he'll kill Mirek."

"Mirek?" Morgana put her hand on Sam's knee. "My cousin? Holy shit, that's right, you mentioned him at the market before your guard came. Mirek is alive?"

Sam picked at a blade of grass, her eyes downcast. "He was a few months ago. Maverick didn't let me see him very often, but he said he'd keep him alive as long as I did what he wanted."

Jack stepped over to them and they all looked up. "We will find him. I promise you. Now, come over here." Jack reached his hand out for Sam and gently pulled her up when she put her hand in his.

Damon conjured a large deck chair and almost fell into it, his feet straight out in front of him. He grasped Morgana under her arms and pulled her up into the chair with him, placing her between his legs. She leaned back against his chest, and he wrapped his arms around her.

They watched as Jack led Sam over to where Ben was sitting in a similar chair. Jack must have just conjured it because Damon hadn't noticed it when they'd walked up. Ben's face was ashen, but he seemed alert.

Reaching Ben's side, Jack faced Sam. "Sam, do you know that your real name is Julia?" Jack's voice was soft, almost soothing, when he spoke. Damon could only imagine what his best friend was feeling. There wasn't a precedent or a rule book on how to introduce someone to a father who thought he'd buried you years ago.

Sam nodded and twisted her hands together. She didn't look at Jack as she traced lines in the dirt with her once-white sneaker. "Mirek told me when I was twelve or thirteen. But I'd forgotten until then."

Ben struggled to stand, grasping on to Jack for assistance. It took a moment for Ben to get upright and face his daughter for the first time in over twenty years.

With all the care of a loving father, Ben put his fingers under Sam's chin and lifted it so he could look into her eyes. "It doesn't matter that you forgot, sweetheart. You were just a child." Ben's voice cracked and he cleared his throat. "It doesn't matter what your name is. You. Are. My. Child. I love you."

"I— I—" Sam's voice choked like her father's and Ben pulled her into his arms.

Damon could hear their sobs and it ripped at his soul. His own throat felt tight as he swallowed against a lump. "You okay?" he whispered in Morgana's ear. She'd never get a reunion with her parents, nor would he with his father.

He felt the back of her head move in a nod against his chest.

"Ben?"

Damon turned his head to see Stella standing beside Meredith. Meredith's power was so strong now, she must have flashed back to Blue Mountain and helped Stella flash the long distance. Since Morgana and Meredith were both orphans now, she understood the importance of this reunion.

Ben pulled away from his daughter just enough for his wife to see who he held. He hadn't bothered to wipe away the tears that streamed down his face amidst the dirt and blood. Ben extended his hand, palm up, to his wife.

Stella tentatively walked the few steps to her husband, taking his hand, and then gasped. Her free hand flew to her face. "Julia?"

Stella let go of Ben's hand and threw herself at her daughter, pulling the young woman into her embrace. Ben's arms encircled them both.

As they watched the family in each other's arms, Meredith walked up to where he sat and conjured her own chair, flopping into it. "Damon, you need to get better at rescuing damsels in distress. You're always getting hurt. First you were hit with magic with Rowena, then you got beat up when you were with Isabella, and now you let a building fall on you."

He heard the teasing in her voice but knew there was also a grain of truth in her statement. He'd do every one of those things again, especially to keep Morgana safe. "I think I'll let you damsels save me from now on. You're all pretty kick ass."

Morgana twisted in his lap so she could see him. "Good idea."

EPILOGUE

*M*organa got in the car and watched as Damon shut her door and walked around to the driver's side. It'd been a month since they'd returned from Mexico and she couldn't get enough of looking at him. He was tall and gorgeous—a great-looking man—but it was what he had inside that she truly loved. She'd learned he wanted to protect her, not control her.

She still couldn't flash and she had accepted that her magic was just different than others. Damon had helped her get her learner's permit and soon she'd be able to drive.

He started the engine and looked over at her, one brow lifted. "What are you thinking over there? Should I be worried?"

She leaned over and kissed the scars on his right cheek. Even with Jack's healing power, he couldn't heal them all the way, and Damon would always have the reminder of what they'd gone through.

When she sat back in her seat, he lifted his palm and scrubbed it along his face. He'd said they didn't bother him, but they were a constant reminder that they'd almost lost each other. She thought they kept him from looking too pretty and teased him about it.

He checked over his shoulder and eased the car onto the road. "Did you notice something with Isabella and Reece tonight? I mean, something worse than normal?"

She chuckled as she thought of her cousin and their new friend. "Not any more than usual. Wanna bet how long it will take for them to get together?" Isabella and Reece had taken to each other like oil and water since the moment they'd met. Reece claimed that they didn't like each other, but Morgana thought they'd be better just climbing into bed with each other and burning off some of the lust that seemed to ignite whenever they were together. Reece and Isabella reminded her a lot of her and Damon. They just had to figure out they were stronger together.

"No way, I'm not taking on that bet." Damon glanced away from the road for a moment and gave her a smirk. "It's not that I don't think they'll end up together, it's that both of them are so stubborn, I don't know how long each one will hold out."

"So true." They talked about others who'd attended the family dinner on the rest of the drive home. Morgana hadn't officially moved in with Damon yet, but they spent most nights at each other's places and tonight they'd decided to go to his place because he hadn't been home for a few days.

Inside his condo, he dropped his keys on the table, took her purse off her shoulder, and picked her up. She cried out and then laughed before wrapping her legs around his waist.

He carried her into the bathroom and sat her down on the counter. "I think we're both dirty and need a shower."

He stood between her legs and she reached up and undid his tie, loving the feel of the silk in her hand as it slid from around his neck. "Is that so? Then you better make sure I get clean."

Leaning down, he nipped at her lips. "I need to see you and I don't want to wait."

Her breath quickened with the feeling of heat that was building inside her. "Then don't."

He waved his hand in front of himself and then her, and they were both naked; the cool air felt good against her flushed skin. When she saw over his shoulder that the chair in the corner was empty, she looked down. Their clothes were in a heap on the floor down at his feet. She teased his lips. "You didn't even fold them."

"Later." His lips descended on hers and he kissed her with all the passion she'd come to crave from him.

He lavished attention on one nipple and then kissed his way to the next. It wasn't enough. "Don't tease me, Damon. I need more."

"I need to see them first." His words were muffled against her skin.

She gripped his hair in her hands and tugged his head back. "You can see them later."

"No."

"Gah, really?" She put on a good pout, but she wouldn't deny him.

He flicked his hand behind him, and the shower turned on before he picked her up. Her core tingled as she rubbed against the hard muscles of his stomach and wrapped her legs around him.

He carried her into the shower stall, and she slid down his body, igniting her further as she stood and he dropped to his knees. Running his hands along her body, he worshipped her, kissing each part of her tattoo. His lips paused about partway down her ribs and she looked down.

When they'd worked together and trusted each other to get out of the building in Mexico, the final two sunflowers on her tattoo changed. Both evolved together as they joined.

It wasn't until much later when they were in the hotel showering, Damon running his soapy fingers along her tattoo, that he'd noticed. The former sunflowers were now two connected puzzle pieces. Just like she and Damon had worked together to get themselves out of the building, and how they'd be for the rest of their lives.

The Day Morgana's Spell Broke

"STOP!" Rowena yelled to the voice in her head, pressing her palms into her forehead, as if she could push the voice out. "Stop! It's too much, let me think!"

The words and visions in her mind disappeared. They'd been coming on and off for months now, but they'd started up again tonight as soon as she'd gone to Morgana's and discovered the spell on her had been broken. The logical part of her brain knew it wasn't a coincidence.

She let out a long breath and conjured a large glass of wine, taking a seat in the overstuffed armchair in her living room. The gulp she took did little to wash away the bitter taste of anxiety coating her tongue. Lifting the glass to her lips again, she forced herself to take a smaller sip so she could fully savor the light, fruity flavors of the pinot grigio—her favorite wine.

She'd consumed too many glasses of the beverage lately, trying to dull the voices and hallucinations in her mind. If she wasn't careful, she could easily drown herself in wine until even it wasn't enough.

As a psychologist, she knew the signs and symptoms of common mental disorders, and although no one was immune, she never thought it would happen to her. At least, she'd hoped it wouldn't.

She looked around her apartment, seeing her favorite things, items she'd collected over the years. Framed pictures covered the walls, and books and other cherished items lined the two large bookcases flanking the far wall. There were candles and crystals, and several packs of beautiful tarot cards on display. Perhaps strange things for a psychologist to collect, but she loved the look of them and the symbolism behind them, whether they were real or not.

Her collection soothed something inside her as she continued to visually scan each item. She took another sip of her wine and felt a sense of calm finally settle over her. More and more lately, she needed things that brought her serenity in order to combat the chaos in her thoughts.

It was subtle at first—a word here, a word there—but nothing very clear or that made any sense. She'd gone to a doctor and had every test under the sun to rule out nervous system problems, such as Parkinson's disease, epilepsy, and brain tumors. That left a whole host of mental health disorders as probable causes.

She'd then seen a psychiatrist, but her symptoms didn't present as an identifiable mental disorder and her psychiatrist finally told her she needed to lower her stress levels. Now she knew what her own patients felt like when she told them that—frustrated and angry.

Putting her empty wine glass on the coffee table, she conjured a small charcuterie board. She'd been as giddy as a teen girl on a first date with the high school quarterback when she'd figured out she could conjure one.

Chewing a piece of cheese, she thought back to the last hour. She'd flashed up to Morgana's apartment when the spell had broken.

The news had been bittersweet. It was fantastic that Molly was still alive, but her brothers Mirek and Taren were dead—she knew that in her heart, although she couldn't have said how she knew. It was likely connected to all the hallucinations she'd been having and the strange words popping into her mind.

She reached forward and picked up another piece of cheese, sandwiching it between two crackers, when something fell off a shelf. Placing her snack back on the board, she got up and walked over to the book that had fallen to the soft carpet.

Kneeling beside the book, she pulled it up onto her knees and lovingly ran her hand over the cover. It was a photo album her mother had made of her and her brothers—the last one she made before she died. Something or someone had knocked the album off the shelf on purpose, wanting her to see something inside. Before she knew she was magic, she would have said it was a coincidence—but not anymore. Perhaps showing her the album was meant to remind her of everything she'd lost.

She put her fingers under the cover to lift it open when the book was pulled out of her hands. A gasp tore through her throat, but before she could react, the book slammed down on the carpet with a soft whoosh. The album's stiff pages flipped open one after the other until reaching the final page. She pulled the book into her lap again, staring at the only picture on the page—a large eight-by-ten-inch portrait of her brother Mirek. It'd been taken when he was ten, just before he died.

Sounds burst into her mind, like static from an untuned radio. The album slid off her knees as she crushed her palms against the sides of her head. "No! I don't understand!" she yelled into the silence.

She closed her eyes as images swam into her mind. They were clearer than they'd ever been before. She saw Mirek on his bike, Mirek kicking a soccer ball in their old backyard, and Mirek swimming at the lake. But it was as if she was seeing them through someone else's eyes, like they were someone's personal memories.

Alive.

The word was spoken into her thoughts as more images of Mirek popped into her mind, like someone slowly flipping through an album. These images were like the others—someone's memories. When the last image hovered in her mind, she sucked in a breath and held it as her hands started to tremble.

He was sitting on a couch and he looked like he was in his late teens. But that was impossible—it couldn't be a memory because Mirek died when he was ten. Didn't he?

Thanks so much for reading *Found in Magic*!
NEXT IN THE IN MAGIC SERIES:
Find out what happens when Rowena figures out where the voice is coming from and who she needs help from in
COURAGE IN MAGIC
https://books2read.com/courage-in-magic

ALSO BY KJ WARAWA

IN MAGIC SERIES

Lost in Magic

Truth in Magic

Found in Magic

Courage in Magic

Love in Magic

Forged in Magic

Forever in Magic

CURSED TO LOVE SERIES

Cursed to Love

Cursed to Dream

Cursed to Wither

ABOUT KJ WARAWA

Paranormal romance author KJ Warawa had worked every job under the sun, including swimwear seller, switchboard operator, legal secretary, sign language interpreter, soldier, massage therapist, and process improvement advisor, before settling into the career she'd always dreamed about: Author.

She still loves processes and spreadsheets, doesn't love massaging feet, and is currently living out her own love story in Alberta, Canada.

STAY IN TOUCH WITH KJ:
Join KJ's Newsletter at
https://kjwarawa.com/free-book/
to receive a FREE book, exclusive deals, special offers, behind-the-scenes info, and learn about new releases, plus more!
www.kjwarawa.com

www.ingramcontent.com/pod-product-compliance
Lightning Source LLC
Chambersburg PA
CBHW030810210726
48290CB00002B/514